MW01167387

Miner's Haven

Elaine Sharshon

AuthorHouse™
1663 Liberty Drive
Bloomington, IN 47403
www.authorhouse.com
Phone: 1-800-839-8640

©2011 Elaine Sharshon. All rights reserved.

No part of this book may be reproduced, stored in a retrieval system, or transmitted by any means without the written permission of the author.

First published by AuthorHouse 3/02/2011

ISBN: 978-1-4567-4470-0 (e)
ISBN: 978-1-4567-4468-7 (dj)
ISBN: 978-1-4567-4469-4 (sc)

Library of Congress Control Number: 2011903854

Printed in the United States of America

Any people depicted in stock imagery provided by Thinkstock are models, and such images are being used for illustrative purposes only.
Certain stock imagery © Thinkstock.

This book is printed on acid-free paper.

Because of the dynamic nature of the Internet, any web addresses or links contained in this book may have changed since publication and may no longer be valid. The views expressed in this work are solely those of the author and do not necessarily reflect the views of the publisher, and the publisher hereby disclaims any responsibility for them.

Chapter One

She stood naked before the looking glass. Her body, grotesque with unborn life, was deathly white. Her breasts, now heavily veined, were beginning to show the signs of small stretch marks as they etched their tell tale patterns just above her nipples. The once slim waist was now budging in all directions, openly testifying to a condition no amount of self reproach could change. Smiling sadly, she spoke to her reflection.

"Becoming a mother is not very becoming to you, young lady. As a matter of fact, you're beginning to look like a pear with legs."

The face in the mirror stared back at her, the smile fading as a small tear began to glisten in the corner of one eye.

"How could you have been so stupid?" she scolded. "Stupid, and now ugly as well. Even dear Papa can't stand the sight of you."

The very mention of her father caused her to cower like some stricken animal, being punished, and unable to fully comprehend why the misdeed was beyond the possibility of forgiveness. Feverish with guilt and confused anguish, she glanced at her thighs, which were slightly parted, then quickly slid one leg closer to the other. Her mind riveted on Papa's brutal words spoken just the night before.

Keep those legs together, and your little bastard in there, for a respectable amount of time. Folks always seem to accept a seven month baby, although it beats me why, but not a single day before, unless you want the whole town on ya. The whole town and every gossipy biddy in it will want to pick your bones if you don't get this lad to marry you. You hear what I'm telling ya?"

With convulsing stomach she had raced to the sanctuary of her own room, shutting out the hatred in his voice and eyes. Now glancing once more at her misshapen form, she turned and threw herself unto the bed, crying quietly into her pillow.

If only she could go back to that beautiful sun drenched day in spring, when a carefree girl swung on the garden gate, dreaming her dreams of love and great lovers. Papa had just minutes before stormed into the kitchen to find her reading, once again, Scott's romantic tale of Ivanhoe and his beautiful Rowena. Knocking the book from her startled fingers, he bellowed.

"Why can't you find something worth your while to do, Jessica, instead of wasting all of your time with your nose stuck into some book you've read over and over again? There's a garden of blueberries in the yard that have been past pickin' for three days, and me mouth's been watering for just about that long for one of your special pies.

Now come on girl, let's git to moving." His arm guided her somewhat roughly to the door where, smiling gently to himself, he watched as she scurried into the garden, filled with good intentions and a resolve to please her father.

She knew he loved her dearly, but his inability to show it frustrated him, forcing him into the role of irritated blusterer, whose rantings could be heard in the next yard. To Jessica, these outbursts had become a way of life, and she neither resented, nor attended them. Absolutely secure in the knowledge of his camouflaged love, she had feigned sleep on many a night as Papa, creeping into her room, had gently pushed away her hair and timidly kissed her cheek. Then certain she could not hear, he would pause in the doorway and safely profess his love.

Isaac Hobbs had allowed Jessica to remain at home when she reached the age of fifteen, partly because he disapproved of schooling for girls, considering it unnecessary, and partly because of his desire to have the pleasure of his daughter's company. His health remained sound, but like all mortal men, he concerned himself with the uncertainty of the number of days allotted to him.

His beloved wife, Mary, had died at the moment of the child's birth, and his affection had transferred immediately from one to the other. Jessica, from that day, had been the only woman in his life, and his love for her had become his contentment, consuming, but never demanding. So it was that his rantings were a vocal denial of his total submission to her desires, and because he could actually deny her nothing, he felt the need to apply an occasional parental scolding, which he assumed, was the right of every child to receive. Never once had he considered her spoiled or strong willed, despite her many and repeated tantrums. When his orders were not carried out, he simply forgot about them, dismissing them as having had no real importance anyway. Her dalliances were forgiven under the guise of having no mother's example to follow, while her increasingly strong displays of temper were considered to show an admirable mark of spunk, and the type of high spirit needed to be a success in today's world. His blinded eyes saw only perfection reborn, miraculously transmitted from mother to daughter, and he chuckled with delight as the brilliant afternoon sun turned the bobbing auburn curls into dancing shafts of fire among the blueberry branches.

The garden was at its best. The heat of summer had not yet laid its claim to brown the grass, and the trees and shrubs held the intense green that only spring rains and mild weather bestow on them. Jessica, forgetting both the blueberries and her father, ambled to the garden gate, and lifted the latch. Stepping on the bottom bar and slightly shifting her body weight, she was able to stretch the gate's heavy spring and swing lazily back and forth. The motion was pleasant, conducive to excellent day dreaming. So it was that while she swung, transfixed in her fantasy of knights in armor, down the hill from the colliery, and into her life forever, swaggered Michael McClellan, the most handsome man she had ever seen.

Michael was tall and heavily built, with hair and eyes as black as the coal he extracted from the mines. He walked with an arrogant air, and the confidence of a man known to be held in high esteem. He never came down from the colliery alone, but was constantly surrounded by laughing companions, who roared at his jokes, and were fascinated by his fabrications concerning the adventurous things he'd done before coming to Miners' Haven.

Every Saturday evening after the paymaster had given out the envelopes, it was Michael's pleasure to invite his friends to a cup at Dougal's on the way home. Most of the men had family responsibilities and could not return the favor, but Michael never seemed to notice as long as he was their center of attention. This, of course, considering a free cup was not that difficult to achieve.

Michael had come to Miners' Haven just three months before from, according to him, all ports in the world. He had put to sea when only fourteen, trying to get to America, but what with a few sinking's and scurvy epidemics, to say nothing of remaining in some ports, which held interests of another nature, it had taken him seven years to reach this country, and in his own words, "settle into the life of a miner." He lived alone on the other side of town, and always wore a sly smile when asked if he were lonely. The men envied his seemingly free existence and particularly his ability to purchase as many tankards as he damned pleased. Each man knew his woman would check every cent in his envelope, and he would be held accountable if more than the price of one tankard was missing. The unmarried men remained at home and were accountable to their mothers, so it was natural for them to envy Michael's life of responsibility to himself only. A man accountable to no one was a rarity in Miners' Haven, most of the men having a never ending stream of relatives, and when disaster struck, each man knew his duty.

Working underground made them ever conscious of danger and death, and they massed together in characteristic animal banding in their efforts to cheat the final predator. What a man gave today he may have to look to receive on the morrow. When crippling injury or death came, no woman felt a beggar, for more than likely her man had already been another's benefactor. When the men left the wash houses on Saturday night, it was not uncommon for them to find their woman waiting with the sole purpose of relieving her man of the biggest part of his envelope and the temptation to tarry overly long at Dougal's, and although it made the men quarrelsome and grumpy, they grudgingly acquiesced rather than face the results of their own weaknesses and a harping tongue. The women respected the perils facing their man daily, and had to admit a week without disaster was reason enough for celebration, and sympathetically saw to it that their men were left with enough money for at least one well deserved tankard before leaving the hill. They also knew that the coming of Sunday and the prospect of spending an entire day above ground, sometimes spurred the men on to festivities that poached heavily on the family income, and thereby felt no real remorse for their heavy handed tactics.

A man with unlimited funds, under these circumstances, was understandably well received, and particularly on Saturday afternoon. The men mulled around Michael good naturedly, happy in the prospect of a trek to Dougal's, and the possibility of being treated to a few extra cups.

Jessica's abundant hair billowed about her face, the errant strands caressing her apricot cheeks as it flowed back and forth with the motion of the gate. Her deep brown eyes stared, unseeing, at the cracks in the garden wall, as a million thoughts of love and romance flitted through her mind. Her gallant knight's mouth pressed against hers, and she felt herself grow dizzy as the length of their bodies touched in an embrace. With parted lips, she sighed and closed her eyes, the better to see her fantasy. The bellowing voice of Michael McClellan interrupted her reverie as he chucked her under the chin, roaring.

"How would you like to pluck this sweet plum, lads?" Then bending close to her ear, he spoke in a low but audible voice. "You're quite a beautiful little piece, my girl, and if you ever need the services of a good man, just remember the name of Michael McClellan."

The men in their joviality at day's end, merely laughed at this banter, waved their greeting to the young girl, and quickly moved on down the hill. Michael's hand on hers had stayed the swinging of the gate, while his laughing eyes held her for a fleeting moment. She had seen him many times before, and had attempted on consecutive Saturday afternoons to be present at the gate in order to catch one more glimpse of her hero. His was the face her imagined lover wore, and now, as his hand rested on hers, she struggled to escape the dream and surface to reality. The warmth of his touch raced up her arm, and a touch of heat turned her cheeks crimson. Then, suddenly, she realized this was not the face of one who loved her, but one who mocked her and looked depreciatingly down on her. She jerked her hand away, causing her feet to slip off the gate's narrow bar with a thud. Her mouth fell open in surprise, her face a study in confusion. Michael, taking a step backward, roared anew with laughter. Then, somewhat ashamed of his manners, he spoke to her softly.

"It was only a joke, my little miss, not worthy of paying it any mind," Patting her scarlet cheek reassuringly, he turned abruptly and followed his comrades down the hill to Dougal's.

Frustration brought bitter tears; she had so wanted to impress him with her maturity and womanliness. She had envisioned their first meeting a hundred times over. She, every inch a lady, aloof, condescending and beautiful in a brand new beige silk dress, with perhaps a bit of lace at the throat. Her hair, of course, would be piled high on her head, like the ladies in the catalogs, with just a touch of paint on her cheeks to insure a healthy color.

Michael would be overwhelmed by her loveliness, stammering as they met, his black eyes brimming with admiration and desire.

Instead he had seen her as she really was, a girl barely past seventeen, and as unworldly as a new born titmouse. If only she had said one intelligent word, or even smiled coyly as cousin Clara had instructed her to do so many times. Total despair gripped her because she feared he would not care to pass the time of day again with a total bumpkin.

In her utter dismay and frustration, she did not see Tom Quinlan watching her from the side walk. His face wore a scowl that was almost obliterated by the carbonite still covering it. Tagging along behind the older men, he had been witness to the entire episode, and was filled with consternation over her apparent unhappiness, which could only have been caused by the unseemly manners of that dirty Irishman. He had loved Jessica for as long as he could remember, and longed only for her seldom given attention, and the comfort her smiles afforded him.

Becoming crippled when a weakened timber had given way, trapping him for hours, despite the strenuous efforts of the rescue crew, he had faced the partial loss of his left foot as being far less important than his many weeks in lost wages. He was, by nature, very shy, and wanting nothing about himself to evoke or attract attention in any way, he soon discovered that a small bag of sand in the empty part of his boot, weighted it just enough to insure better balance. After all, insignificant accidents in the mines were many, and soon forgotten. He was not about to become a constant reminder.

Now, looking at Jessica, a fierce protectiveness filled his every fiber, and forgetting his reticence, he pushed open the gate and limped to her side.

"Don't fret, Jessie," he dared. "That man is nothing but a lowly Catholic, with not a lick of decency in his whole body. He's a man interested in only his own comforts, and has no business even speaking to one such as yerself." His hand reached out to comfort her as he continued.

"He's accustomed to women on the town, and--"

A voice he didn't recognize cut through his words, and he realized it was Jessica, speaking in a tone he had never heard before. With one movement she had wrenched her arm free of his touch, and turned full around to face him. Her innocence did not allow for the comprehension of his words, but her vanity disallowed his commiseration.

"What does someone like you know about a man like Michael McClellan, except jealousy," she shrieked. "And if he were the worst of everything you say he is, I can still manage to take care of myself, thank you, Tom Qinlan, and I don't need you're butting in." Pausing to twist her mouth in disgust, she added cruelly. "And you can just take that look of pity off your dirty face, I'm not the cripple, you are!"

The electrified look on his stricken face slowly registered on her mind, forcing the bitter taste of self loathing to rise in her throat. Hatred vanished from her face, as it crumbled into a mass of sorrow.

"Forgive me if you can, Tom," she muttered. "I can't imagine whatever made me say something like that." Stumbling out of the garden and up to the house, she paused at the kitchen door to turn and wave weakly as a shower of sadness dampened her cheeks.

Tom's eyes darkened as an uncontrollable anger rose inside him like an evening tide, sweeping away his good judgment in overwhelming waves of urgency. Without giving any thought to his inferior strength or affliction, he arbitrarily decided he must openly face this man who had brought such agony to the only joy in his dull life, and castigate him before the very men who had seemed so eager to approve of his chicanery, and debasement of their neighbor's daughter.

Running blindly down the hill, and accelerated by his need for acrimony, he was momentarily able to forget his handicap, and give vent to his pressing need for satisfaction. Like all men down through the ages who had ever been bent on the preserving of a woman's honor, he felt magnanimous, and satiated with self righteousness. Reaching the swinging doors of the saloon, he staggered against them, almost losing his balance, and causing them to swing wide as they announced his presence with a resounding smack.

Dougal's was the men's sanctuary, and though shuttered and dimly lit to escape the attention of meddling Prohibition Inspectors, there was always a warm welcome at the front door, and bootleg whiskey at the back. Dougal's would have to close down every now and again when warnings filtered in from surrounding counties, alerting him to the presence of an enforcement agent in the area. The fear of heavy fines and possible imprisonment sealed Dougal's doors, but never his lips, as he expounded, to all who would listen, on life's injustices. Loudly crying out to God for mercy and the right to make a living, he would bang the bar with clenched fists, imploring the heavens to let him live long enough to see an end to all of this foolishness. His supplications went unheeded. It would take almost fourteen years of mass murders, increased prostitution, smuggling, bootlegging, the birth of speakeasies, and the entire country roaring wildly, before this useless law would be overturned. The general public, never having been convinced that the consumption of alcohol was a crime, became a nation of criminals by the time the government, staggering under the influence of the depression, finally repealed the Volstead Act in order to regain the liquor traffic profits.

Dougal's had expertly assessed the situation when he complained of being punished, while gangsters were rewarded, and the government itself losing a billion dollars a year in lost tax revenues. And all of this to placate a bunch of teetotalers, who never did come to realize they had served only to increase drunken driving arrests, arrests for drunkenness, and even escalated the death toll from alcoholism with their unsuccessful attempt to halt the flow of happiness. After one dry week, the miner's thirst, like the rest of the nation, seemed almost insatiable, and Dougal's income really never suffered from the seven day drought, regardless of his perpetual complaints.

Most of the men took advantage of the wash houses the companies provided on the surface of the mine. Here they were able to remove their dust laden clothing, placing their shoes in one of the rows of galvanized iron buckets, and their discarded garments on hooks attached to each bucket's bottom. These containers were then suspended near the ceiling on locked chains, allowing them to dry and ready themselves for the next day's use. Showering, and again donning his street clothes, a man could leave the mines as clean and presentable as workers in any other industry, and above all would better appreciate his stop at Dougal's, where he could readily recognize the man whose back he was playfully slapping.

Tom, being very young, and not yet a drinking man, never joined in the Saturday night ritual at the wash house or at Dougal's, so when all heads turned to the still blackened face, it took a few minutes for the men to realize it was Tom Quinlan who stood in the doorway. Finally one of the men raised his glass in surprise and asked,

"Aye, is it young Tom Quinlan come to drink a cup with us? Begorra, are ya marryin' Tom, or what is it you're here to celebrate?"

Ignoring the man, Tom strode directly to Michael, striking him full in the face with an open hand. There was a sudden intake of breaths around the bar, and as the astonished men watch, Tom began punching Michael, his arms flaying about, as he stood with both feet seemingly anchored in one spot. Michael overcame his surprise within a few seconds and, because of his height was able, with one backward step and one outstretched arm, to hold the angered boy at bay as he muttered.

"Come on now, boy. You'd best let up before you hurt yourself

The words only served to spur Tom on, increasing the fury of his attack, while he grunted with the effort of each and every swing. Michael casually looked about the room with quizzically raised brows as he successfully held young Tom at a safe distance. The entire scene grew comical, and a few of the men began to snicker softly. Then, as if by signal, they were all laughing uncontrollably and slapping their hands on the bar and each other.

The young man's anger ebbed with exhaustion as he wearily stepped back to look at Michael. The sound of their laughter beat against his ears like the whir of bats in a belfry, and he raised his arms, as if warding off an attacker, then again faced Michael with a look of pure hatred. His labored breathing over powered the menacingly low tone of his voice as the room stilled and everyone present strained to hear his words.

"You're a man without principle," he uttered gutturally. "Lower than the lowest shaft in the hill, nothing but a conceited braggart who thinks he can buy a man's friendship with the price of a tankard." Feeling the bubbling beads of anxiety bursting upon his upper lip, he quickly dragged the back of his hand across his mouth before continuing. "You have no real place here among us, and you know it, and we've all had to suffer through your crowing while you tried to find one. Ever since you came to town you've strutted your wares like a banty in a barn yard, but just because the hens on your side of town are interested doesn't mean anybody wants you over here." His voice dropped even lower. "If you ever so much as dare to look at Miss Hobbs again I swear I'll kill you and consider it, not only a good deed, but a benefit to the community."

The perspiration now flooded his coal dust laden face, rendering his streaked expression almost pitiful despite the splinter of fire still glowing in his normally docile brown eyes. Maintaining what he considered an intimidating, steadfast stare, he backed slowly out through the swinging door, like some old time western gunfighter, leaving his embarrassed opponent standing awkwardly alone in the middle of the bar room floor.

The men shuffled their feet, unable to look at Michael or each other. In a way the boy was right, Michael was certainly not one of them, and never would be. His very presence denied one of their own a job, and his being Catholic was something, until now, they had chosen to overlook. After all, he wasn't one of them bead handlers, and never wore any nonsense around his neck to blatantly remind them of his difference. At the end of the day all the other "Kicks and Pollack's", as was fitting, went down the opposite side of the hill to their own end of town where newly arrived immigrants struggled against too much Americanism by still speaking their native tongue, and pleasuring themselves with long standing customs and handed down recipes, guarded and preserved as treasures from their home land. The homes in this section had originally been owned by the coal company in the days when Miners' Haven was little more than a mine patch. Having been hastily constructed, and without conventional household facilities, they were set up in long rows of simple design, and then enclosed by crude, unsightly stockade type fencing, which turned out to be a considerable fire hazard as well as an eye sore. As the town grew and the companies lost control of housing and supply stores through long overdue legislation, the fences came down and the homes were sold to whomever could afford to make the purchase along with the necessary improvements. Many of the new landlords converted the rows to more practical rooming houses with a minimum of innovation and an eye to the maximum return on their invested dollar.

All were clapboard, and sat directly, without benefit of lawn, on small cobbled walks, lining narrow one way streets. In their very midst they erected two churches, one Orthodox, and one Roman Catholic, which they managed to fill to overflowing every holy day and Sabbath, keeping them poor in purse, but fulfilled in faith.

Although, never actually decreed by some silent understanding, the main street had become the dividing line. The entire populace shopped there, shared the same movie houses, and together, even deposited their savings in the same City Bank, but there the sociability ended and the battlefield began, with Catholics on the one side of town, and the Protestants on the other. Only Michael had cared enough to dare and cross over this biased line of prejudcialness.

All these thoughts and others darted through the men's mind, as they found themselves forced into a position of side taking and decision making alien to their nature. Michael had proven himself to be a good friend to many a man at this bar, loaning them money when necessary, without the pressure of a certain repayment time or the encumbrance of the fear of divulgement, which weighed heavily on their unconquerable innate pride. His unflagging good nature and enjoyable personality had also contributed mightily to his unconditional acceptance, but Tom, despite his youth and evident lack of charisma was, after all, born in Miners' Haven, and, not unlike themselves, a son and grandson of a mining man, but above all, though few would utter the thought aloud, a Protestant. One by one they hastily gulped their drinks, making excuses about the nagging woman who would be waiting for them, and then slowly drifted out of the saloon with dampened spirits, feeling their usually festive Saturday had been turned into a dismal affair. Not one soul had gotten in his cups, and even if they had, the entire affair had been just too sobering, and they resented this unwelcome intrusion on an occasion they had anxiously looked forward to all of the working week.

Finally Michael stood alone at the bar, the boy's words echoing and reechoing in his ear. He was, he knew, everything the boy had accused him of being, and for the first time in his life he decided to give a thought to the why of it. In a voice, louder than usual, he ordered another drink from a self conscious Dougal's, who had busied himself by gathering up the speedily abandoned mugs. Gulping with a new found thirst, he motioned for another while his thoughts drifted to a childhood his mind had seldom focused upon. He could not remember his parents, having been raised in a small Welsh mining town by his maternal grandmother, a silent withered old woman, who told him only that his father had been an honest and good man, perishing long before his time from some undiagnosable malady that had left him weak hearted and bereft of his senses. Whenever he had questioned her concerning his mother, she glared at him and found some arduous task for him to perform, and so he soon learned to curb his curiosity in favor of not having to suffer the wrath of his grandmother.

When he was but twelve the old woman died without ever having said one loving word to her only grandchild, and he whispered a daily rosary for her intentions, hoping the silent world to which she had gone, had made her happier than the comfortless one she had left behind.

Upon the day of her funeral, the above ground boss came to the grandmother's small rented cottage and offered Michael a job at the colliery and a garret room in exchange for all of the old lady's meager furnishings. The boy, relieved of the prospect of being completely alone, and even more fearful of being sent to the orphanage at Weigh scale, eagerly agreed, without assessing the value of his inherited possessions, and the very next morning began his job as a breaker boy. Seated on a backless wooden slab near the coal chutes he gazed out at an endless stream of coal headed in his direction. From this never ending ebony flow he was expected to, with a flick of his wrist, remove all extraneous pieces of slate, rock, wood or any other foreign matter that had accidently mixed in with the coal from the point of its extraction to its arrival in the bin before him. The breaker lurched and groaned ominously as it shook under the weight of another wagon load of coal being dumped at its tipple, which then roared over a screen of mine rails to be fed into a gluttonous maw of revolving rollers, and crushed and separated into various sizes of steamboat, broken, or egg. Finally, moved by gravity alone, it descended through the chutes, sprawling in front of the poor slate pickers with the need for its purification. After only the first few hours of his nine hour day, the pain in his fingers had become excruciating. The excess rock and slate had torn away the tips of his skin, leaving them raw, bleeding and aching to his very elbows. He sometimes faltered, then stopped completely, only to feel the bite of the hickory stick used by the pusher boss to urge the boys on as he shouted, "Come on now, lads, don't let a bit of the red tips hold you up. You got to keep working on them bins, lads if you want to earn your way here." Shaking the stick vigorously, he would admonish the boys further. "Pick them bins clean now, lads or I'll have to march your asses out of here without you're getting your pay voucher for this day." Unclogging a chute with his multi-purposed weapon, he would then slam it against the bins, jarring the boys to diligence.

For these valiant efforts he received equal to thirty cents a day, half of which had gone to pay for his board and scanty, unembellished lodgings. By the end of the second year he was working underground, which served to consume him with a desire to spend the remainder of his life on top of the good earth, despising his mole like existence, with the ever present terrifying dangers from fire and gas, of rotting timbers, sudden floods and suffocating dust. If man had been meant to burrow through the ground like some animal all of his life, it stood to reason God would have had no reason to create the beauty of sky and sea, flowers and mountains, and a sun, whose rays were seldom felt. The sea had always held a special fascination for him; possibly because he had never seen it, so shortly after his fourteenth birthday, armed with the determination of youth, and twenty dollars in cash, he set out for the coast, signing on as cabin boy to the first schooner that would have him.

His first five days aboard were spent in the hold, where the swelling of every wave in his heretofore beautiful sea, filled him with nausea and a sickness that made him look back, with longing, to his former occupation. The captain, a merciless brute of a man, had ordered him beaten daily as a purge against what he considered to be laziness, but the mate appointed to carry out the punishment felt a twinge of pity at the sight of the young green face, and instead, lay cool rags wrung from sea water, on the boy's fevered brow, sponging the cracked lips with some foreign tasting liquid, while repeatedly assuring Michael he would live to see land again. When, on the sixth day, he was able to rise up on somewhat wobbling legs, the mate, displaying a broad toothless grin, roughly slapped his rump proclaiming, "Aye I knew from the first ye were a stout lad that could do it. I'd say you're a lad that could do whatever year a mind to, and don't ever ferget it." Winking knowingly, the old mate playfully punched his shoulder, grinning even wider.

` It was Michael's first experience with anything even remotely resembling praise and he reveled in the sensation of it, swelling with haughty pride and the pure joy of unexpected and unsought acclaim.

The jet black eyes, somber for so long, were scintillated at last by the unimaginable delight of another person's recognition, and the acknowledgment of his possible worth. Vowing never to disappoint the mate's confidence in him, he vigorously applied himself to the fulfillment of this well intentioned pledge and, under the older man' tutelage, quickly became astute at knot tying, correct soundings, manipulation of the rigging, and every manner of seamanship. By the time they had made port twice, his unerring determination to succeed, and do justice to the old mariner's faith in him, had paid off in substantial dividends, and he knew himself to be as worthy as any man jack aboard the vessel.

It became his life style to excel in all things, and then wait for the anticipated and always wondrous sound of praise. If at times, his attempts were less than his idea of perfection, he bragged about them none the less, proffering the thought anything he did would always be impeccable and faultless. He soon discovered that people were willing to believe whatever you, yourself projected to them, without too much investigation into what was truth. Everyone admired self confidence, probably from a lack of their own, and enjoyed associating with persons of accomplishment, whether real, or imagined. So he matured, striving ceaselessly for the esteem of his comrades, their approval and advocacy being the main sustenance of his otherwise drab and lonely life. It was the closest thing to love he had ever known, but had the fates been kind enough to allow him a look into his future, with a view to the extent and inundation of the love he would one day be subjected to, he may well have found more solace in the ambiguity of solitude.

Chapter Two

The fortunes or misfortunes of men's lives are sometimes decided by a single incident. If Michael, on that day, could have known of Jessica's love, he would have had the choice of deciding to return it or completely ignoring it and either decision would have changed their destinies, allowing both of them a chance at a happiness that was to be endlessly sought after and eternally denied. Unfortunately he was not conscious of the tear filled eyes watching him from the window as he, trying to ward off the unfamiliar sensation of depression caused by Tom Quinlan's unprovoked attack, whistled softly to himself and began the long walk home.

He had accustomed himself to the laud of his associates and despised the hollow sinking feeling that had relentlessly churned within him since the young man's horrendous public denouncement of him. Feeling his cheeks flame anew with the remembered agony of the embarrassment surrounding the encounter, and his inability to cope with the verity of the accusations, he had stood momentarily outside of Dougal's establishment, vainly trying to compose his thoughts and regain control of his heaving innards. Even his sour faced, churlish grandmother had never chastised him in the presence of others, but had rightfully confined her limitless criticism and perpetual nagging to the privacy of their small cottage, But now that young fellow Tom, had deeply wounded his self esteem today with his unrestrained need to malign him, and even more disquieting was the fact that he had definitely sown the seeds of doubt that, soon enough, would sprout into buds of disrespect in his fellow workers. Rehearsing the dismal scene one last time, he breathed deeply, then plunged his doubled fists into his pants pocket with a firm resolve to expend no more energy on an incident that could not be changed no matter how much effort he devoted to it at this moment. Eventually, he prophesied to himself, he would find a way, not only to regain, but to magnify all the regard lost to him this day at Dougal's. By the time he was half way home, the importance of the episode had become somewhat dimmed by his uncanny ability to optimize almost any situation, and his whistle had become loud and cheery.

Jessica had stared at the spot on the hill long after Michael had vanished behind it. Anguish flooded her mind like an angry wave, leaving gullies of pain, and rivulets of despair. She had finally realized her opportunity with him, and had acted like some diffident school girl; tongue tied, mouth agape, and performing her final humiliation by falling awkwardly off the garden gate. Wringing her hands in defeat, she paced unhappily about the room, then stopped suddenly to evaluate her appearance in front of the looking glass. There could be no doubt about her beauty, she assured herself, forcing the unruly auburn curls behind her ears and leaning closer to the mirror to better examine the large slit of her luminous eyes, with their exciting flecks of burnished gold. Dilating the fine nostrils of her delicate nose, she turned sideways to make a study of her flat stomach, and amply curved posterior, pouting as her eyes fell upon, what she considered to be, an inadequate bust line.

Gazing distractedly at her image, an idea began to slowly take form in her mind. Dreaming a dream doesn't make it come true, she decided, but action, with the help of a few conspirators, just might turn her dreams into a reality sooner than she thought possible. With renewed confidence she smiled at the girl in the mirror. There would be no more room for mistakes this time because she would consult her cousins first, and they, of course, would know exactly what to do.

Clara and Molly Benfield were two of the luckiest single ladies in all of Miners' Haven. By merely sitting on their front porch swing on Saturday afternoon, they were able to flirt with every available bachelor in town, as their house sat conveniently next to Dougal's. The sisters were, to say the least, not comely, both possessing light colored hair, faded blue eyes, and the jaundiced sallow complexion that usually accompanies coloring of this type. Their voices were as shrill as excited magpies and they seemed constantly to be giggling behind their kerchiefs at some continuing silly secret between them. Despite these drawbacks, the sisters did have outstanding figures, without the assist of a single stay, and all the men leaving Dougal's, whether single or married, enjoyed stopping by for a word with the girls in the hope that either one or the other might lean over the banister and reveal the voluptuous sights beneath their bodices, which always proved to be more than worth the price of idle chatter.

Clara and Molly were ever popular with the young men, mostly through the efforts of their mother, who took great pride in the never ending attentions the townsmen showered upon her two buxom daughters.

Annie Benfield, widowed many years before, had devoted much of her time trying to insure her girl's future by instructing them in, what she considered, proper and lady like husband hunting procedures. She had patiently instilled in them every womanly wile, from the coquettish tilt of the head, to the inviting sultry look of the siren, guaranteed to ignite interest through its hidden, but never to be delivered promise. Tempting was permissible, acquiescence, punishable.

Unwilling to indulge in these practices herself, Annie had always feigned a lingering bereavement for dear John, her husband for about as long a time as it had taken to conceive and give birth to their two pale children. The union had been most unhappy because of John's need for a time table type of existence, with a strict regimen of dinner precisely at five, bedtime not one minute beyond nine, and the exclusion of all visitors both Saturday and Sunday afternoons. These times had been set aside for the punctual performance of Annie's connubial duties, scheduled to begin exactly at two. Luckily for Annie, the man's nervous and exacting nature, and inability to deviate from his structured life of discipline, eventually affected his health, and she found herself widowed before she had reached the age of thirty. Undeterred by her disagreeable experience, she steadfastly maintained that marriage was a noble institution, but contented herself with the conquests of her daughters, as she ambled through each day at her own leisurely pace.

Generously, she plied them with every new scent or artifice the market afforded, then enthusiastically encouraged their study of the simple directions included in every package, sitting back to languidly enjoy their delight with, and eventual application of, this latest acquisition.

Clara and Molly, both avid students of pomposity, thought nothing of spending hours over their paint pots, each trying to outdo the other with a new slant to the brow, or a more muted shade to the cheek. The girl's were extremely vain, motivated by their mother's continuous flattery, and it's vindication by the fawning attention of the miners, which was theirs to receive every imbibing day of the week.

Both girls sat preening at their vanities, carefully eyeing their reflections for any flaw in their makeup, oblivious to a pallor that no amount of fakery would ever be able to alter. Their pale fingers fidgeted and fluttered from powder to paint, dabbing fruitlessly at cheeks already caked from an over abundance of application. A light tapping at the door frame mercifully interrupted their assiduity, and they turned in union to find their cousin, Jessica, timidly standing in the doorway.

"Aunt Annie said I could come right up." She spoke apologetically. "I was wondering if you would mind giving me a little advise, and some help, with a matter that's become quite important to me."

The sisters turned to each other in utter disgust. Since the day that Jessica had turned twelve years of age, their Uncle Isaac had managed to perpetuate this unwelcome intrusion into their lives every few weekends, indirectly seeking their aid in the imparting of information an adolescent girl should certainly be privy to if she were expected to remain toward. Their understandable resentment to this unwanted responsibility manifested itself in a total unwillingness to confide in, or even counsel their innocent young cousin, beyond the explanation of the monthly cycle, and that, only when it had become expedient to do so. Neither Molly nor Clara had experienced even the slightest twinge of conscience for their neglect, in spite of knowing full well what had been expected from them. In truth, they were but girls themselves, intent upon their own existence, and the world's revolvement around them, selfishly ensconced in their own problems, and without the slightest interest in someone they considered to be a mere child.

Molly, the elder sister, pressed a tissue to her freshly painted mouth, stood up, and tried to smile sweetly. "Dear cousin, Jessica," she whined, "I am really pressed for time at the moment, but Clara, who is actually more your age anyway, will be happy to help you, I'm sure." With a malicious grin she turned in the direction of her sister and continued. "If there's any question she doesn't have the answer to, please call me. I'm only as far as the porch swing away."

Jessica's eyes followed her cousin admiringly as Molly waltzed out of the room with the identical demeanor employed by all of the story book princesses the young girl had ever read about. Cousin Molly would never be tongue tied by any man, she thought with envy, because she was as self assured, poised and glamorous as any of the elegant older ladies posing for the new spring catalogs, and actually had superseded the majority of them when it came to an effectual chest measurement.

Clara's impatient voice interrupted her thoughts. "Well, on with it, Jessie, I haven't all night either, you know." Her words were staccatoed by the final drumming of the overused powder puff against cheeks already caked with subterfuge.

Jessica rushed over to the vanity and quickly seated herself beside her cousin. Now that the time had come to present her petition, she became flustered, her features flushing with the perplexity and complications of her unspeakable and tumultuous longing. Her voice was almost inaudible as she lowered her eyes and stammered simply.

"I want a man."

Clara's eyes narrowed in surprise as she closely scrutinized Jessica's expression, studying her obvious discomfort suspiciously. Was it possible that this child had been feigning innocence all the while, toying with their inadequate, but none the less, good intentions, and was now ready to boldly flaunt her mundane knowledge beneath their unsuspecting noses? Cursing Molly for her ill timed absence, she nervously patted her faded saffron locks into a flatter, less bouffant coiffure, deciding she would have to attack this problem slowly, and with diplomacy, until she was able to discern the real reason for her young cousin's unwanted visit. Reaching out, she placed her pallid hand over Jessica's and asked calmly,

"Did you have any special man in mind, sweet cousin?"

"Oh, yes," answered Jessica breathlessly, and the long pent up words began gushing from her like the torrents from a waterfall. "I'm sure you must know him, Clara. It's Michael McClellan, the tall handsome one with the real black hair and eyes. The one who goes to Dougal's every Saturday afternoon."

They all go to Dougal's every Saturday afternoon, ninny, thought

Clara as she stole a sidelong glance at herself in the mirror. Already relieved by this flood of adolescent prattle, she tried forcing herself into a pretense of interest, but found it difficult, knowing this childish crush would eventually dissipate itself when the poor girl's attentions were not reciprocated. She herself had experienced several such episodes a few years back, but had long since learned to harness her emotions while she waited for the right man to release them. Pursing her lips in silence, she listened patiently as Jessica continued.

"Oh, Clara, I just want him to take notice of me, that's all. He did stop by our gate once but I was so dumb struck I acted stupid and made a fool of myself, when all I really wanted to do was to be as grown up and as beautiful as you and Molly."

Clara automatically preened, glancing once again into the mirror to verify Jessica's assessment.

"I thought if you would lend me a dress, maybe something a little more mature than Papa allows me, and perhaps show me how to fix my hair in a more becoming manner, like the way yours is tonight. I would love to wear my hair up in big curls on the top of my head like that, it's so sophisticated. I swear you're more lovely than the ladies in the catalog."

Obviously Jessica's only reference to beauty was dependent on Sears and Montgomery Ward, thought Clara, but accepted the compliment as her just due, while hoping for a swift end to this boring conversation.

"If you wouldn't mind giving me a few lessons, especially in the application of a bit of make up, maybe one Saturday I could sit on the porch with you and Molly and try to get him to take notice of me again. What do you think, Clara?"

Looking down on the abundant auburn hair, the flawless ivory skin and full, sweetly curved lips she had to wonder who the man was who had resisted so much beauty. The glow of love had imparted a most becoming gleam of animation to Jessica's features that had never been apparent before, and Clara immediately despised her for it. She did not dare to admit that this sudden, unwelcome rancor had been brought, about by pure and simple envy, for that would have necessitated the further examination of Jessica's attributes, and worst of all their ultimate comparison to her own, and so she chose to label her ill will as righteous disgust with an interminable situation that had been unfairly fostered upon her and her family. At last the little pest was growing up and she still maintained this annoying habit of belaboring her kin with every manner of personal problem. Well if she was ready to throw herself at the very first chap that met her fancy it was certainly not Clara's duty to try and dissuade her, but neither was it her obligation to assist in this futile pursuance at her own and Molly's expense. She was not about to share the advantage of the front porch with this one, cousin or no.

She moseyed to the window, gazing up at the ever growing culm bank whose daily accumulation of coal dirt and sludge carelessly draped itself over every inch of available ground, creating a mountain of mourning that gradually encircled half of the town. Her mood was as black as the hill's top, when finally, she spoke.

"Not only will I make you beautiful, my dear, but I will personally arrange for you to meet your young man on Saturday after next."

Jessica excitedly opened her mouth to proclaim her gratitude, but Clara swung around to face her with a warning.

"I must insist that you do not tell your father about this meeting. Men so seldom approve the attention given their daughters by other men, or at least, so I'm told."

Clara's barb of insinuation that she too had been underprivileged by the possession of only one parent, bounced off Jessica's armor of elation without notice as she stood in the center of the room, hands clasped tightly together in the sheer joy of anticipation.

Clara sighed audibly. "Just plan to spend the evening here as you've already done a hundred times before, and I'm sure no one will be the wiser, understand?"

"Yes, of course I understand, but I just can't believe it's finally going to happen." Jessica's face was radiant with her new found happiness as she ran across the room to fling her arms about her cousin.

"I should have known I could depend on you Clara. Heaven only knows what a help you've already been to both Papa and me." The luminous brown eyes hurriedly blinked away their excess moisture. "And, of course Molly and Aunt Annie too," she amended quickly, feeling the need to placate. "I really don't know what would have become of us without all of you to rely on all these years, honestly I don't."

Clara patted her arm gently, smiling to herself. "And you can rely on us still, pet, although you've become so grown up, I could almost predict this may be the very last time."

The following weeks dragged out endlessly, but Jessica, determined not to be thwarted a second time through her own inexperience and naivety, devotedly ignored the colliery whistle on successive Saturdays, praying her absence would be noticed, and her final long awaited for reappearance, rewarded by his relief, and joy at having found her again. Their next meeting would be spectacularly different from their last, and she dreamed about it daily, with every dream diverse from the last. All of them, however, somehow relegated him to a position of supplication, while she, regal in every way, condescended to respond to him only after she felt he had paid sufficiently for having embarrassed her at the garden's gate. Nevertheless, by the time their meeting again was finally at hand, she had forgiven him so many times in fantasy the actuality of it had lost its importance, becoming buried beneath the mounds of nervous apprehension and joyous expectations.

Humming happily to herself, she crammed the drab clothing she was certain not to wear, into a small bundle and tucked it under her arm, then flying down the stairs she stopped briefly in the kitchen to kiss her father good bye, and playfully tweak his freshly trimmed beard.

Isaac stood shaking his head in utter amazement as he watched his daughter race down the street to Annie's house. Most suggested excursions to the Benfield's had been met with howling protests, bouts of pouting, and finally, silent submission. This time, however, Jessica herself had surprisingly initiated the overnight visit, and he, of course, ever mindful of the need for girl talk, had heartily approved. This thing about a woman's continual change of mind must actually begin in the cradle he decided, since his little girl, although guilty of the trait, still had quite a way to go before she could be considered a woman. With one more shake of the head he picked up his momentarily discarded newspaper and turned his attentions to subjects more easily understood.

The two sisters anxiously awaited her. Clara had confided to Molly their cousins astonishing request, over emphasizing Jessica's desire to inject herself into their advantageous realm, and omitting most of the young girl's compliments and earnest yearning to emulate them, in the fear that her sister's unbridled vanity might affect her better judgment, subjecting both of them to an infringement they could ill afford. Once it was decided there was a definite lesson to be taught here, and above all, the positive establishing of the correct pecking order, the girls gleefully set about to enjoy the rewarding job as taskmasters.

Molly had wisely arranged a date for herself and Clara with two of the younger lads regularly stopping by the porch to chat, then shyly suggested they might take a walk up Raspberry Hill, knowing full well it was an invitation they could not resist. The boys grinned mischievously at each other, nodding in instantaneous agreement, for a walk up Raspberry Hill had become notorious as the pathway to extensive necking, experimental fondlings and other pleasantries their immature bodies, until now, had only fantasized over. Their eagerness became quite apparent when Molly, suddenly pouting in dismay, remembered a guest they were obligated to entertain for the week end, and petulantly began to apologize for her need to cancel what she was sure would have been a very enjoyable evening. The boys doggedly determined not to be cheated out of such an auspicious opportunity, readily agreed to supply the interfering young lady with a partner of Molly's choice, falling prey to her plan, and solidifying the certainty of the next step in her well planned scheme. Smiling with satisfaction, she purred.

"I think she might enjoy Michael McClellan, I've heard he's very entertaining. But, then he does live on the other side of town, and perhaps you're not well acquainted enough to solicit his company for an entire, evening with someone he doesn't even know. I don't want to make this difficult for you boys."

Then wearing what she considered her most beguiling smile, she had slowly moved forward to remove a stray leaf from beneath the porch swing, permitting her beaus ample view of her favors. A trip to the next county would not have proved too difficult at that particular moment, and both boys began babbling at once in an effort to assure her that Michael McClellan's presence was a problem they could handle. Armed with the sword of excitement and the spear of anticipation, they ambled down the street, unable to believe their good fortune, and ready to do battle with any and all obstacles that dared stand in the way of their enjoyment the following Saturday night.

Both Molly and Clara had trekked to Raspberry Hill with several of the young men in town, but because of their mother's tutelage and their own keen interest in the securing of a husband, the girls and allowed only enough petting and promiscuity to wet a man's appetite and insure his attentiveness, but never enough to be bantered about town and ruin their valuable reputation.

They loved sneaking into the stilled house at evenings end, and slipping by Annie's door to their own oversized bedroom at the rear of the hall. Once inside their private chamber, they would roll around on the large single beds, laughing and exchanging their night's experiences, candidly assessing them as possible future prospects or discard-them on the mounting heap of one time fruitless encounters. Again tonight they were to be deprived of this pleasure, stymied once more by the presence of Jessica, but they consoled themselves with the idea that the evening's outcome would be well worth the sacrifice.

Clara was the first to hear footsteps on the wooden porch, and almost simultaneously, a frantic tapping at the door. Before she was able to release the latch, the tapping sounded again, and as Clara opened the door, Jessica burst in, circling about the room, singing jubilantly.

"I'm here, I'm here, I'm finally here!"

Clara hastily jumped to her side, clapping a warning hand over her mouth, and scolding in a whisper.

"Do you want to ruin everything with your big mouth? Mother's in the kitchen with Mrs. Quinlan, and if she ever even dreams that you're going out with us tonight, she'll skin us all alive." Dropping her hand she glared at Jessica in disgust, then silently motioned her to follow.

The cousins tiptoed up the stairs and down the long hall in time to see Molly add a final touch to her toilette, as she sat grandly before her vanity mirror. As the girls cautiously closed the bedroom door she turned and rested her freshly painted nails over her adequate hips, like someone who was about to take charge.

"So this is our little lady in love," she smirked, eyeing Jessica up and down. "Well I'd say we've got quite a job ahead of us this night if we're expected to transform her into some semblance of loveliness, wouldn't you agree, Clara?"

Now that their young cousin had entered into the full light of the brilliant room, her own natural beauty had caused their painted faces to appear almost grotesque. The prolonged excitement had gradually tinged her normally delicate cheeks with a very healthy and most becoming apricot glow that was considerably enhanced by the flashing fires and expectant twinkle in her already luminous dark brown eyes. The sisters looked at each other and nodded in unspoken agreement, determined now, more than ever, to see to it that this little trollop be privy to a well deserved lesson in humility. Driven by jealousy and the need to avenge themselves, they chose not to examine motives they considered vile and beneath them, focusing only on what was the obvious solution, and definitely in the best interests of their cousin.

Clara busied herself with Jessica's hair, piling it high in big puffy curls, as had been requested, but pulling it back severely in a manner she hoped would prove to be most unbecoming. Molly had generously laid out a light weight summer wrapper, with a neckline so revealing, even the sisters had not donned it till now, but as Jessica ecstatically pulled the garment down over her not fully matured body, it had only become enhanced by the promise of womanhood beneath it, docily falling into flattering folds, without even a suggestion of appearing licentious. The applied eye make up served to transfer her already thick lashes into lush black fans, that either fluttered against velvet soft peach cheeks or ostentatiously bordered wide slit, radiant orbs of luscious chocolate. By now the effulgent unruly hair had already begun to mutiny against its unfamiliar restrictions, returning to its usual framing of her flushed face with shimmering copper tendrils.

Molly and Clara stood scowling at Jessica with open resentment as she gratefully admired her refection in the vanity mirror.

"I do look quite grown up, don't I?" she asked, unable to relinquish the pleasurable sight of her own reflection. Then totally forgetting her cousins willing assistance, she stood enchanted by her own transformation. Abandoning all thoughts of gratitude, she pirouetted slowly, viewing her pleasing projected image from every possible angle.

"I almost can't believe my eyes," she breathed.

"Nor can I," answered Molly, her voice heavy with frustration. "But I do think we need just one more touch."

Whirling to her jewel case she quickly retrieved a pair of hideously dangling purple earrings and, with one motion, swung Jessica around, clamping one monstrosity on each ear.

Satisfied she was on the right road, she purred. “Now just one more thing and we’ll have it perfect.”

Reaching into the top drawer she found exactly what she was looking for and pressed a rouge of vibrant red to Jessica’s lips. The slash of color clashed violently with the girl’s natural hues, and the vivid, almost obscene shade of the earrings, hanging on her already too full lips like some grotesque gaping wound, totally obliterating the loveliness of her features.

Stepping back, Molly smiled wickedly. “Now I’d say that’s more like the effect we’ve been looking for. What do you think, Clara?”

A malicious light danced in Clara’s eyes as she automatically followed her older sister’s lead and agreed. “Yes, I’d say that’s exactly what we were looking for, and I can hardly wait till he sees her.”

The very thought of it forced her to giggle into her hand, but Molly’s stern glance quieted her immediately, and before Jessica could turn back to the mirror, the sisters, one at each arm, propelled her out of the room and down the stairs.

As the three girls neared the prearranged meeting place they could distinguish two men bending over a third person sitting on the curb with his head cupped in his hands. One of the men, glancing up, hurriedly walked toward them, and Molly immediately recognized him as Jim Bolen, her partner for the evening. Jim, talking rapidly, tried apologizing, while simultaneously denying all liability for Michael’s obvious insobriety, for it had become quite apparent, but to only two of them, that the man perched on the gutter was considerably in his cups.

Jim, ending his swift speech, pointedly reminded Molly that he had not faltered in the difficult fulfillment of his end of their bargain. He had gotten Michael here, as agreed, and did not expect to be held responsible for his condition. Resting his eyes temporarily on the slatternly looking woman standing only a few feet away, he was almost tempted to add that Michael’s present state might actually be a genuine advantage, but promptly rejected any negative comment that well might incite Molly to anger and jeopardize his long overdue evening.

As the girls reached the curb, Michael warily raised his already aching head, and with bleary, blood shot eyes, managed to smile negligently in their general direction. A resolute Jim Bolen mumbled his way through the embarrassing, but necessary introductions as Michael, reluctantly rising on wobbly legs, clasped Clara's conveniently close arm in error, and whispered some garbled pleasantry in her shocked ear. Stunned and confused the poor girl could only wonder at her sister's spontaneous reaction as Molly immediately stepped forward to forcibly remove Michael's tenacious grip from her arm and vehemently turn him around to face Jessica, stating simply,

"This, Mr. McClellan, is your partner for the evening."

Molly, puffing slightly from this unexpected need for exertion, placed a protective arm around her sister as she cast a critical eye in Jim's direction, silently reprimanding his lack of support, then settled down to enjoy the evidential rebuffing of her over inflated cousin that she assumed was imminent.

Michael stared for only a moment as he tried to focus clearly on the young lady Molly had indicated was to be his companion for the night. The arc light's unflattering glow greatly magnified the hideous slash of color predominating her entire face, and the long shadows cast by the unseemly ear decorations only served to increase their ugliness. A half smile played about the corners of his mouth as he recalled the lads devoted fervor as they struggled to entice him to leave the pub with a guarantee of a wonderfully entertaining night and the company of one of the town's most promising young beauties. Rapt in their vivid description of the womanly pulchritude he could expect, and caught up in their boundless enthusiasm, he had finally succumbed, agreeing to accompany them to wherever it was they were going, only to discover he had been put upon by these two wily chaps, and actually used to further their own prospects for the evening. His eyes unwillingly fastened on one of the unsightly earrings, and he cringed inwardly. Surely the pub he had been tempted into leaving held out better and more respectable opportunities than this. Realizing all eyes were upon him, and expecting some type of protestation, he decided upon another course, and smiled broadly. The young men had had their fun at his expense, and he could not deny it, but he was not about to let them wallow in the joy of having bested him, he would enjoy the evening in spite of them. With a reassuring pat to his pocket flask, he bowed mockingly in front of Jessica, and in an exaggerated, gentlemanly tone, pronounced two words.

"My lady."

Having forgotten to remove his cap, it immediately tumbled from his head, rolling across the cobbles to rest at his fair maiden's feet. Pretending to grope around on the darkened street, he allowed his flailing hand to stroke her ankle and move indelicately up her leg before retrieving the wayward headpiece. As his eyes once again reached the level of hers he winked knowingly, carelessly tossing one massive arm around her diminutive shoulders. Leaning heavily upon her, and without another word, he dragged his unsuspecting accomplice in the direction of Raspberry Hill.

The Benfield sisters had remained speechless, almost spellbound by this unimagined turn of events. Their intention had been for Jessica to be snubbed in a manner that might lessen her self esteem, and most definitely diminish her desire for a spot on their prestigious porch. They turned to look at each other in muddled confusion. Molly hurriedly excused herself to scamper after the receding figures. Teaching her a lesson was one thing, but allowing her to run off alone with an obviously drunken man was certainly not the answer to the proper schooling in humility, besides, an indiscretion of this magnitude would never be condoned or even tolerated by her mother. Visibly winded by the time she caught up with the fleeing couple, her words came out in short spasmodic spurts.

"Jessica,--please,---I-must talk to you for a minute." Seeing her cousin's hesitation, she insisted. "Come dear,--it will only take a moment."

"Make it just a moment then answered Michael as he plopped unto the grass. "I could not bear to be denied her beauty for very much longer than that." Then leaning back on both elbows, he laughed derisively, and began whistling the currently popular ditty, "Ain't She Sweet?"

Molly, beset by a multitude of conflicting emotions, threw Michael a look of extreme distaste and began addressing Jessica sternly.

"I really don't think you should go with him, Jess. For one thing it's not fitting and proper for a girl your age to run off alone---"

Fear and disappointment took hold of Jessica as Molly's voice droned on, numerically listing one reason after the other why she should reconsider the continuance of this evening with Michael McClellan. An indiscernible line of determination settled slowly over her lipstick laden mouth, as she vowed not be stayed by Molly or anyone else now that her long awaited for dream was about to be realized. Everything was happening precisely as they had planned and now Molly was about to spoil everything with her whining objections to a tryst she, herself, had implemented. What in the world was wrong with her anyway! Taking a deep breath she opened her mouth to interrupt, but was interrupted herself by the expedient arrival of Jim Bolen.

"Molly, dear," said Jim, "the night will soon enough be over, and we'll not have spent any of it together. Surely your friend here doesn't object to being alone, and speaking for myself, I'd relish it." Leaning closer to her ear and lowering his voice, he spoke confidentially.

"I've something important to converse with you and I thought tonight just might be the right time to do it." His small giggle was very tight and caused him to clear his throat nervously.

Molly's heart convulsed, wildly thudding against the becoming silk paisley shirt she had saved especially for this evening. Struggling to glean the true intent behind these words, she bestowed her most winsome smile on young Jim, almost convinced that his excited, moist eyes and agitated tongue, flicking repeatedly over his dry lips, could only be indicative of one thing, an impending proposal of marriage. There was just no other explanation for any man's being as jumpy as poor Jim appeared to be at this moment, she decided with delight. Molly was well past twenty, and although she would never admit to it, had given considerable thought to that fact. She had had her fair share of attentions from many of the young lads, but even the slightest hint at matrimony had sent them scuttling back to their mamas, who were happy enough to have them for the much needed additional income. When a young couple did marry these days, they were expected to abide with the in-law whose situation was considered the most dire. This arrangement proved to be reciprocally beneficial for the first few years of the youngster's marriage, and seldom presented any major problems because of an uncomplicated and practical view of life, and the acceptance of its many injustices that was shared in general.

Jim's father was still alive, working the mines beside his three sons, and making Jim a perfect catch for Molly who could remain in her own home to look after her widowed mother and steadfastly dedicate all her efforts to the difficult task of marrying off Clara. Vaguely she wondered if her sister would resent having to relinquish the sharing of their beautiful large bedroom, and immediately shrugged off the thought, focusing on the present dilemma of having to choose between attending Jim Bolen's pleadings, and it's possible outcome, or extricating Jessica from any further involvement with Michael McClellan, and its probable outcome.

The now benevolent street lamp spewed a shower of golden radiance on the normally lusterless crown of curls perching precariously near her eyebrows. Snuggling against Jim's shoulder she whispered huskily.

"Please, just give me another minute, Jim. Believe me; I'm as anxious for us to be alone as you are."

The young man, engulfed in an urgent inane desire to loosen that precious, shimmering mass of tresses, could only rewet his lips, and answer.

"Please hurry,"

Pulling Jessica aside she felt no compunction about dispelling her responsibility.

"Look, Jessica," she whispered, "All you have to do is allow a few kisses and a pat here and a pat there. Do you know what I mean? Just learn how to play the game, because the men all love it, but whatever happens, don't go all the way. Do you understand what I'm telling you?"

Jessica, stupefied by this conversation, could only answer with a question. "Have you ever gone all the way, Molly?"

For a fleeting moment Jessica thought Molly might strike her, but ever mindful of Jim's presence, Molly quickly regained her composure, merely answering in a whisper of obvious irritation.

"Of course not! What a total ninny you are."

Her face, covered with a mask of sheer disgust, magically transformed itself into the perfect picture of sweetness as she turned around to again face Jim, then slipping her arm through his; she strode off down the hill without another thought to her cousin, or the consequences of her decision. Not unlike Jessica, she too, had waited a very long time for a moment like this, and would not be denied. Still mulling over her cousin's words, Jessica stood marveling at the bobbing locks as they left the circle of light and promptly returned to their typically faded lemon hue.

"I'm going up to the top, are ya with me or not?" called Michael as he started up the hill without waiting for her reply.

It had taken but a second for her to reach a decision, and she began running to catch up. This side of the hill was completely unmarred by refuse from the mines, and held the only truly green spot in all of Miner's

Haven. It also held the town's cemetery, which seemed only fitting. Those who had suffered from the dust of coal throughout their entire lives should unquestionably be granted their freedom from it in death.

When Jessica at last reached the top of the hill, she found Michael already seated under its largest tree, his coat, gallantly spread out on the grass, lay ready for her arrival. Just wait until Molly hears about this, she thought, elated over her decision to follow him. He is truly my own knight, gentlemanly, and even more handsome out of his dingy every day miner's clothes. Wanting to appear as ladylike as possible, she gracefully seated herself beside him and watched, her eyes suffused with love, as he removed the top of the flask and helped himself to a long pull. Then pushing the bottle in her direction, he belched softly, and wiped his mouth with the back of his other hand. Wondering what Molly would have to say about this, she resolved the question by deciding not to tell her. After all, it was clearly an occasion to be celebrated; she told herself, pressing the bottle between her painted lips, and allowing the fiery liquid to fill her mouth. An unexpected burning crammed her throat, surged; to her stomach with the searing heat of a branding iron and simultaneously paralyzed her knees.

While she sat pondering the question of why anyone would choose to willingly burn their innards to this degree, Michael bent over and kissed her still damp lips.

Blushing in the darkness, she felt her body heat accelerate under the pressure of his mouth and pulled away from him that she might fan herself with the corner of his jacket.

"Our very first kiss," she breathed, "And in a beautiful spot like this." Pointing eagerly, she indicated the tiny valley below. "Just look at it, Michael. You can see in all directions from here, and from this night on it will always be our own secret and special place to remember." The jacket fluttered back and forth like a banner of conquest, forcing

Michael to moan, inwardly. Why was it women always had to have a commitment or insist on some sort of silly sentiment before they could make love? He had to surmise that any small token of tenderness somehow insured them that their virtue remained, at least partially, intact, and thus became man's eternal cross to bear. Only the town women remained consistent by demanding only money, and he felt Jessica had grossly over stepped her bounds, but answered with all the sincerity he could muster.

"Ah, yes my love, it belongs to us. But now what about what is supposed to belong to me?"

He kissed her with a savage demand that was surprising, but she gloried in the meshing of their mouths, despite his increasing ardor. Having envisioned this scene a myriad of times, its actuality and final consummation had already exceeded her most outlandish imaginings. Returning his kisses with ever increasing emotion, her eyes widened in surprise as she felt his strong hand tentatively exploring her tiny breast. Wondering if this was the pat here and the pat there Molly had tried to warn her about, before rushing off in the opposite direction with Jim Bolen, she suddenly realized Michael's curious fingers had invaded her blouse, and were deftly kneading her hardening nipple. Astutely judging this to be far more than should be expected from her, she tried releasing herself, and struggled against him as he buried his face in her partly exposed bosom, and groaned with the delight, of devouring her.

Although he considered her protestations feigned, he was, none the less, delighted by this diverse, provocative behavior, and found himself stimulated to greater heights by her every act of resistance. In her desperate desire not to displease him, Jessica had merely tugged at her bodice, gently pushing his hand away in the hope he would soon tire of this patting business and return to being the gentleman she had so admired at the outset of the evening. Instead, finally wearying of this contest, he pushed her to the ground, leaned over her menacingly, and growled.

"Are you and I supposed to be playing some kind of game, my lady?"

This abrupt change in his demeanor frightened the young girl, and yet she groped frantically for some intelligent reply that would not again relegate her to country bumpkin status. Resolute in her determination to make a lasting impression, at any cost, she gratefully remembered Molly's words, and weakly repeated them.

"Yes, I just want to play the game."

Momentarily taken back by this strumpet's unceasing audacity, his patience at last gave way to angry persistence. "Well the game and you both be damned," he snarled, as he re-covered her scarlet lips with his, and with one sweeping motion of his massive hand, brutally brushed aside her protective clothing, penetrating her deeply.

A piercing pain welled up inside her, causing her to moan against his open mouth, and violently raise her body in a futile effort to escape it. Michael, mistaking these acts assigns of extreme passion, spent himself in only a moment, liberating her lips and relaxing atop her tense body. Gradually his breathing became more even and just when she thought she could no longer tolerate his weight, he rolled over unto his back, appearing to fall asleep instantly.

Jessica's shaking hand timidly slipped between her legs in puzzled wonder. Modesty dictated the immediate rearrangement of her undergarments, and prudence demanded the striving for control of her confused thoughts and rampant emotions. Lying quietly beside him on the damp grass, she attempted to sort out the reason for this unforeseen behavior, and the pain and disappointment it had inflicted upon her. Basic animal instinct had held out a more enjoyable prospect than the dismal agony and bitter distress she now suffered. If only Cousin Molly could see me now, she thought. I guess this must have been what she meant by going all the way, because there certainly can't be any further to go than that. Extreme youth allowed her to regard these musings with bold humor, and she smiled up at the starlit sky with undaunted juvenile satisfaction.

Stealing a sidelong glance at Michael, she noticed that he lay pathetically awry, his pants and underwear hanging indiscriminately about his knees in a most unkempt fashion. Never having seen a man's body before, the unexpected sight of it fascinated her. Gingerly raising herself into a sitting position, she bent slightly forward, as it was difficult to see clearly in the dim light under the tree.

Jumping back in dismay she heard Michael question drolly.

"If it's a repeat performance you're after, lass, I'm not quite sure I can promise much of anything. It's been a long night with many, too many cups, but then I'd never want it to be said that Michael McClellan doesn't aim to please his ladies."

Sighing, he placed on arm around her small waist, dragging her slowly down to him. This, time his mouth was tame and teasing, lingering, on her fearful cheek adoringly, his patient tongue languidly running across her bared shoulder, gliding very gradually down her velvet throat. By the time his searching lips had reached her breasts, her body had come alive with an uncontrolled fire that soon rekindled his own. His great hands were now everywhere, ecstatically probing and poking into every inch of her body, as she squirmed beneath them with deliciously growing urgency. This time as he entered her she stifled a moan of exquisite pleasure against his shoulder, and giving herself up completely, allowed the night to explode about her, bursting into indescribable pangs of pleasure, and exhilarating her to the ultimate joy known only to a woman in love.

They came down the hill together, Michael quiet and exhausted, sullenly allowed his damp coat to drag along in the grass behind him, as though its sodden weight presented more of a burden than he could bear. While she, blinded by her own exultance, babbled incessantly about future plans, as totally unaware of his silent sulkiness, as she was that her ramblings clacked hopelessly against ears that had made themselves impervious to the sound, of her voice. Confiding to him how very important Isaac was in her life, she described her father minutely, detailing all of features and faults, expounding at great length about his surface gruffness, and the many reasons for it. It was imperative that Michael understood him, for after all, it was only reasonable to assume that the two men would now be spending much of their time together, and she was trying to insure their compatibility.

Alive with the treacherous joy of believing their love to be mutual, she literally danced back into town, spinning about every now and again with the spontaneity of a small child, enthusiastically advancing every new thought as it entered her mind, never once waiting for, or needing his response.

As they again reached the circle of light at the corner, Michael stopped abruptly muttering something about the very long distance he had yet to go, and putting his hand politely to his cap, walked off rapidly in the opposite direction without another word. Having anticipated some elongated and rapturous type of farewell, embellished with words of endearment and pledges of fidelity, she could only stare after him dumfounded, stunned by his failure to insist on a time for their next meeting, and his obvious unconcern about seeing her home. Paramount in her list of disappointments was his indelicate omission of even the smallest, but traditional, good night kiss. Watching him disappear into the darkness, she could only console herself with the knowledge that nothing in this life is ever perfect. Besides, maybe Molly had warned him about being seen by Aunt Annie, and so he had merely adhered to her wishes, and after all, hadn't he told her himself how very tired he was? She conceded contentedly that he had every right to be.

Appeased by the probability of this rationale, she started home, humming cheerily to herself until she reached the steps of the infamous porch. Quietly entering on tiptoe, she stealthily made her way up the stairwell and down the long hall to her cousin's room. Undressing hurriedly in the dark, she was surprised to discover that neither Molly nor Clara had reached home before her. A glance at the porcelain clock on the vanity told her a mere two hours had passed since she had left this very room. But what a glorious two hours it had been, she thought, snuggling on the tiny cot in the far corner of the room. Her entire life would be different now, she told herself. Naively she construed the word love as meaning the beginning of all things bright and beautiful. Not too far into her future she would look upon it as an inescapable bane, whose poisonous arrows of jealousy and distrust had made all things bleak and desolate.

Running one hand along her still tingling body, she, unknowingly, gloried in the emotions of a woman's fulfillment.

"Michael, Michael," she whispered to the empty room, allowing the very sound of his name to excite her, satiating her with a renewed longing to be with him again. This time, happily, the meeting would not have to be contrived, for Michael, like she, would be anxiously looking forward to their next encounter. Being an innocent she felt no shame or remorse for having followed the dictates of her body, but a nagging instinctive concern warned her she should not confide this night's happenings to either of her cousins.

Her relaxed body had barely begun drifting into a state of limbo when a sudden thought thrust itself into her almost unconscious mind with brilliant clarity, and she smiled. At last she knew more than Cousin Molly.

CHAPTER THREE

As the garden's grass and flowers wilted under a relentless summer sun, so Jessica's hopes withered under Michael's complete indifference. Not once since their night on the hill had he passed by the house, nor had he gone to Dougal's on Saturday evenings.

At first she thought him ill or perhaps injured, but cautious inquiries soon dispelled both of those ideas. She had spent the first few weeks gradually eliminating every possible reason why he had not attempted to see her again, eventually concluding he had not wanted to.

She tried vainly to recall any action of hers he may have found objectionable, perhaps a word which had offended him. No, he had seemed very pleased, indeed, with both himself and her. She did remember his ill manners by not seeing her to her door like any true gentleman should, but he had complained of being tired, and no wonder. She giggled aloud, and the sound brought her back to reality. This was certainly not a matter to be laughed at. Soon her condition would become apparent to Isaac and she would have to confess her lover had deserted her after only one evening's entertainment.

She groaned inwardly with humiliation and self pity, cursing herself for a fool. If only she had taken Cousin Molly's advice and been satisfied with a pat here and a pat there. Her superior education was becoming quite a burden.

She lay on her bed, listless from the heat of the day, while fantasies of Michael with another woman played against her closed eyelids. Perspiration appeared above her lips and her body tensed simultaneously with hate and longing. Slowly she rolled on her side. A bitter smile curled her lips as an all too familiar flood of nausea assailed her. As usual she had known half a situation, how to recognize a pregnancy, but nothing about how to prevent one.

Not one thing in her life had ever been complete. She had known only half a family, was given half an education and was now involved in half a love affair. Her half, silently screaming for one who was oblivious to her. Perhaps if Mama were with her things might have been different. Most certainly her mother would have imparted some wisdom that would have prevented her folly. Perhaps, like Mama I will die giving birth, she thought. Perhaps it was foolish to wait. Slowly she raised herself on the edge of the bed. Thoughts of escape through death scurried into her mind and were immediately rejected. How often she had heard the saying, "The coward's way out," she shuddered to herself. "God" she thought, "How much courage it would take to cease to be. To never breathe, nor hear, nor speak another word." She was not prepared to explore the ambiguity of eternity.

She eased her body over unto her back praying the movement would not resurrect the waves of nausea that seemed to assail her every change of position. The moment she relaxed Michael's handsome features began focusing in her mind's eye with a clarity that made her tingle with the feel of his nearness. Once again the sweet odor of his pompade covered hair filled her nostrils as his tongue gently teased her swollen breast. Her mouth pursed with the remembrance of his acrid liquor laden kisses and her ever eager responses to them. Her lips parted ardently as the weight of his strong body pressed against her, making her reach out to draw him even closer, to hold him forever next to her heart. Two short blasts from the colliery whistle promptly dissolved her reverie propelling her abruptly back to reality. She heaved a heavy sigh, not only for the loss of her luscious abstraction but because she knew the two short blasts was the forecast for yet another rise in temperatures. This damnable debilitating heat had already sapped all of her energy, leaving nothing but weakness and exhaustion. Raising up on one arm her gaze fell upon the tilted full length mirror. Her usually bouncy ringlets had turned to sodden masses pressed flat about her ears and forehead. Small daubs of brown appeared painted beneath her sunken lifeless eyes. Thanks be my love cannot see me now, she thought. He most certainly would not recognize the beauty of Raspberry Hill. Innocently, she wanted always for him to remember the way she looked that night.

Their night. A night she found herself living over and over. A convulsive yearning left her trembling with desire. A desire that was soon to be dispelled by a more pressing exigency. Anxiously groping for the chamber pot beneath the bed, she wretched miserably as quantities of distasteful bile pervaded her mouth, dripping in disgusting strings unto her night gown. Silently she screamed his name again and again until the horror of the moment subsided, only to be replaced by the old horror of her loneliness and abandonment.

Sprawling across the bed she tried to control the rapid, rasp-like pants of her breathing. The damp gown now clung to her body like a piece of extra sagging skin. With revulsion she whisked it off, flinging it as far away as her diminishing strength would allow. Slowly she examined her still beautiful ivory colored body, touching her stomach with trepidation and wonder.

The sensation of her touch immediately transferred her thoughts to Michael, and she wondered if he could possibly be thinking of her this very minute, perhaps as tortured as she, afraid to approach her again, knowing it was his insistence that had led to their indiscretion. Rationality dictated he had to be experiencing the same wondrous recollections of their shared intimacy.

She scowled for a brief second, taking time to label whatever were the reasons for his continued silence as unfathomable. Youth, springing to her rescue, allowed her to remain undaunted in the belief that love eventually vanquishes all things, vindicating the Pope's contention that hope springs eternal in the human breast.

Jessica's one regret was Isaac Hobbs. There had never been secrets between them, but then nothing of consequence had ever occurred before. Their relationship had been built around the comforts each provided the other. He, the bestower of love and security, she the companion, and pride of his life. She was about to strip him of the latter gift.

She began pacing about the room, frantic with indecision. If only she could contrive some manner of allowing her father to come to the realization of her situation without her having to speak. Then suddenly she plopped back down on the bed. The answer was so simple she couldn't imagine why she hadn't thought of it before. She would go to her cousin's house again, but this time to see Aunt Annie.

Isaac Hobbs was an extraordinary looking man. His hair and beard, white as driven snow, curled softly about his face and head, while his ice blue eyes peered from beneath shaggy brows, fierce as an eagle's. He seemed constantly to shift his pipe from hand to mouth, and though its presence pleased him, it remained unlit. He always wore faded red suspenders and pin stripe shirts whose vertical lines elongated his already tall, sparse frame.

He had had a wonderfully happy childhood, a roguish youth and, as befitted an only child, never thought of marriage until both his parents had gone to their great reward. Isaac and his bride had reached their middle years when the advent of Jessica's arrival Presented itself, and they prepared for it with wonder and eagerness. Their union had been short but ecstatic, a time Isaac always remembered with love and tender passion. Their temperaments were so perfectly suited, they had been able to anticipate and comply with each other's wishes without utterance, and this very compliance had always been the sole satisfaction of their life together. Each was a reflection of the other's happiness.

Jessica's arrival and his wife's demise caused Isaac to put away his miner's clothes forever. The using of his, up to now, well guarded inheritance, would insure them both a comfortable future, and his decision to direct his full attention to this new found responsibility had never once been regretted in all these years.

Now as he sat sternly at the kitchen table, his icy glaze fixed upon an ant, painstakingly trying to pull a crumb through a hole in the, wainscoting on the wall. The insect's arduous labor and continued patience fascinated him, and his stare intensified on the spot, directly above his sister-in-law's head.

Annie's voice droned about his ears like the disquieting hum of hornets about a hive. She had begun her tale calmly, with a softly modulated voice, but Isaac's cold, glaring eyes, which seemed to penetrate her very soul, along with the sordid details of her account, had caused her to become extremely agitated. Her voice had become almost shrill, while her trembling fingers constantly smoothed the oily hair drawn carelessly over her ears. Her timorous eyes darted helplessly from father to daughter, her face flushing with excitement, as she rambled through her well rehearsed recitation, longing only for its end, and her release from this miserable scene.

The ant suddenly disappeared through the crack and Isaac forcibly relinquished the spot and directed his gaze to his nieces, Molly and Clara. The girls flanked their mother at the table. Mascara rivulets etched crevices on their highly powered cheeks, while their crumbled kerchiefs dabbed with clock like precision about their swollen, colorless eyes. They looked from their mother to Isaac with imploring expressions in an apparent effort to gain sympathy for their good intentions and betrayed trust.

"God," thought Isaac to himself, "If what Annie's saying related to one of these strumpets, I would not feel a moments surprise, but Jessica---" His head automatically turned to the corner of the room where his daughter sat with downcast eyes, the luster of her hair forming a burnished mantle about the bowed head and sagging shoulders, the consummate picture of forlorn beauty and innocence.

Isaac was forced to turn his attentions back to Annie as she restlessly continued, "And you know, Isaac, that poor Molly's been spoken for and plans to wed Jim Bolen the first Saturday in September." Both hands now pressed against the greasy head in futile consolation. "How can we face this scandal, which I'm sure will affect the marriage plans? I can't bear to see Molly's opportunity forfeited because of Jessica's indiscretions." Looking to her daughter for support, she found it as the girl, emitting a long sigh, soundly blew her nose.

"It just isn't fair, Isaac. We've done nothing except try to help you raise her, and now our thanks will end up being having to share the shame she's inflicted on the whole family."

Still holding her head, she rocked back and forth. "You must do something, Isaac. Isaac, do you hear me, are you listening, Isaac?" Her voice had reached an almost hysterical crescendo as her flailing hands finally clapped together to gain his attention.

Rising wearily from his chair, he appeared taller than ever as he loomed ominously over the three women, still seated at the table. Looking first at one and then the other, he spoke in a low, but firm voice. "Go home women, and take care of your own house, and I will take care of mine."

The women, glancing uncertainly at each other, tried to decide whether or not to further their plea, when, unexpectedly Isaac, leaning both hands on the table, almost shouted into their faces.

"Go home I tell you! Go home!" His shaggy brows had drawn together over eyes of glinting steel, encouraging the women to spring from their chairs and into the garden.

Stopping just outside the door, they caught their breath, and stood shaking their heads in shock and disapproval of Isaac's demeanor. After all, they were the offended, not the offender. His daughter's sluttish behavior would reflect on them, the ones who had done nothing but try to help, and had tried to help for the better part of her life. Hadn't he always sent her begging for every scrap of information that had really been his duty as a father to impart? He had forever shifted his unsavory parental duties onto his sister-in-laws family, but such were the ways of a thankless relative. They had received rebukes rather than the gratitude that was most certainly their due. From now on it would be exactly the way he wanted it. He would have to take care of his own house. Smugly they left the garden, happy with the knowledge there would never be another encounter with Isaac Hobbs. He was a man without reason.

Isaac walked the short distance across the kitchen to his daughter, his heart bursting with pain, his long legs heavy with the weariness of grief. Looking down on the only reason or meaning to his life, he asked uncertainly. "I need to know if what was said be the truth, child?"

Jessica raised her eyes to meet her father's as tears of shame rained unabounded, hampering her reply. "The only truth that wasn't told, Papa, was that I love him. I love him very much." She continued to look into his face, hoping to find just one glimmer of understanding perhaps a spark of forgiveness, but the blue eyes remained emotionless, and as cold as steel.

Abruptly and with one spasmodic motion, he struck the pleading face with a force that pummeled her off the spindle backed kitchen chair and unto the floor. Without another word he left the room, his pipe held tightly between clenched teeth.

Jessica, unable to move, more from shock than actual inflicted injury, crawled into a small corner and huddled there, stroking her blazing cheek, whimpering like a chastised puppy.

Jessica sat on the porch swing listening as the whistle announced another day's end at the colliery. Soon she would enter the kitchen to prepare supper and Isaac, as though compelled by silent agreement between them, would move immediately to another part of the house.

They had willingly avoided each other since Aunt Annie's visit, both filled with shame, and regarding their separate destructive acts as irreconcilable. The uncontrolled striking of his most precious treasure had immeasurably oppressed him, while she, fearful of additional reprisals, or even worse, the advent of recriminating conversation, had remained uncommunicative, spending endless hours in her bedroom to escape any possible summons. Gradually this solitary chamber had become her sanctuary, and his punishment. Trust, an important link in the chain of their love, lie broken in a chasm of doubt which widened with the passing of every silent day. Their unfamiliar roles as adversaries weighed heavily on their consciences, but neither father nor daughter was able to cross the incredulous breach between them. Finally, prodded by the shackles of indecision, and the whip of desperation, Isaac scrawled an almost demanding note to Michael, requesting him to call Sunday afternoon, then secretly began to plan his strategy.

Michael leaned against the breaker re-reading Isaac's note. He had just left the mine shaft elevator, and his eyes squinted together in an effort to keep out the still bright light of the afternoon. Tom Quinlan had approached him just as the lunch whistle blew, rudely thrusting an envelope into his blackened hand, muttering,

"I've got a message for ya, Mick."

Tom's eyes stood out in his dirty face, distended with hatred and loathing. His lips stretched across his teeth, and for a moment Michael, with relief thought the boy was about to smile. Instead, the young mouth simultaneously emitted a whistling sound along with a large ball of spittle, which landed, with deadly accuracy, directly on the tip of Michael's boot.

Tom's eyes never left Michael's face as he stood ready for any eventuality, daring the older man with a stance of knotted fists and sneering lips. Michael's knuckles turned white as his grip tightened on the handle of his lunch pail. Realizing he was being deliberately goaded into another confrontation, an almost irresistible urge to oblige the young fellow flooded through him. The insolence was more than any man should have to bear, and especially the man whose ability to extinguish that sneer with but a single blow, was indisputable.

As Michael returned Tom's steadfast stare, his anger slowly ebbed and, surprisingly, he found himself experiencing a pang of pity for the arrogant young man whose crippled foot sank into the coal dust beside his own. He could not raise his hand against him, but instead allowed his gaze to fall to the desecrated spot. Then, resting his weight on his heel, he carefully examined the toe of his boot, and a broad smile covered his face, and his voice was filled with good humor when he spoke.

"Well I've no doubt that it," he pointed to the drying ball of saliva, "will surely make it shine. Thank you, lad, for both services."

Touching two fingers to his miner's cap and tucking the envelope into his breast pocket, he walked off to have lunch with his friends, leaving young Tom completely abashed, but filled with resolve. He now had two scores to settle.

Michael had avoided the Saturday night rituals at Dougal's since the initial episode with Tom. In no way did he want to involve him-self in a situation that would affect his popularity with the men, for he had sensed an uneasy strain in their comradery since that evening. He had been offered a representative position with the union if he could rally the, men to new loyalty, which was not an easy task. The strikes had been many and long, each time promising magnanimous rewards, which seldom materialized. It had taken the UMW from 1893 to the First World War to gain their goal of industrial democracy. This was accomplished only through wise leadership, a banding together for strength, and a public that was finally sympathetic to the labor movement.

In September of 1900, John Mitchell, then president of the UMW, had ordered a general strike, demanding union recognition, wage increases, labor and management arbitrating committees, along with the right to employ check weighman. This would mean every miner would be assured of the proper credit for his own coal production. The walk out was called for only after the anthracite operators had totally ignored Mr. Mitchell's invitation to attend a convention designed to amicably discuss and adjust the many and varied grievances.

In a spectacular show of collaboration, 150,000 men heeded the call, forcing the companies to comply by the posting of notices offering a wage increase of 10%, Mr. Mitchell's original demand. By October Mitchell called off the strike, gaining only a few concessions and waiving his demand for recognition. Although the union gains were small, they had at last succeeded in organizing the hard coal industry as men clamored to join their ranks, swelling the union's membership beyond even their own anticipation. A decided victory for labor.

In May of 1902, Mitchell again pressed for a wage increase, along with a 20% reduction in hours of labor, not to affect the earning of employees paid by the hour, day or week. As always the union vied for the incorporation of an agreement between themselves and the operators on conditions of employment, wages and the adjustment of grievances, which would have greatly reduced the continual work stop-ages. As always the operators refused to discuss rate increases, and once again Mitchell called a strike, with once again public sentiment and solidarity behind him. But as the idleness dragged through the summer and into fall, public fears of a coal famine and soaring prices tended to somewhat dampen their stalwart support of the miners, and by October President Teddy Roosevelt summoned both Mitchell and the operators to a White House conference.

John Mitchell, in his wisdom as a leader, was willing to submit his beloved UMW to third party arbitration. The operators however, labeling the union a lawless body, vowed not to arbitrate under any circumstances, with what they considered to be a band of criminals. Unfortunately bitterness through the long strike had manifested violence and the destruction of company property. The usual vanguard of pumpmen, firemen, and all those necessary to protect the mines from damage were called away from their posts for the very first time during a strike, and the National Guard had been summoned by the Governor to preserve order and control chaos.

The President, in his notoriously flamboyant manner, then threatened to send in 10,000 troops, seize the mines, and operate them for the government, a desperate move, which drove the reluctant operators to the arbitration table.

This act on the part of government set a precedent. The Anthracite Coal Commission, appointed by President Roosevelt, would set the stage for all future agreements governing labor relations in the coal mining industry. For the first time, industrial disputes were being decided on merit, and not by the dictum that management was forever infallible. Despite this victory, it took until 1916 and a bevy of joint sessions or work suspensions for the operators to finally recognize the UMW.

When the war ended and the lads returned from serving the colors, everyone feared a lack of work would result, but prosperity continued as the demand for coal seemed ever increasing. The men found themselves working less hours a day and collecting higher wages than ever heard of in the history of Miners' Haven. By 1920 the United Mine Workers Union had advanced its demands to cover time and half for over time and double time for Sundays and holidays.

A new bank had been erected on Main Street just prior to the great conflict, and already many of the families had opened modest accounts, a feat impossible to attain until now. A second movie house had also made its appearance, and men and women alike thrilled to the talents of Dorothy Dalton as the "Home breaker", and the antics of Mickey Normand in "Ss Hopkins". The local paper advertised a Chandler roadster a man could buy for only $1,895, and real silk shirts were featured at the downtown Emporium for only $7.95. Its pages also lauded the success of Prohibition in obstructing the flow of alcoholic beverages, while it sounded warnings regarding the overflow of oil in the fields of Texas. The industrial production of the nation was rising to new peaks, and though the miner remained, as always, at the bottom of the financially rewarded heap, his fortunes had vastly improved. Life was good and contentment filled men's hearts, while a full larder filled their bellies.

Michael, like most of the young men, felt there were still better things in store for all of them. The town needed its own hospital accommodations. The fifteen mile distance to the State Hospital was too far to allow for the proper care of injured men requiring immediate attention. The loss of life and limb would be stemmed immeasurably with the advent of adequate facilities. Moreover the men needed medical plans in order not to deplete their life savings when disaster did strike, and pensions to insure a carefree retirement, independent from the charity of relatives.

Like all noble thoughts, they were easier to conjure up than they were to fashion into reality. The old timers were happy with their lot, and the grumblings of the younger men irritated them. Young folk were all alike, lazy, and always looking for a handout, without too much expenditure on their part. The old men knew what it was to work sixty hours a week with only a pick and black powder, to drive the mules, hitched in tandem, sometimes pulling as many as twenty-five carts at the same time. The drivers spent their underground life with these poor beasts, teaching them to chew plug tobacco and enjoy a beer for lunch. Pampering them with chocolate candy and sugar lumps, administering horse liniment rubdowns to both themselves and their charges. They reasoned that what was good for mule was good for man, as they both shared the pain, aches, injuries, and ever present fear of death.

The old timers considered this generation soft and demanding, allowing themselves to be influenced by the despotism of the union, when they had already attained more than their fathers and grandfathers before them. Tempers ran high and many a family stood divided by their unwillingness to reflect on the other's view. What had been good enough for the fathers and, now, not good enough for the sons, was a sentiment scoffed at by one faction and sworn to by the other. The children, fulfilling the legacy passed down from the Garden of Eden, found their parents old fashioned and unable to recognize their needs. The parents, likewise, found their children ungrateful and almost beyond their comprehension.

It was into this arena Michael had chosen to enter, dedicated to pleasing both generations, striving for better working conditions and an improved quality of living, without biting the hand that feeds. The company had become slightly more generous as their profits mounted, and Michael only wished to pressure as long as everyone benefited. Already he had been paramount in reaching a tentative agreement regarding a local hospital. Whatever the miners, both union and nonunion donated, would be matched, in kind, by the company, construction to begin on a lot obtained through the generosity of the bank's president. Most of the men were in favor of the proposed plan, and even some of the retired miners had expressed a desire to make a contribution, knowing full well it was the only possible deterrent to the flow of fatalities. To this date every one million tons of produced anthracite had been paid for with the lives of five miners.

Michael reread the note as he neared Isaac's house. He had heard it whispered that Mr. Hobbs had retired at an early age, being a man of considerable wealth. He was cheered by the thought that he was about to receive an extensive donation, once again ingratiating himself to both the men and the union.

Isaac pushed open the huge sliding doors and motioned Michael inside the parlor usually reserved for Sundays, holidays and special occasions. The odor of moth crystals, stealing from beneath the mohair cushions, drifted about the musty room, which felt damp despite the summer heat. Michael, appreciating the grandeur of the delicate lace curtains and heavily fringed velvet drapes, eyed the small inlaid top tables, laden with exquisite porcelain and China figurines. The collection, which had belonged to Isaac's mother, sat protected behind each table's petite filigree railing, and had been, next to Jessica, Isaac's most prized possession. In one corner stood a highly ornate treadle organ, and just above it, in a scrolled gilt frame, hung the portrait of a breathtakingly beautiful woman, with copper colored hair and a complexion to match the freshness of dawn. A faint spark of recognition stirred in Michael as the enchanting lady in the painting stared back at him.

"Jessica's mother," said Isaac softly. "Quite a resemblance, wouldn't you say?" The blue eyes seemed to grow more intense as he smiled with nostalgia in the direction of the picture. Both men receded into their own thoughts momentarily, Isaac, recalling some treasured memory from yesterday, and Michael, trying desperately to sort out his muddled memories surrounding the girl named Jessica.

His Saturday nights had become an endless succession of bawdiness and booze, with one face fading into the next. He had found a more compatible bar in his own end of town where he was never judged by another man's religious convictions, and the women were interested only in his pleasure and their purse. The arrangement had suited him well enough for him to decide to visit Dougal's only when it was prudent for him to do so, diplomatically dispensing a few free rounds in order to better emphasize the union's positions.

He glanced back at the portrait, his mind denying, despite the resemblance, that the girl he vaguely remembered as Jessica could, in any way, be related to the dignified lady whose soft brown eyes smiled into his from the life like portrait on the wall. If, indeed, the girl on Rasberry Hill were related to this woman, he had been much deeper into his cups than he cared to admit.

Isaac rocked dreamily back and forth, abstractedly pulling on his unlit pipe, as he reflected on the unalterable fate that had taken his wife, and brought he and his daughter to their present circumstances. He knew now that a father's love could not replace a mother, and the confidences shared between women was a thing apart, and perhaps to be envied. It could be the only possible reason his own daughter had opted to confide in that imbecilic Annie Benfield and her equally idiotic offspring, with never a thought to divulging to him the most important advent in her entire life. Somewhere, in the most distant part of his mind, a note of jealously sounded, and he dismissed it as an errant piano player dismisses an incongruous chord. His wondering mind was so weary and heavily laden with grief, that he had momentarily forgotten his guest, starting at the sight of Michael, stiff and uncomfortably seated opposite himself.

Struggling, he regained his composure, bringing himself back to the situation at hand. Dexterously shifting his pipe from one corner of his mouth to the other, Isaac calmly started to speak while he allowed a condemnatory expression to descend upon his features.

"I suppose you're well aware of the reason you've been invited to my home today," pausing, he leaned forward menacingly. Many a time lately I've wished myself a younger man, and our meeting not taking place in a sheltered parlor."

He watched in amazement as Michael smiled broadly, nodding his head in complete agreement. The old man's brows shot up in surprise as he stared blankly at the open mouth. This man is impossible, he thought. How could she have been so blind? He must be a total rake, without an honest intention in his entire body. My poor baby, used by this ruffian because I have never warned her against the powerful physical needs of men, and the binding duty of women to be repulsed by them. Clearing his throat exaggeratedly he forged ahead as fingers of fear constricted his voice.

"What are your thoughts in regard to marriage, Michael McClellan?"

The unexpected question reduced Michael's wide smile to a tight grin. Moving uneasily in his chair, he answered. "Well, I guess to avoid it as long as possible, Mr. Hobbs. Why do you ask?"

Ignoring the impertinent question, Isaac's voice rose angrily.

"But you have no qualms about seeking its comforts, as long as you can escape its responsibilities. Is that it, lad?" He focused his full attention on the young man now, straining to keep extraneous thoughts from his mind.

Michael's back stiffened as he sat upright and tense in the mohair chair. His recollection of Jessica was obviously quite correct and this man was trying to trap him because of his wayward daughter. He was not about to be taken in. It was clearly evident to him that this poor father was being hood-winked into thinking his daughter was the essence of innocence, when in fact, if his memory still served him well, she had possessed some expertise. Despite his sympathy for Isaac he was not about to become someone's benefactor over one night of folly. Accenting each word, he answered firmly.

"I do not seek, nor ever have. I only accept what is offered and assume it's been offered before, as any man might."

Isaac's brows lifted once again, a silver gleam filling the translucent blue eyes. God, he is going to deny her, he thought, and we are going to do battle over my beautiful Jessica, whom even the angels would look upon with desire. All I've heard of this man must be untrue. He is without honor, a scoundrel or worse. Grinding his pipe between his teeth, he almost spat the words at Michael.

"I've heard the Catholic dog jumps over the log to get a piece of meat on Friday, but why is it always a Protestant piece they're after?" His look defied the young man to answer as his brows knotted in repulsion.

Michael's black eyes smoldered. He was certain now of his position, and as much as he admired this man, he was not ready, out of admiration, to commit his life to Isaac's daughter.

A dog, whether Protestant or Catholic, accents any bone that's dangled before him like the lure on the end the fisherman's line.

Isaac, finally grasping Michael's innuendos jumped from his chair, "Bastard!" The rocker bobbed frantically to and fro, emitting a shrieking sound alien to the tranquility and beauty of the room. The old man's eyes were wild with disbelief, his face a mask of incredulity, as he repeated, "You are a bastard!"

Michael rose to his feet with slow deliberation. He felt sick at heart that a man such as this should be dragged to this depth of degradation by his wanton child, but he dared not let pity cloud his better judgment. The maelstroms and pitfalls of everyday living were numerous enough, without the need to deal with the quick sands of marriage. Looking directly into Isaac's eyes, he answered sarcastically,

"I would suggest you direct that sentiment to your new grandchild, sir."

Isaac, swaying back and forth as though his body had received a physical blow, was unable to cope with the unraveling of events so contrary to his planning. His face turned as white as his beard, and his pipe dangled precariously between his open faded lips. To Michael's horror a tear began to glisten in the old man's eye, and his desperate voice, croaking with the effort to suppress his sobs, questioned piteously.

"So you would deny her then, and bring dishonor to my house and my beloved Jessica. Is that to be your answer, Lad?" Isaac strained to hear the words as Michael's lips began to move, but a whirring sound blocked them out. The room began to diminish in size, as blackness crowded into the corner of his eyes, and the brightness shining thru the curtain transformed itself into a sliver of sunlight, then suddenly went out.

Jessica was the first thing Isaac saw when he opened his blood shot eyes. An incessant dull pain pulsated through his brain and a disorienting weakness assailed his frail, tired body. To his surprise he found himself lying on his own bed, the counterpane neatly folded about his feet. A flutter of anxiety passed over him as he felt the peace of the room incongruous to his state of mind. A sense of foreboding overcame him as he tried to recall the reasons for the disquieting alarm nestled in his subconscious, threatening at any moment, to burst upon his memory. He tried staying all extraneous thoughts by again glancing at his beautiful daughter who sat quietly dozing on the chintz chaise lounge near his bed. Her abundant hair fell about her shoulders in a shawl of bronze, her small breasts rising and falling in the relaxed rhythm of deep sleep, known only to the very young. Thick lashes fanned her rosy cheeks, which still held a flush of excitement from the afternoon's commotion. Her moist lips were slightly parted, and as Isaac watched, her breathing seemed to quicken. He imagined her mouth curling wantonly, her tongue flicking over lips, dry with the thirst of desire. She seemed transformed before his very eyes, and he marveled at the tricks an old man's mind could fall victim to. Michael's unsavory remarks repeated themselves to his now conscious mind, and he recognized them as the reasons for his corrupted senses and inability to think clearly.

Sitting upright in bed, his eyes distended in their effort to plainly see the girl seated beside his bed. Then just as he was about to call out, the bright brown eyes flew open and his darling Jessica, dimpling with a smile of relief, threw her arms around his neck, sobbing with happiness.

"Thank heavens, Papa, you're all right. Dr. Salters said you would be, but my goodness, you gave us such a start. I don't know when I've been more frightened, seeing you lying there on the floor like that. Oh, Papa, I thought for a minute you were dead and I'd never again have the chance to say how much I love you." Pulling an arm's length away, she whispered, "I do love you so very much, Papa."

The warmth of her brown eyes seemed to melt the icy blue of his as he replied weakly, "And I you, lass, and I you." Exhaustively he searched her face for any signs of licentiousness, then relieved at finding none, was content to bask in the glow of her adoring eyes without shame or censurable guilt for having doubted her.

They sat on the bed, each transfixed by the other. Each silently projecting their love, each thinking the other could never really understand, but experiencing the intensity of their own feeling and having the satisfaction of knowing it had not be denied.

Jessica slowly slid one hand from behind her father's neck, gently tweaking the snowy bearded chin.

"You're the slick rascal, aren't you?" she said. "Why didn't you tell me that you and Michael had gotten together? I couldn't believe my eyes when I saw him here in our very own parlor getting everything straightened out at last." Her eyes were pleading, Oh, Papa, when you get to know him better you'll be able to see why I fell in love with him, just wait and see."

The old man, despairing, blinked stupidly and was incapable of reply. What could have happened to precipitate all this rapture, he wondered, when Michael had disclaimed her just a few hours before. Anguished and confused he was about to speak when Jessica scolded.

"You know, Papa, surprises are wonderful for me but awfully hard on you, and I don't want you ever again to do anything that affects your health, no matter what happens, understand? The doctor said it was a simple fainting spell, but we're not taking any chances. I want you well, enough to enjoy your first granchild. I want you to hear the word Granpa."

The intensity of his misery magnified as she kissed him lightly on the cheek and began to waltz around the room.

"The best part of all, Papa, is that the date we set is the very day cousin Molly's getting married." She ran back to the bed, her eyes wide with excitement and almost savage glee. Then gazing out the window and into the distance she became engulfed in her own dire emotions, oblivious to all things now, save the overwhelming need for retribution growing within her

"You could almost call it fate," she murmured. "I will be making my own announcement at dear cousin Molly's reception."

Her eyes glazed over with some hidden satisfaction, and her features once again held that wanton expression Isaac thought he had imagined a few moments before. The old man twitched involuntarily, his lips trembling in disbelief.

"I will steal her own show from under her very homely nose." The very thought of it so stimulated her that she began giggling wildly, twirling about the room in ever widening circles.

Her laughter filled his ears leaving his heart as empty as the tomb. Confusion buffeted his brain as he tried to grasp the import of the words revealed by this now giddy young girl dancing joyfully around his bed. Her transformation from bitch to beauty preyed upon his mind, testing his sanity. A slight tremor passed over him as he had listened and watched without really comprehending anything, except that through some miracle, Jessica and Michael were to be married. Perhaps he had misjudged the lad's intentions after all. No, he was sure he had not. He knew men quite well, and this lad had no intentions of giving up his freedom for the comforts of only one woman, no matter how beautiful she was. He had lied to her to escape the sight of a sick old man and his damaged daughter. Probably they would never catch glimpse of him again. Slowly he closed his eyes, rendering the sight of Jessica's rapture invisible. How would he face her hysteria when the cruel truth was finally exposed, and she stood alone and helpless, her temporary happiness again eradicated by Michael's indifference. His face became tight and grim with smoldering rage at the very idea of any man exiling his beloved Jessica to a life of shame because of his vile and unthinkable rejection.

His passion ebbed quickly, leaving only the thought of death and its welcome release from a life that suddenly seemed unbearable. He was extremely weary, and longed to end this struggle with peaceful sleep, perhaps somewhere in that twilight to recapture the love lost to him so long ago. To once more know the certainty of unconditional love, and the wonderful warmth of sharing it with another. In the darkness of his closed lid, a vision faintly began forming, with auburn tresses that flowed gracefully about a creamy throat and perfect shoulders. Plainly now he saw the soft smiling brown eyes alive with affection and fondness, their glow of admiration inviting him to her. Struggling to capture her lips, he gasped in disappointment as a slight pressure on the bed beside him caused the fantasy to vanish, forcing his attention back to Jessica.

Taking his limp hand and pressing it between her own, she smiled sweetly, saying, "Papa, there's just one more thing I have to tell you about, and then I want you to rest. The doctor says that's your very best medicine and, of course, we must abide by whatever he says. Do you feel well enough to talk a few minutes more Papa?" It really can wait until tomorrow if you'd rather."

Isaac, although now completely immersed in his own misery and self pity, could not deny that expectant expression. "I'm just fine," he answered gallantly, assuring himself as well as her.

Pleased at the prospect of getting this subject behind her she readily plunged forward. "Well since we've never been much on church going or any kind of religion for that matter, when Michael suggested Father Regan marry us I saw no harm in it, and I agreed." She lowered her eyes, fearful of his reaction, while she secretly acknowledged to herself that it would not really matter. The decision had been made and would remain unalterable. She was not giving up the man she loved over some theological premise which, in her mind, was questionable at best.

"I'm going to have to go to Father Regan and study the catechism." She peeked at him, alert for any signs of resentment, and seeing none, hurried on. "I will have to promise that the child will be raised a Catholic and taken to mass on Sundays and holy days of obligation. And, Papa, I will have to keep these promises if I am to be a good wife to Michael." The brown eyes beseeched his understanding.

Isaac's hand tightened on hers, his eyes widening with surprise. Jessica became frightened as his face turned ashen and he strained to sit up. All these words could only mean the lad was really going to marry her after all. The very thought of it flooded him with jubilance. If all this could be believed it would mean a surcease at last, a happy fulfillment for his deserving daughter, and a much needed respite for himself. Hoping he was not premature he gratefully thanked the God who presided over all churches without prejudice.

"What is it, Papa, did I do something wrong? Tell me, Papa, please what is it?" Jessica was almost screaming in alarm.

Isaac collapsed back against his pillow, heaving a heavy sigh of relief. He lowered his eyes to the small hand so tightly holding his, and began patting it abstractedly. "It's alright, my darling, you did right." Then almost to himself he added, "No man should be expected to give up everything. We're gonna have to do some giving up ourselves.

Jessica grasped his arm, uttering a cry of delight. Then laying her head beside him on the pillow, she whispered in his ear, "Oh, Papa, I'm so glad you approve. I can't imagine what I would have done if you hadn't."

CHAPTER FOUR

Michael, trudging wearily homeward, cursed himself for a fool, trying to rationalize how he had committed himself to a woman he barely knew, and most certainly did not love. How in God's name had he come to ask a perfect stranger to become his wife? His mind riveted on the word perfect as he began restructuring the dismal scene he had left behind.

The crashing sound of Isaac's body falling to the floor had brought Jessica racing to the parlor. Her apparent joy at the sight of him and dismay at the sight of Isaac had tended to throw them both into confusion as Jessica vacillated between her pleasure over his presence, and her concern for the condition of Isaac.

Michael watching, became entranced as the afternoon sun formed cataracts of copper in the radiant unruly mass of curls bobbing about her stricken face. Her constant moving between the men ignited leaps of fire in that flowing mass of red and a slow incessant burning in his loins. The flowing grace of her gestures awakened in him a profound appreciation for her beauty, making him realize he had been grievously mistaken. This delicate and lovely girl had fallen victim to her own innocence and a drunken fool.

Somewhere through her continual babble there ran a thread of responsibility that tightened around Michael's conscience and, for the first time in his life, he felt a squeeze of shame for having caused this comely creature even one moment of agony. Observing the girl as she frantically patted her father's cheek, pleading for forgiveness and his return to consciousness, he could no longer suppress his feelings of guilt, knowing an act of his had brought both father and daughter to their present deplorable predicament.

He escaped momentarily by running for Dr. Salters, but once Isaac was settled in his bed and the doctor had left a reassured Jessica, they faced each other again, she, with a definite advantage.

Flinging her arms about his waist, she purred her contentment that he had finally come for her as she always knew he would. She considered him her destiny and had trusted God to see to its fulfillment. Her head rested below his chin and the sweet fragrance of her hair flooded his nostrils. A rain of protest splattered weakly against his reason. She must not be allowed to consider his appearance as any type of reuniting, when, in truth, his real concern should be a respectable escape, but unable to shatter the moment, he remained silent, enjoying the heady aroma of her nearness.

Her body moved against his as she continually poured out her gratitude over their being together again, and dazzled by her beauty, he cursed himself for being a brute and for ever having mistreated a lass as sweet and lovely as she, through his drunkenness. He tried once more to remember that fateful night on Rasberry Hill but the memory of it was vague, clouded and very distant. He would have to admit he was just too drunk to remember, but the stirrings he felt within himself denied she could not have been worth remembering.

Jessica suddenly raised her head and whispered huskily, "Please kiss me, Michael." Only too eager to satisfy her command, his head bent forward, and as their lips met he felt a moments recollection that was soon distorted and forgotten by his present, pressing needs.

Slowly, reluctantly, she pulled her mouth away. Her voice was low and trembling, filled with anticipation and longing. "I can't wait for us to be together again, Michael. I love you so."

"We are together now," he answered, and pulled her roughly to him, covering her mouth salaciously. Her lips parted beneath his, quickening his already throbbing pulse. Pushing her towards the mohair sofa, his lips and tongue caressed her neck, while his hand found and explored her breast, hardening her nipple between his anxious fingers. Unexpectedly her body arched away from him, and much to his surprise, she bolted upright with an urgency that astounded him. Tears washed over her face as she jumped from the sofa and began agitatedly pacing the floor, sobbing quietly to herself. Momentarily stunned, Michael moved to her side, asking, "What is it, Jessica. What's wrong?"

She wheeled about to face him. "What's wrong?" she sobbed. "You really don't know do you? You're so blinded with lust that you can't even see that it's just like before all over again. You didn't come here to ask me to marry you at all, did you?" she asked with dismay. "No, of course not!" she answered herself in a positive tone. "You came to take advantage of me one more time, without a single thought to how much you have already injured me and my entire family. How can you be so insensitive and cruel?"

He opened his mouth to speak, but she continued without pause. "You're like some scavenger, come to prey on a young girl's affections. A girl who has already given you all her love, and above all her trust, and you have chosen to misuse them both." Her shoulders sagged, and her long sigh whispered about the room.

"Michael, Michael, for so long you have been my shining knight. Am I now to discover your armor is rusted with deceit?"

He wandered vaguely how he had managed to remain unaware of this girl's all consuming infatuation. Her dogged insistence in the veracity of her love was beyond his understanding. They were strangers, and worlds apart in every aspect.

Jessica, nauseous with the fear of losing him again, and sensing his doubt, wrung her hands, crying, "Dear God! You have brought me to the depths of disgrace, and my father to the depths of despair, and still your only concern is for your own satisfaction." She turned away from him. "I knew the day you stopped by the gate you were probably not worthy of me or my love, but that night on Rasberry Hill I thought you had proved me wrong. We were truly together in the way man and woman were meant to be together." Her voice softened, "And my heart tells me you could not just have pretended to care."

She turned to him, her eyes radiant with enchanted yearning, the sensuous full lips carving out her words of pleading. "If your only reason for staying away this long was our age difference, or the difference in our ways of life, believe me, they don't matter, Michael. Nothing matters except that you have come for me at last, and I have waited, knowing that you would."

Merciless and unspeakable guilt forced him to frown with self reproach as he nibbled gingerly on his bottom lip, trying to suppress his response. How could he possibly tell her his visit had merely been to swell the coffers of the union, void of any thought of her or knowledge of her situation. Cursing the deep tenderness and pity her words evoked within him, he cringed as she began to speak again.

"Michael, please don't make me feel as though I must prove my gratitude for your decision to come back. Let me feel like a woman, complete in the love of her man. Am I really asking too much from the father of my child?"

Tears formed diamonds in the corners of her widening brown eyes as her amber brows arched in a pitiful expression of explicit and desolate pain that brought a pledge of fidelity and a promise of marriage to Michael's lips.

After multiple reassurances from Michael and the finalizing of the wedding plans they stood together at the front door, reluctant to say goodbye. A contented silence fell between them as Jessica once more nestled her fiery head beneath his chin, cuddling against him like a small child seeking comfort. Michael, at least a foot taller, towered over her, feeling protective and very masculine, despite the sensation of excessive strength he felt exuded from her.

Playfully toying with the collar of his worn shirt she raised up gleaming eyes that held a promise he knew he wanted her to keep. Crushing her body to his in a ferocity of lust, he moaned into the copper curls, smothering her against his massive chest. She moved to touch his cheek and lips with gentle fingertips, her firm small breasts hardening against him.

"I promise you'll not be sorry for being my man, Michael. The warmth of my love will surround you like a welcome blanket in the dead of winter. All my days will be devoted to your happiness." Her eyes narrowed almost imperceptivity, a glint of steel cooling their usual soft warmth.

"Our lives are one now, sealed together by this unborn life within me." She pressed his hand to her womb. "But even that seed of our love will never interfere with our destiny, which is to be together forever."

The word forever echoed and reechoed about every corner of his mind, considerably lessening his fervor. Kissing her almost shyly he had to wonder how suffocating that blanket might become. Even the longest winter ends.

Michael let himself into his small rented room and leaned wearily against the closed door. His eyes swept about the unembellished lodgings, and he could not resist comparing them to the beauty of the Hobb's splendid parlor. All he possessed and acquired in his entire lifetime could be tucked into one drawer of his cupboard, and was of no real value to anyone but himself.

The worn bedsprings sang their usual song of protest as he lay down to reconsider his situation. To live in Isaac Hobb's house could only increase the esteem of his fellow workers. He told himself his opinions would carry more weight if they appeared to reflect the opinions of one of the town's most respected and admired old timer, and possibly, could be the trick needed to turn the heads of the obstinate older men.

Isaac, before his retirement, had become fire boss at the colliery, which demanded his lone entry into the mine by two o'clock each morning. It was then his duty to enter every working place under his protection, checking for any dangerous conditions, including the dreaded formation of gas. Slowly raising his safety lamp to the chambers roof, he would watch intently for the tell tale blue cap forming over the flame. Should it appear, he would hurriedly place a barricade across its entrance, and if it were free of this evidence, he merely chalked his initials and date on the face of the coal, announcing safety to the men whose lives depended on his thoroughness. Returning to the main mine entry, he would make his report and the workers, confident in his assessment, would proceed to their assigned chambers. The men trusted and relied on his abilities and good judgment, forming a strong basis for bonds of respect and loyalty. Bonds never to be forgotten by those whose jobs were made safer by his astute reckoning with any signs of danger. Yes Isaac Hobbs would be a definite attribute. Of this there could be no doubt.

Even the position of spokesman for the union might be viewed more favorably in light of his improved social position. The final star in his crown, of course, would be his entirely new and unique status for having successfully circumvented the barrier of religious prejudice. His marriage to a Protestant would give him the advantage of seeming completely unbiased, enabling him to approach both factions with an equal attitude, unmarred by the stigma of partiality. Never once did he consider the promises he had extracted from Jessica as any form of bias or obliquity.

The overall picture appealed to his better judgment and he began to wonder if she, not he, had become the forfeiter. In return for the loss of her maiden hood, the lending of all her family's comforts and influence, she would receive a man who would rather bed than wed her.

Deciding it was definitely she who was to be pitied, he graciously resolved to always treat her with a constant and consistent degree of respect, totally concealing his deficient love.

He smiled judiciously in the dark, and his bed groaned anew as he rolled over unto his side. Sympathy and charity raced for first place in his thoughts as he pictured a forlorn and defenseless Jessica. Perhaps the same fate had befallen his own mother, and was the reason his grandmother had always shown such displeasure at the very mention of her name. Woman were forever persecuted for their carnal enjoyment, he thought, wishing for a son. But even for the male there were dues that had to be paid if a man was to remain honorable. His child would at least have the benefits and stability of being raised by its own father, and the thought precipitated earnest emotions of paternal protectiveness for his unborn offspring.

Thinking again of Jessica, he mumbled into his pillow, "Poor, sweet lass," then tried giving himself up to sleep, but somewhere in some secret chasm of his mind, a furtive probe of fear released itself, and though he countlessly reassured himself through the endless hours of the night, he could not escape the feeling he was falling victim. To what, he did not know.

Rising to a morning filled with the promise of a beautiful day, he marveled how dawn's light had a way of dispelling the forebodings that crept into a man's mind in the darkness of night. He scoffed at himself, saying aloud, "It's a pity when a man who lives each day with danger can be frightened by a wisp of a lass, barely seventeen."

Inserting one leg into his work pants, he stopped short as the meaning of his words descended upon him. Here was the secret fear imprisoned in him, escaping through his own lips, released like a prevailing spirit to haunt his thoughts and demean his manhood. What was there about this seemingly innocent girl that was so consummately disquieting? She had successfully manipulated and wielded him into doing her bidding through her relentless and downright unyielding persistence, despite all of his reservations and discontent. Yet all the while she had appeared so vulnerable and helpless, so exposed, dependent and weak. Being an uneducated man the incongruity baffled him. He was not wise enough to understand such excessive love, or how to guard against its bitter consequences. Instead he chose to revel in its flattery, accepting its devotion as his just dues, and the preservation of his superiority.

Glancing back to the window and the glory of the rising sun, his thoughts brightened. I've got the bachelor jitters, he told himself, but marriage like religion, is not a belief, but a way of life, and few men survive without the benefit of both. His mind envisioned Jessica as she administered to Isaac, her face filled with tears of regret, knowing her improbity to be the cause of her father's undoing. Surely she was a selfless, dutiful and contrite child, and would remain so as his wife.

"Aye," he spoke aloud, without conviction, "I couldn't have done better if I had planned it this way myself."

Chapter Five

Annie Benfield's house was filled to overflowing with well wishers and celebrants from Molly's afternoon wedding. Everything had gone according to plan, including a pleasant day, with now, just the right touch of evening stir to suggest the coming of fall. The many guests who had been witness to Molly's final conquest spilled out of the house and unto the front porch, raising their glasses in continual toasts to the happy couple. The bride, resplendent in Annie's creation of traditional white satin, lace and seed pearls, was almost radiant, despite her usual natural sallowness. For the first time her cheeks held a glow emerging from joy, rather than from a jar, and her eyes sparkled with delight and anticipation whenever they found sight of her new husband, Jim Bolen.

Clara, relieved at having Molly no longer in contention, surrounded herself with every available bachelor attending the reception. Determined to follow in her sister's footsteps as quickly as possible, her small lively eyes darted wildly from one eligible man to the other, her yellow tinted face keen with interest in their every spoken word.

Gifts crammed the buffet and dining room table so that securing a morsel of food was no easy task. Jessica, waiting while Michael ran the gauntlet of people and presents in an effort to retrieve some small refreshment, smiled viciously to herself as she watched Clara's animated features, and obvious desire to please the gentlemen. Enjoy the party while you can, dear cousin, she thought, because I'm about to put a bit of a crimp in it very shortly.

The reception had been in full swing several hours now, and most everyone was well on their way to a gala evening. Her eyes, darting fruitlessly about the room in search of her father, noticed Tom Quinlan staring at her in a most discomforting manner. Walking directly over to him, she questioned in a most demanding tone.

"Have you seen my father?"

Tom, still staring at her, seemed filled with frustrated anger as he blurted out, "I can't believe I seen you come in here with that rotten Mick. Please tell me my eyes are getting dim, or tell me I'm going crazy, but don't tell me it was really him!"

Jessica's arms crossed belligerently in front of her as the toe of one dainty foot impatiently tapped the floor. "You have got to be the most exasperating boy in Miners' Haven, Tom Quinlan. To answer my question with a question of your own is ill-mannered, but to interfere in other people's business is unpardonable. I shall have to have a talk with your mother regarding your evident lack of etiquette, my lad."

Tom, who was at least three years older than Jessica, felt the heat of embarrassment rush to his face as he noticed some of the nearby couples cease conversing in favor of eavesdropping. His ever present awareness of his lameness and habitual striving for ambiguity, always left him discomfited with even the slightest amount of attention. Now, unguarded, he felt open to attack, and the need for retaliation forced him to speak.

"Your father left over an hour ago. Praise be he was spared the sight of his little girl throwing a toe tapping tantrum." Glancing at the onlookers, he rolled his eyes heavenward, shaking his head from side to side disparagingly. Vindicated by their giggles, he quickly scurried into the crowd, avoiding further observation or confrontation.

Alone with her small audience, Jessica chose to ignore Tom and concentrate on her real reason for attending this detestable affair. A bright smile flashed over her face, as she licked her lips in anticipation. Adding a note of conspiracy to her voice, she whispered, "Follow me if you want some real excitement." Then turning abruptly, she made her way into the dining room, her curious comrade's close at her heels. Pushing a surprised guest from one of the high-backed cane chairs, she stood upon it, calling lustily for quiet. The din in the house was vociferant, and a few minutes elapsed before she was able to capture everyone's attention. When, at last, she felt all eyes still capable of reasonably fair vision were upon her, she began in a loud clear voice.

"My dear friends, it would have so pleasured my father to make this announcement, but as you all know, he has been unwell lately and had to retire early this evening, so I take it upon myself to pass on to all of you this good news." Clearing her voice with importance, and making sure she had captured her audiences' full attention, she continued. "All of you here tonight are lucky enough to be celebrating not one, but two wedding feasts. Because of my father's ill health we were unable to be as elaborate as dear cousin Molly, but she, in her charity, was sweet enough to schedule her wedding to coincide with mine. It is her hope that as married women we will be even closer than ever before."

Looking directly at her ashen faced relative, she nodded slightly and smiled. "We have been more than just cousins, each to the other, for if it had not been for Molly's interest, and my eagerness to learn to be just like her, indeed, neither of us might have been wed this day." An undeniable strain of sarcasm tainted her words, and a slight stir rustled through the crowd. "I lift my glass to sweet cousin Molly and to her groom, Jim Bolen, but above all I raise my glass to the handsomest of men, my own new husband, Mr. Michael McClellan!"

Tom Quinlan stood inconspicuously at the rear of the assemblage, mouth agape, as a momentary silence of expectancy and awkwardness descended like a pall until a voice, thick with intoxication, rose from somewhere in the back of the room.

"Happiness to Michael and Jessica, a sweet lass if there ever be one!"

The revelers, pleased for the relief of the unwanted tension, rose to the occasion, each trying to reach her side, then plying her with every good wish and heartfelt congratulations. Michael, his hands laden with food and drink, stood inside the kitchen door in confounded silence. The significance of Jessica's speech had turned his face somber with disbelief and doubt. Dazed, he stood watching her gleeful acceptance of everyone's admiration, unable to fully comprehend exactly what had prompted this obviously exaggerated display. A voice, heavy with hatred, penetrated his stupor.

"The dirty little slut," hissed Molly. "She's going to steal away my wedding day and make it her own with her slippery tongue and flaunting manners. I won't have it, I'm going over there and rip that ugly red hair of hers right out of her damned head and stuff it into her cocky mouth!"

A restraining hand forced Molly to turn to her mother. "No, Molly, don't let her destroy one of the happiest days of me life by creating a scene. Can't you see you'd be doing exactly what she's expecting you to do? Ill not allow you to be goaded into some kind of shameful exhibition. No, child, there's a time for all things, and this is not our time. Creating misery for others only begets misery for oneself. Soon everyone will be able to see the reason for her sudden marriage, and the tongues will fly all over town, but you, Molly, will still be respected, and above all, married to a man who truly loves you. Her days of wretchedness will not be long in coming, so don't fret, my darling, we will soon have our day with her. Mind what I tell you. Now let's join the others and congratulate her like the ladies we are. It's the only weapon we have against dimming her satisfaction, believe me."

Molly relaxed somewhat, but a note of rigidity still edged her voice, "I can't tell you how much I look forward to having that day, Mother. It will give me indescribable pleasure." Her ample bosom rose and fell rapidly as she tried mastering her malignity. The look of concentrated hatred dissolved into a dismal smile as she dutifully followed Annie to her triumphant cousin's side.

Michael had moved away from the two women, wishing only to be shed of all he had seen and heard. With thumping heart, his mind renewed its persistent warnings of things he did not understand nor wish to recognize about this woman child who was now his wife. Father Regan, totally captivated by her charm and eagerness to learn the catechism, had shaken Michael's hand with warmth and enthusiasm.

"You've got yourself a fine woman here, lad," he had bellowed, beaming at the girl who stood marveling at the new circlet of gold on her left hand. "One who'll make you proud and give you many children.

Looking at Jessica in her simple ecru pongee dress, decorated only by the brilliant copper collar her unloosened hair had formed, he had felt a swelling of pride and felicity that was totally dissipated now, as he longed only for his escape from her brazenness.

Looking frantically around the crowd for his wife, he vowed to take her home and impart his first lesson in remorse, but, without warning, his friends pounced upon him, and before long they had found his sought for escape in the innumerable cups pressed into his, not entirely reluctant hand.

Molly and her eager groom had long since departed when Jessica finally persuaded Michael it was time to tread past the few doors to their own home. Michael's mood, altered by his excesses, was expansive, and he crooned a lewd Irish ballad about the beauty and modesty of all young brides. Jessica impatiently shushed him into silence as he stumbled up the porch stairs and entered the house, creeping quietly past Isaac's door to the place they would now share.

Looking about him, he decided Jessica's room could not have been better suited to her. It abounded with ruffles and lace in beauteous shades of rose and lilac. Delicate rose patterned paper clad the walls, and the sweet scent of lavender seeped from beneath the cup-board door. The intricate design of the crochet bedspread fell in a flurry of pink tufts and tassels. A large circle of fringed carpeting spread from beneath the bed, it's deeply crushed pile emitting as many different shades of rose as the glass bowl of dried flowers adorning the bureau.

Despite all its outward frills and elaborate trappings he could not help but notice its need for one vital focal point, one outstanding feature to tie it all together. There was nothing to define it as beautiful or ugly, overdone or too simplistic. It was a room that portrayed welcome, without real warmth, beauty without really being beautiful, forever lacking that one intangible element necessary for its completion.

Jessica carefully folded down the bedspread and began undressing hurriedly. Her fingers trembled over the tiny pearl buttons on her dress as she cast an expectant glance at Michael, who remained standing at the bedroom door. An unpalatable sensation churned within him and he felt diseased and ill from all this lurking femininity. Striding to the bed he fell upon it fully clothed, trying to conquer the nausea pervading both mind and body, smothering every fiber of his manliness. His eyes opened finally to a vision in pure white silk and lace. The gown, as sheer as gossamer, illuminated all her beauty, and stood before him, needing only to be desired, but his condemning eyes saw only her overly pink cheeks, and found them offensive. Lowering them he discovered her rosy nippled breasts, already swollen to accommodate the demand a new life would make, and he cringed instinctively. She sank slowly beside him on the bed, and to his complete dismay, her velvet like skin reflected the lamp's peony colored glow, drowning him in a world of roseate.

Blessedly the room fell into darkness as her hand touched the daintily sculptured light resting on the night table.

My wife, he thought, and I know her scarcely better than the child she carries. All the depression and doubts of the past weeks converged on him now, and he knew a smothering of spirit. Like the almost bawdy looking lamp beside the bed, something in himself had been extinguished. Brooding, he examined a hard suspicion that her true character traits of cruelty, falseness and hypocrisy, had been covert, and very well concealed by her acts of innocence, sweetness and sentimentality. Ever deepening depression subjugated him to emotional havoc, a condition almost alien to his personality.

Remotely he felt her head come to rest upon his chest as, deftly, she began undoing his stiff wedding shirt. Then gradually relaxing, he recognized, and allowed himself to succumb to the beginnings of a familiar aching, as her fingers gently, but persistently, traced tiny patterns across his naked chest and waist. Her soft breath next to his ear caused his own to quicken as she raised her head, anxiously searching for his lips. Then without warning, the nausea returned.

Springing from the bed, he followed her hurried directions, and sped down the hall to the water closet. Retching and cursing himself for a fool, he came to realize his sickness did not come from over imbibing, but from the disgust that stemmed from his own weakness, always enabling her to be the conqueror, and himself the conquered. If he were to retain one shred of his own self respect he must start, this very night, to be master, at the very least in his own bedroom. Straightening up with extreme effort, he trod laboriously back to their room. Jessica rushed to his side with obvious concern.

"Are you alright, my darling?"

Grinning tightly he casually walked to the bed, answering, "Remind me not to compliment your Aunt on her cooking." I believe it was a mite of indigestion from those sausages, but it's all passed now. Come to bed, lass." His hand patted the spot beside him, and Jessica, needing no further invitation, smiled her pleasure and speedily joined him.

Suffocating him with her nearness, she cuddled as close as was possible. "It's our wedding night, Michael, a most important occasion. The most important occasion of our entire lives." She tried snuggling even closer.

"Aye, weddings are always important occasions, there's no denying that, lass," His voice turned stern, "But tonight is Molly's wedding night and hers alone." The rusty head moved against his chest as he persevered. "Your's was celebrated over two months ago on Raspberry Hill and since, as you yourself pointed out, she was good enough to share her wedding day celebration with you, I think it best if we leave the wedding night festivities to her. Good night, my pet."

Releasing himself from her embrace, he immediately turned over, pulling the muslin sheet up to his chin, despite the still warm room. He lay perfectly still, anticipating her reaction, but as seconds turned to minutes, and expectation to fatigue, he drifted into a dreamless sleep, comforted by his firm action and its quelling result. Sleeping soundly, he was disturbed only by the unfamiliar feeling of having to share his bed.

The brightness of the morning told Michael he had slept well past nine. To his relief the bed beside him was empty and smoothed so neatly one would never have suspicioned he had not slept alone. A pitcher of fresh water stood on the bureau, complete with wash cloth and towel. His laundered shirt hung on the clothes tree, and clean socks peeped from his highly polished boots beneath it. As he surveyed this homey scene, a wide grin spread over his features. Then slapping his knee happily, he spoke aloud.

"Sweet Mother, it's determined she is to do her wifely duty, if not in way, then another." He laughed with triumph and felt better than had in over a month. Taking extra pains with his hair and shave, as befitted any spanking new groom, he descended the stairs with a bouncy gait, feeling able to handle any situation now.

The kitchen was filled with the unmistakable odors of home baked bread and the scented steam from boiling black coffee. Isaac dozed in the rocker near the window, while Jessica busily scurried about, shaking up the coals in the kitchen stove and checking the rising loaf. Raising her eyes at the sound of his footsteps, she rushed with apparent delight to bestow a morning kiss upon him.

"Papa and I thought you were going to sleep the day away," she chided,

"But, of course I know how exhausted you must be." She wore a coy expression and a slight flush came to her cheeks as she dropped her eyes with what Michael assumed was meant to be modesty.

The sound of his daughter's voice had roused Isaac and he nodded and smiled knowingly. "Ah yes, the spirit of youth is always remembered with envy, and the older one gets, the more envious he becomes. Come, sit down, lad, you're probably starved."

Michael wishing to protest against being either tired or hungry and in particular against the assumed reason for both, but he knew Isaac would never be able to understand his not having bedded his obviously adored daughter now that it was his legal right. He stole a sidelong glance at his wife whose profile held a suggestion of smugness while she carefully poured his coffee. An unmasked glint of malice danced momentarily in her eyes and Michael, in an attempt to extinguish it, openly blessed himself before partaking of his food, willing to forsake this ritual while living in this Protestant home, he now found it a useful protest against her domination.

Pretending not to notice, she gushed over him. "Papa has some wonderful news for us. I'm sure it will make us even happier than we are now, if that's possible." Her eyes held and bore into his with exaggerated looks of devotion, as she emphasized the last three words. Michael clenched his fist beneath the table, wishing earnestly for the satisfaction of being able to slap her taunting face. Within himself he damned her and called upon the Saints for some kind of justice. Somehow she had won again, and they both knew it.

Isaac coughed lightly, interrupting what he thought were two young lovers entranced with the sight of each other. He spoke gently, with affectation, "Son, I know I'll be proud of having you in the family. I've heard it said that you're an honest and hard working man, but sometimes given to over partaking of the cups." He continued with gentle candor. "A fault, lad, that's been known to many a man, but one that, can be overcome if the flesh is willing." The grey brows knitted together briefly. Nevertheless I'm still of a mind to put my confidence in you and your willingness to assume your new responsibilities of devoted husband and father. The clear blue eyes rested on his darling and his beard parted with a smile of pride that intimated, for Michael to be anything less, was beyond his conceiving. Looking back to Michael, he continued.

"As a token of gratitude for the happiness I know you'll bring to Jessica and the babe, I'm giving this house and all of its contents to you children as my wedding gift. I ask only to remain within its walls until my death." T'was a bargain no man could refuse and an insurance policy for the future happiness of his daughter.

Michael, stunned by such generosity, spoke hesitantly. "I, of course, am very grateful, sir, but being almost strangers as we are, perhaps you should wait until we know each other better. It would give me a chance to prove my worthiness, and possibly spare you a disappointment. To give another man your life's possessions is not to be taken lightly."

Isaac sucked his unlit pipe, carefully watching the glistening black eyes for signs of greed. "I'm glad you're wise as well as honest, it's a good combination, lad, but you see I have a reason for what I'm doing, and maybe I'd best tell you about it. "If you and Jessica can be free of the monthly expense of having to pay rent to some uncaring landlord, those monies could be applied towards savings. Savings that would be put into a special account for the little one." Leaning back in his chair, he tugged at the faded red suspenders, smiling. "When the lad's eighteen he's automatically guaranteed a college education if he feels the need, or better yet, he could start his own business and be his own man. A great opportunity for any young feller with even the tiniest spark of ambition. I'd like to die knowing there's one Hobbs gonna be working above the ground."

His face became serious. "From the day I left the mines I never once missed it, and always pitied the other men, having to spend their lives covered in filth, clawing out the black diamond's day after miserable, day, their perpetual back breaking labors interrupted only by death. I've never thought for a moment it was in God's plan, it always seemed more like something thought up by the devil himself to me." He regarded Michael sorrowfully. "Let an old man die content knowing my own granchild will never have to suffer the drudge of being a miner."

"Well, its right you are about that, Mr. Hobbs, answered Michael bleakly. "Many's the time I've longed for a different life myself, but it's all I know 'cept the sea, where a man can die from loneliness and the want of a woman."

A sudden movement in the corner of the kitchen reminded him that Jessica was still present and somehow his own words became an embarrassment to him as, tilting her head to one side, she kissed her fingertips, and blew in his direction. Be damned to her, he thought, as he turned his attention back to Isaac.

"What manner of business do you think a man could turn a profit in these days, Mr. Hobbs?"

Isaac squinted his eyes as he scratched his wiry white beard. "Well," he answered thoughtfully, "if I was a young feller looking for the almighty dollar, I think I'd open a hardware store and fill it with everything a man needs to keep his home in good repair, so's he wouldn't need outside help. Then I'd lay in a goodly supply of tires and automotive gadgets for all them new cars that practically everybody will be driving soon." His eyes had shrunk to two small slits of concentration. "With that in mind I'd install a gas pump outside the store, and whatever else those contraptions are gonna need to keep them on the road."

Thoroughly impressed, Michael became enthusiastic. "I wonder why nobody ever thought about this before. What an idea! There isn't a well stocked hardware store for at least twenty miles around here. Most everybody does their buying from the catalogs that take forever to get here and then is usually the wrong merchandise when it finally does get here. Aye, it sounds like a capital idea for any lad." His tone had turned dreamy.

The two men fell into silence, Isaac picturing a successful, ambitious young man, proud and independent of the mining company, while Michael mentally stocked the shelves, his mind running rampant with plans and unexpected new ideas. Jessica began to giggle as she studied the expressions of concentration covering the men's faces. Then unexpectedly she began laughing out loud as their startled eyes turned to her. Gasping for breath and holding her stomach she tried to talk.

"You men are really so ridiculous! Sitting here planning something to happen twenty years from now, when by that time there'll be five hardware stores, and who knows what else around here." Having herself under control at last, she leaned over the table looking from one to the other, her eyes flowing with tears of amusement.

"There's just one item you're forgetting, my plotting twosome. I'm planning on having a girl." She straightened up and walked from the room, but they could still hear her stifled laughter as she left the house through the side door.

When Michael entered the bedroom that night he found Jessica lazily paging through the latest fashion magazine. The small circle of light from the lamp revealed a plain blue muslin gown that completely camouflaged her figure. Even her hair had been tied back in an austere manner that seemed to coincide with her mood. Michael had remained downstairs listening to Isaac reminisce about the old time mining method and dangers that men no longer faced. Isaac had been animated as he told how many a beautiful canary had sung its last song in the mines.

"We'd take 'em down in wee cages and set them in the middle of the chamber while we picked away. At the first sign of their getting sluggish or fallin' from the perch, we hightailed it out of there cause you knew damned well the gas was coming from somewheres. But times changed and now we got all kinds of detecting devices, which is a wonderful thing. Aye, a wonderful thing. But you know, lad, there's no modern devise that's as sure fire as the instinct of a rat, and how they all know when it's time to exodus before a squeeze. Have you ever been in a squeeze, Michael?"

"No, sir," he answered, shaking his head solemnly, "and pray to God I never will be. It must be pure hell to be trapped like that."

Isaac's mind's eye could still see the particles of coal being forced out from the pillars as the supporting timbers began to buckle, crushing slowly beneath the weight of the sagging roof. His ears still echoed with the thunderclap sound of the fall as the rush of the concussions air blew out his head lamp, and he lay alone in the dark, groping blindly for the touch of his fellow workers. The small glow from his relit lamp exposed the apprehensive faces of the men around him, and he gratefully thanked a merciful God for their survival. Beckoning them to follow, he had moved along the face of the chamber next to the thick vein of coal, their only hope being to reach the heading which was usually driven into solid coal and would not be damaged by the fall. Their flickering head gear had gradually revealed the carnage of torn out walls, and loaded cars, lifted and thrown from their tracks by the tremendous gush of air, littering the mine with dangerous debris.

Isaac encouraged the men to continue despite the cracking and loud crashing noises of the still falling roof on the level below. Frozen with fear and almost void of mobility they gingerly picked their way under precariously leaning slabs of slate and perilous hanging pieces of roof. They climbed hills of rock and rubble, and crept through apertures barely large enough to admit them, their trembling bodies wet with trepidation, and bathed with the putrid smell of terror. Weak with exhaustion and on the verge of collapse they had finally reached a place of safety, only to be told that the fall had covered over thirty acres and would forever serve as the final resting place for at least ten men.

The chimes of the grandfather's clock tolled the hour and Isaac started in surprise. Good Lord, man, I've bent your ear all evening, and you probably dying to take your leave. His blue eyes sparkled with moisture. "I'm grateful to ya, lad for putting up with an old man's loneliness."

With all the sincerity he could muster, Michael answered, "It was purely a pleasure, sir, to listen to you and to have had this talk. Let's hope it's the first of many. Young men get lonely too, you know," he added sheepishly. Their eyes held, filled with the knowledge that since time immemorial, men have always needed the company of other men.

"You're a good lad, Michael, and I thank ye." Isaac rose slowly and drifted up the stairs, leaving Michael no alternative but to follow. He had remained below, feigning interest, and trying to postpone the inevitable confrontation with Jessica. Yet, somehow, as the evening went on the old man's conversation had intrigued him and he found himself genuinely interested in his tales, forgetting both the time and the one who waited for him.

Now as he crawled into bed, she lay docily beside him, her profile etching itself into his eyes as they accustomed themselves to the darkness. "I'd like to know why you ridiculed your father at breakfast this morning?" he asked quietly. "Sometimes dreams are all an old man has left, you know, and I can't imagine why you would want to deny him his."

Her head turned little by little to face him. "Is that what you think I did, ridicule my father?" She hesitated, "Yes, perhaps it would have seemed that way, but it was just too funny, both of you pondering over something a million years from now, and both so serious about it. Here I am with an unborn baby and you two have him running a hardware store." Raising her hand to her mouth to smother a giggle, she suddenly burst into unanticipated tears.

"Oh, Michael" she moaned. "I'm sorry. You know I wouldn't want to do anything else to intentionally hurt my father. God know I've done enough hurting to last him his lifetime. Maybe I have a twisted sense of humor, but it just struck me so funny I couldn't help it. I'm really sorry if you think I did anything wrong. I didn't mean to, Michael."

Raising himself on one elbow, and satisfied with her being contrite, he gathered her to him tenderly. She really is just a child, he thought. "Hush now, you're absolutely right when you think about it." He smiled down at her. "Maybe your father and I have no sense of humor at all."

They began laughing softly together, and her tears vanished like drops of water on the sand. They held each other close. They made love. They were happy.

The arrival of winter found the three of them well settled in particular patterns regarding one another. Michael, having developed a fondness and respect for Isaac that he had never know for his own father, willingly spent most of his leisure time entertaining and being entertained by the older man. Isaac, though well pleased with his new in-law, continued to dote on Jessica, inquiring daily with concern for her health, and praying nightly for her safe delivery, unable to erase the memory of her birth. While Jessica's attention focused entirely on Michael, longing constantly for the sight or touch of him, ever mindful of his presence, avowing her love in her every action and invariably searching for its reciprocation.

This then was their circle of love, each dependent on the other, yet not one returned in kind. Like all human relationships, theirs were evolving into positive, specific patterns of behavior, and like all humanistic patterns, once established, would be all but impossible to alter. Man, with his tendency towards being habitual, easily falls prey to the comfort and safety of repetition, finding change distracting, unnecessary, and most times, impossible to accomplish.

By Christmas Michael had wearied of Jessica's never ending demands and his own acquiescence. Regardless of his resolve, she seemed always able to arouse his interest with some new ploy, until he fell victim to his own desires. He began looking forward to the baby's arrival as a respite, or at least a temporary cessation in this all too over abundant flow of affection.

Like all winters, this one proved interminable, denying forever the promise of Spring. The sludge covered mountain rose, purified by the onslaught of winter's storms and the silence that covers a snow covered world. The men walked down from the colliery, bodies bent against the savage winds, their voices muffled behind up turned collars and protective scarf's.

Michael was extremely grateful this day to be living in the Hobb's home, as it was the very first one leading down from colliery hill. The men waved an envious, if not too enthusiastic farewell, and continued trudging homeward. Michael's raven hair had turned silver with the falling snow by the time he opened the garden gate and stood clutching the lapels of his coat where, again, a gnawing ache had begun in his chest. It was a familiar twinge that had started with a flu weeks before, and since he had been unable to dislodge either, due to the relentless weather, he chose to ignore them both and petition heaven for an early spring. Removing his work clothes, he huddled near the kitchen coal stove trying to diminish the icy cold penetrating every bone in his body, and he shivered convulsively. The pain in his chest became aggravated by the suddenness of heat in the room, and he began a cough that soon turned into racking spasms, leaving him weak and more chilled than before, despite the beads of sweat dotting his forehead. Pulling his kerchief from the pile of work clothes in the corner, he shakily wiped his eyes and mouth, coughing once more into the damp hanky before tossing it back again among the dirty wash. It lay in a wrinkled ball, hiding it's dark secret well within its folds. It was laundered and back in the cupboard without anyone having discovered its maze of tell tale blood.

BOOK TWO

Chapter One

It was the last Sunday in March and a fierce wind whistled about the eaves, penetrating every crack and crevice of the house with its icy breath. Jessica moved restlessly on her bed. Despite the chill of the room, perspiration lay heavy on her brow as she felt the beginning of another pain and stiffened to steel herself against it. She had been in labor for over five hours and the increasing crescendos of pain were becoming almost intolerable. Tossing from side to side she buried her face into the mattress and moaned anew.

"You're doing very well, my dear," encouraged old Doc Salters, as he gently forced her unto her back for one more examination. "Just a little while longer now, we're almost there. Yes, indeed, we're almost home now."

Flashing him a look of hatred, she mimicked "We're almost home now. What the hell do you have to do with it? I've been pushing and squeezing for hours while you sit there nodding and smiling. For God's sake, can't we get this thing over with?"

Another pain assailed her and she bore down with all of her strength, wishing only to expel the cause of her torment. "Ah, that's my brave girl," cooed the doctor, patiently ignoring her outburst. Now I think just another contraction or two will do the trick. Are we ready?"

"I don't know about you, doc, but I've been ready all day. Oh, God", her voice trailed off as she concentrated all her efforts in one determined direction, stifling her scream against the back of her hand.

Annie Benfield stood in the far corner of the room docily holding a steaming kettle of hot water poised over an empty bowl, as she waited for her instructions. Her muddy brown eyes gleamed with satisfaction as Jessica writhed and thrashed on the bed, unable any longer to control her screams of unendurable agony. Well the little slut is sure paying for her sins now, ain't she, Annie thought, without pity. Like all good and sanctimonious Christians, she was firmly convinced that all suffering was the work-of the Lord.

Wiping Jessica's face with an already overly damp cloth, the doctor suddenly exclaimed, "That's my girl, just one more push and we're all done! Ah, that's the good girl, now we can just relax. Oh my dear, you were meant for having babies." He motioned mechanically to Annie for the water and clean towels. "Yes, it's very seldom I see a woman give birth as easily as you, Jessica. I'm sure there will be many children in your future, and heaven grant us they may all be as beautiful as she is."

Jessica lay panting, her eyes closed, listening without interest to the prattle of the old doctor. Slowly her lids parted only to behold a grotesque, blood smeared form, somehow suspended in mid air, wrong side up. The mouth suddenly opened, emitting a protesting howl as the doctor applied a resounding smack to its posterior end. Her last thought before slipping into an almost comatose doze was that the purple, mottled creature dangling above her had been unbelievably ugly.

When next she opened her eyes both she and the room had been somewhat tidied up, while Annie Benfield still busied herself gathering up the last of the soiled linens. Pausing near the bed, the old woman whispered, "You got yerself a fine little girl there, Mrs. I only hope she grows up to be exactly like her mother." The woman's face was innocent as she hurriedly bustled out of the room, dragging the huge ball of laundry behind her, leaving Jessica to wonder if her words had been meant kindly.

Both Isaac and Michael stood huddled over the small bundle in Michael's arms. They spoke in soft but excited tones, their faces exhilarated, yet filled with awe, as they smiled down on this new life, this beautiful miracle released from the hand of God.

"All that attention for the finished product, and no consideration for the producer almost seems unfair.."

At the sound of Jessica's voice the two men rushed to her bedside, Michael brushing her cheek with a kiss, while Isaac, pressing her hand between his, allowed the tears of joy to splash, unashamedly, over his face and disappear into his sodden beard. Michael, still bending over her, began pulling the pink coverings apart.

"Have you seen her yet, Jess? She's like a rosebud, all pink and cuddly soft, like a tiny marshmallow."

Jessica abruptly waved him away. "I've seen her, Michael, I've seen her. Now put her in the cradle and come sit with me, please."

Michael stood up; smiling as he noticed four little fingers had entwined themselves about one of his. It was as though the tiny fist held his heart, and he felt a pang of love so intense it closely resembled pain.

"My darling little Maggie," he whispered, then, conscious of everyone's eyes upon him, he spoke sheepishly. "I'd sort of like to call her Maggie, if it's alright with you, Jess." Her intense stare made him feel foolish and he explained haltingly. "It was my mother's name, Jess, and since I never knew her at all, it would be kind of nice having a Maggie around I could get to know." The wee body wriggled against him, yawning. "One I intend to get to know very well."

Jessica favored him with a consenting smile and he flushed with pride as he placed his new found treasure in the little bed that had once held its mother. The down covering the tiny head was already black as the night, while the contour of her face was but a miniature replica of his own reflection. Aye, he thought as he pressed his huge thumb against the silken cheek, I'd have the devil's own time denying this one. Sweet Mother, she's the most beautiful child I've ever seen. The indirect compliment to himself caused him to smile. Well, truth was truth, and nothing could be the help for it. Raising his eyes to the bureau's mirror for affirmation, his smile widened. Damned if we're not two pretty good looking rascals, Maggie.

The doctor, still putting away the tools of his trade, interrupted Michael's private joke. "Your wife did very well by you, Mr. McClellan. Having a lusty man about like yourself, I'd say there'll be no problem filling this house with young ones." Winking at Isaac, he turned his attention to the pale figure on the bed. "And, of course, you'll want to nurse the babe I'm sure, so I'll leave these pills to-----"

"But, of course, I do not wish to nurse, I'm sure," she snarled. "I am the one who gave birth here today, doctor, not you, and I know how I feel, which is rather poorly if you want to know the truth. I've never felt so weak or so---"

"Well that's perfectly normal, my dear. Giving birth is no easy job, but it will only take a few weeks of rest and you'll be right back on your feet again, believe me," He smiled knowingly.

"I do believe you, doctor," answered Jessica peevishly. "But for now this child has completely sapped my strength by her refusal to enter this world hours ago. You don't seem able to understand that I have endured more pain this day than I have ever suffered in my entire life, and now you're asking me to drain myself further by nursing her. I don't have the strength for it. I just can't do it."

The doctor chuckled. "That poor baby had almost as hard a time being born as you had having her, dear lady. I know this hasn't been easy for you, but most of it is because you're so very young. Please be assured that nursing is as good for you as it will be for your baby. It's nature's way of protecting both of you, and particularly the child, from disease and---"

"Doctor, doctor," her tone was nasty, "let me put it in a way you'll be able to understand. Right now I'm only interested in one thing, and that thing is getting well and returning to a normal life as quickly as possible, which does not include baring my breast every four hours. Do I make myself clear, doctor?"

The snap of his bag punctuated the doctor's reply. "Perfectly." He strode angrily from the room as Isaac, murmuring his apologies for his daughter's behavior, and begging his understanding of the impetuousness of today's youth, pursued him down the hall.

Jessica, relaxing, turned to Michael, stretching out her hands and smiling. "Come here, my darling."

Hesitantly he walked to her side, completely bewildered by her rapidly changing mood and her ill mannered haranguing with the elderly physician. "I don't understand why you refuse to nurse the child when the doctor says it will give her a better start in life."

Making room for him on the bed beside her, she sighed. "These old fashioned doctors are such a bore. Everyone knows nursing went out with the middle ages. Modern women have found today's formulas to be more than adequate and besides, they're interested in keeping a reasonably trim figure despite child birth. They don't want to look like their mothers, all saggy and out of shape before thy're forty."

Michael, unconvinced, shook his head in chaotic amazement. "I think maybe you're father's right, Jess, you read too many books. Books are only another person's opinion, you know, and not necessarily the last word on any subject. They're written to give you food for thought, not rules to live by. What's good for one person could be totally bad for another."

"I know you're good for me," she answered. Then looking into his eyes and discerning his still lingering confusion she tried diverting his attention by laying an open palm along his whiskered cheek. "I think Maggie's a sweet name, and your reason for picking it, even sweeter. Maggie McClellan, it has such a nice sound, I just love it." she hesitated only a moment. "Just as I love you, Michael." Pulling him down, she kissed him so passionately he could not resist mocking her.

"It would seem your strength has not been sapped as thoroughly as you would have us all believe, young lady."

"My energy is limitless when it comes to pleasing my husband." She tugged at his shirt front, her lips parting expectantly, awaiting his embrace.

"You would please me most at this particular time by resting." Gently releasing her grasp he strode to the cradle, lifted it and it's contents, and headed directly to the bedroom door. "I will take the child below so she will not disturb you further." Pausing in the hall, he cast an unconcerned glance at Jessica, his lips twisted in a forced smile. "We both wish you a speedy convalescence."

The sarcasm in his voice hung over the room like a pall as the door closed firmly behind him.

By the end of the first week Maggie developed severe colic which was to persist for almost three months. Michael had placed a cot, the cradle and a rocker in the small room behind the kitchen that, until now, had held only a treadle sewing machine and a neglected basket of mending. The long nights turned into weeks of rocking and walking the floor with the sick child. Sometimes when her pains subsided, he would snuggle her close to him on the cot, using the warmth of his body to soothe her agonies, until dawn's light foretold the beginnings of another day.

At first Jessica was too weak to assist with the child's care, but as the weeks went by she remained in her room throughout the night, immune to the infant's cries echoing up the stairwell, battering against her closed bedroom door. Day's end found her defeated by the endless barrage of bottles and diapers, and although Isaac was an invaluable aid to her, the baby's constant clamor set her nerves a jar, and she soon found herself detesting the sight of Maggie's contorted and protesting face.

"God, how I wish she'd never been born," she shouted above the persistent wailing. Isaac stopped his pacing to try shifting the child into a more comfortable position, and ease his daughter's despondency.

"Try not to be so upset, Jessica. Many's the babe gits the colic, but both parents and child somehow always manage to live through it. Just remember, we've only to listen to her complaints, but she, poor thing, is suffering the pain of it."

Jessica slammed the tiny brush inside the baby bottle, twisting it spitefully. "There isn't a pain in the whole world like the one she gave me, and now she's ruining my life as well. Old Doc Salters would get a big laugh out of seeing his lusty Irishman now, sharing a room with a squalling brat, in preference to a room with his own wife." Tears of self pity flooded her eyes, and she busied herself over the sink to hide them.

Isaac, walking up behind his daughter, kissed the thick auburn hair and affectionately squeezing her arm. "It's because you're but a child yerself ya have no patience with her, and as for Michael, he knows how hard this has been for you, and how hard you have to work every day. It's his love for you makes him take care of Maggie night after night so's you can git your rest."

"Love of me, or love of Maggie?" She turned and a cloak of pity draped itself about his heart as he watched the luminous brown eyes spew forth the gloomy liquid of grief. Balancing the babe on one hip, he reached out to gather up the weeping girl, but she resisted, turning away.

"I know the lad would not deliberately hurt you, if he but knew your feelings. Can't you bring yerself to talk with him about it?"

"What do you want me to do, sneak downstairs in the middle of the night, like some tart after her lover?" she sobbed. A tear dropped from her chin and sizzled on the coal stove. Isaac watched as it bounced about the lid, then sighing answered.

"I would have you walk down, a woman well within her rights to seek out her husband. A husband, who, I'm sure, will be delighted with her coming. You're a winsome lass, my pet, and the man hasn't drawn breath yet that wouldn't be pleased to find you at his door." Pulling his kerchief from his overalls, he gently dabbed at her cheeks hoping his words could stop the flow of dejection.

Slowly digesting her father's remarks, and deciding to act upon his suggestion, she was able to face him refreshed in spirit. "Oh Papa, you always have a way of making things come out right, just the way you did that Sunday Michael first came to the house. Where would I be without you? She tried to embrace him, but he still held Maggie and she could not encircle them both. She smiled up at her father, "I guess I'll have to get accustomed to her being in the way."

They laughed softly together, Jessica looking forward to following her father's advice, and Isaac, in retrospect, wondering if he had created the beginnings of still more unhappiness. The only thing he had done on that fateful Sunday afternoon was to send a note, instigating it's occurrence, and Jessica, entirely on her own, and by whatever means, had managed to accomplish it's most satisfactory conclusion. Tugging on his suspender he reflected that this time his encouraging words would be the instigation, but once again, she, and she alone would be the sole perpetrator of it's happy or unhappy outcome. The loosened suspender snapped into place as he released it to scratch his head. More and more often lately he found his daughter to be unpredictable.

Jessica had waited until the clock tolled eleven, then donning her woolen wrapper, quietly descended the stairs. A welcome warmth emanated from the banked coal stove as she padded through the kitchen and on to the small room beyond. Michael sat dozing in the rocker, the sleeping child still cradled in his lap. His head was tilted back against the chair, the dimly lit room revealing a gray pallor she had not noticed before. Blue shadows lay deep within the hollows beneath his eyes, and his breathing seemed short and irregular. Frightened, she stepped closer, peering down at him and the now peacefully sleeping Maggie. It was becoming painfully obvious that this new comer was leaving her mark on all of them.

Michael stirred as she carefully removed the baby and replaced her in the cradle. Surprise prompted him to ask, "What are you doing here. Is something wrong, Jessica?"

"Only if it's wrong for a wife to wish to be with her husband after such a long time. I've missed you, Michael," she whispered, not moving from the cradle's side.

His hand passed over his face in an effort to come fully awake, while a thousand pinpoints scratched discomfort in his chest. Trying to delay the inevitable piercing spasm, he dragged himself to the cot and lay down, grateful for it's comfort, and his liberation from the rocker. Jessica, misinterpreting, smiled.

"Papa was right; he said you'd only be too glad to see me." She giggled, then lowered her voice, asking, "Shall I turn out the light, Michael?"

Preoccupied with his ever increasing suffering, he abstractedly answered in the affirmative. Her unexpected presence on the cot startled him and he began coughing violently. Placing his hand across his mouth, he could feel the sticky fluid covering his fingers, and ran to the kitchen to cleanse himself. By the time he returned, Maggie's wails had begun to fill the room. Automatically he started toward the cradle, but Jessica, intercepting him, grabbed his arm, swinging him about to face her.

"I want you to come with me to our room right now. You've spoiled her," a trembling finger indicated the direction of the cradle, "to the point where there's no living with it, now I demand some of your attention. As a matter of true fact, I deserve it, damn it, I'm your wife, and you're living down here like a monk, it's unnatural."

"No more unnatural than for a mother to refuse to nurse her own baby." His voice was weary, holding a note of regret for having spoken.

"So that's the way of it then," she sneered. "All this while you've held that against me, but not being man enough, you've never spoken your mind, holding your grudge against me in silence."

"I've not held it against you, Jess, but I do feel if you had nursed her she wouldn't be having to put up with this colic business. There's nothing in life gives a young one a better start than mother's milk."

"Mother's milk, my foot," she snorted. Let me tell you something Mr. Know It All, I just finished reading in the Journal that there's just as many breast fed kids with colic as there are bottle fed! I can show you the article."

His look was pleading, "It's not too late to start, even now."

She backed away from him, struck dumb by his suggestion. Her pupils dilated with anger as she began laughing wildly, shaking her head from side to side. Reaching the doorway, and raising her brows over eyes filled with repugnance, she asked, "And would you have me moo as well, Michael?" She whirled from the room, leaving him alone with his still fretting daughter, his pain, and a sense of nagging foreboding.

Chapter Two

Summer found both Michael and Maggie enjoying improved health, lessening the tensions that had satiated the house. Maggie now occupied the bedroom adjoining that of her parents who, try as they may, could not rekindle their need for each other. It eluded them like a memory, sweet in retrospect, but impossible to recapture. Though yearning for a return to the short lived happiness they had known, not that long ago, each saw the other as the perpetrator of the problem, and neither was able to initiate the first overture that would bring harmony. Instead, they built a wall with bitter bricks of silence, held together with the mortar of snide remarks, demeaning innuendo and deliberate unconcern, until it's height seemed insurmountable.

Sheer boredom forced Jessica to finally take an interest in her daughter. Maggie was fast developing a personality, knowing with baby instinct how to amuse or gain attention, and her beauty, as Michael had admitted to himself many times, was without equal. Even Jessica marveled at the perfect bow of her lips and the luster of the jet black tufts that had begun to curl about her faultlessly shaped head. Contradicting the general law of nature, her eyes were as blue as her grandfather's, and twinkled with irresistible merriment.

Michael stood unnoticed at the garden gate, watching mother and child pleasuring each other as they sat together on the lawn. The baby, still unsteady, was supported by Jessica's arm, and as she bent to press her mouth against the soft down on the infant's head, Michael's heart constricted with the memory of a picture that had hung in his lonely room.

The Madonna and Child fused together with the sight before him and so powerful a feeling of love convulsed him, uncontrollable tears sprang to his eyes, momentarily blinding him to the almost sacred scene. Blinking rapidly he pushed open the gate, determined to tell Jessica of his feelings and perhaps begin to right their lives, but as the warning screech of his entry sounded, Jessica's face turned cold as the metal beneath his hand, and she rose quickly, preparing to leave.

"I've lost track of the hour," she apologized politely. "I'll start supper right away."

His answer stayed her. "There's no need. They've called an important meeting tonight and they'll be serving sandwiches and beer, which will be plenty for me. I'll take your father with me and you'll not have to fuss at all. Let's just both sit here together for a bit and watch the little lass." Reaching for her hand, he plopped down enthusiastically greeting an oblivious Maggie who was busily admiring her own toes, contentedly addressing each digit in typical baby gibberish.

Reluctantly Jessica had seated herself opposite him on the blanket in time to hear him whisper, "You're so beautiful, just like your mother." Experiencing a stir of response she wished to deny, she stubbornly turned her profile to him, demanding, "Why would you want to take my father along tonight? He hasn't worked in years and I'm sure he doesn't care a fig about your union and it's gripes."

"Your father cares about everything, and especially you and your happiness."

Reaching across the blanket, he touched her shoulder timidly, "I care about your happiness too, Jess."

She faced him defiantly. "Next thing you know you'll be telling me you love me."

Hesitating only a moment, he tried to reassure her. "Of course I love you, Jess. You're the mother of my child."

She stood up, smoothing her wrinkled skirt with exasperated, jerky movements. "Michael, Michael," she sighed disgustedly, pointing to Maggie. "She is supposed to be the result of our love, not the cause of it. She started towards the house, but he bounded in front of her, blocking her way. The earnest black eyes bore into hers.

"I wish you would wait up for me tonight." Groping once again for her hand, he continued. "I promise it won't be late, we should reach home no later than quarter past ten." Waiting expectantly he realized he had sounded somewhat the beggar, and found it necessary to toss her an offhand alternative. "Of course if you're tired, I understand. It's entirely up to you."

Trying to suppress her eagerness she searched his face as though looking for her own answer. "I'll wait."

The meeting to take place this night would, unfortunately, seal the doom of the mine worker forever, forcing the American consumer to seek fuel more reasonably priced, and most certainly more reliably produced.

In April of 1922 the union, now under the leadership of John L. Lewis had called a general strike which was to last one hundred and sixty three days, and become the first time since 1912 that miners had refused to remain working during negotiations of a new wage contract, when promised retroactive terms to the old contract's expiration. One hundred and forty thousand men had stood idle while the union made demands for a 20% wage hike, overtime, double time for Sundays and holidays, and complete recognition of the union. By strike's end their deprivation had gained them only Congress's promise to create an investigative Coal Commission whose sole purpose would be to delve into, and report upon every phase and facet of the mining industry. Meanwhile the miners had returned to work without the companies ever having met one single union demand. Each man had suffered almost eight hundred dollars in lost wages, while Mr. Lewis had gained a better bargaining position for the union in the bituminous fields through his previous, cagey maneuverings to insure that wage agreements covering both hard and soft fields would expire simultaneously. With smug self satisfaction, he had boldly announced at a national convention in the later part of 1921, that he considered this uniform expiration an achievement of no mean consequence, and one that would allow for the full measured influence and economic power of his great membership to be utilized for the achievement of "our ideals".

One year later, one strike later, and an additional eighteen days of idelness, finally netted the men a 10% wage hike, but little else. Now, with the passage of a mere two years, the workers would again be asked to lay down their tools, striking for the recognition of a union whose additional wage hike demands could not be met by the companies without dire affects on the consumer, and, of course, eventually the industry itself. For reasons difficult to fathom in retrospect, the men would cling to their leadership with blind trust, marching without discernment into the valley of diminishing demand, to eventually become an almost forgotten force in labor.

Isaac shoves the afternoon paper across the kitchen table with disgust. "Your man Lewis asks too much when he expects the companies to collect his union dues and then turn them over to him like some dutiful child."

Michael scanned the screaming headlines declaring Lewis's insistence on the check off system, and immediately became defensive. "These funds are a necessary evil, sir. How else could we organize other coal fields or get money for the attorney fees needed to fight these wealthy companies and get the men what they're entitled to receive. In Illinois alone the union spent over $800,000 in defense fees for the Herrin massacre trials. No man has the means to do battle with a company on his, own so it lies with the union to see to their preservation." He nodded firmly. "And that they do, sir, yes indeed, the union surely takes care of it's own."

"And it's own pockets too, I'd suspect." Isaac's thumbs hooked into the faded red suspenders stubbornly as he leaned back in the kitchen chair, eyeing his son-in-law warily. "I've never seen no public accounting for all these monies they've collected so far, and neither has anyone else that I know of. Don't seem right to me that they don't have to report to their contributors what they've done with their money." A challenging spark kindled in the center of the astonishing clear blue eyes. "This here check off system, so long fought for by the union, doesn't only make the company collect the dues to swell it's own revenues, but helps them to create a closed shop by making the worker afraid not to join the ranks for fear of retribution from the labor organization. I agree with the company that it ain't right to compel membership on any man because it's a form of enforced taxation, and dreamed up by your sterling leadership for it's own gain, if you ask me."

Michael's genuine fondness for the old timer permitted his continued patience. "Well, I must disagree with that, sir. Mr. Lewis is one of us who knows firsthand from his own days of working the mines, all the injustices we've had to suffer. His only concern is for making our lives better, and I, for one, think he's doing a good job of it."

The old man snapped his suspenders and stood up, wagging one bony finger under Michael's nose. "Well, just let me tell you this, lad, if he calls another strike there ain't nobody's gonna be the better for it except him, who'll get just what he wants, and what he wants is pretty obvious. It's more and more power that he wants, and mark my words, son, winter's not far away and if he goes calling for another walk out the public's not likely to be sympathetic to those of you who allow them to be cold all coal burning season and then turn around and ask them to pay higher and higher prices for the privilege of staying warm. No siree, they won't let you get away with it."

Michael rose, forcing himself to smile as he good naturedly patted his father in law's shoulder. "Everybody has a right to their own opinion, sir, and everybody else has the right to try and change it. That's why I'm glad you're coming along with me tonight to the meeting. Maybe you'll hear some things that will change your mind."

Isaac, disappointed by this sudden termination of their conversation, answered meekly. Well, I don't suppose my opinions are worth a hill of beans anyway since I haven't set foot in a mine for almost twenty years." An unexpected inspiration brightened him momentarily. "But neither has your man, Lewis, and he's loaded with his own opinions."

Michael laughed heartily as he retreated to the back stairwell. "I'm sure everybody will be pleased with your attendance, and more than willing to listen to your respected opinions. Let me just wash up a bit and we'll go put it to the test."

Isaac shook his head in silent rebuttal. This new young breed of mining men, who used continual work stoppage as their big stick of protest, would surely bring about their own downfall. The union, he admitted to himself, had most certainly brought about many much needed changes, but their ever increasing demands must eventually bankrupt an industry that can no longer sustain increased production costs without penalizing the consumer, a consumer who was already blest with a growing number of alternatives. For the first time in his life he was grateful for being old.

Michael was well pleased with the seemingly endless stream of men entering the hall. Isaac, sitting next to him, waved cheerfully to the many familiar faces in the smoke laden room. Many of the older men stopped to chat and shake his hand, and the stimulation of participation in something outside his own home rejuvenated him in mind and spirit. Laying his wrinkled hand on Michael's knee, he leaned toward the younger man in order to be heard above the din of male voices.

"It was very kind of you, lad, to think to bring me along. It does a man good to know he's not been forgotten by his old friends." Gently squeezing Michael's leg, he added. "And his new ones as well."

Michael affectionately patted the withered hand, but guilt paralyzed his tongue. Regardless of what he had told Isaac he knew he had brought the old man along to further his own ambitions by cashing in on his father-in-laws popularity and using it to his own advantage, and could not bear his gratitude. From the very beginning of their relationship he had done nothing except exploit the older man in situation after situation. The goodness in man is as fragile as the shell of an egg, he thought. One small crack of ambition allowed the seepage of greed and corruption to slowly ooze over it's pure cover until the sticky mess obliterates all good intentions and self denial. The agony of his thoughts caused him to forget the swirling crowd, while the hall and it's contents blurred before him, and he felt the saber of death piercing ever deeper into his chest. I will make amends to both father and daughter, he silently promised himself. Please God, let me find the way. Then as an afterthought he added dismally, and if it be thy will Lord, the time in which to do it.

The heat had become oppressive, and all too familiar bands of discomfort had begun to twist about his chest. Suppressing a persistent urge to cough, he walked to the center of the platform, calling the men to order in a strong voice, despite his miserable anguish. Within a few minutes all had found seats and anxiously waited to hear the proposals about to be set before them. Raising his arm in a gesture demanding silence, Michael smiled at the upturned faces as benevolently as any preacher on Sunday morning, and introduced Jeb Walton, friend to every mining man, and sent to Miners' Haven as representative for Mr. Lewis himself. The men responded with light applause, more out of respect for Mr. Lewis than in appreciation for the stranger who stood before them.

Jeb Walton was a huge man with a shock of red hair that stood straight up, like the bristles on the back of a porcupine. His brows were bushy, with the same wire like hairs that made them appear constantly raised over piercing sea green eyes. One corner of his mouth had been twisted up by a falling slab of slate that would leave him smiling, without mirth, through eternity. The deep lines in his cheeks added to his diabolical appearance, as he gazed about the room without speaking, and each man had the uncomfortable feeling that he was able to look into, and read their very souls. Without warning his massive hand slammed against the podium with the authority of a thunderclap, bringing his audience to rapt attention.

"Aye, lads," his raucous voice boomed, ricocheting off the walls, "It's glad I am to be here for it's plain to see there's not a faint heart among ya, and by the time we've finished this night, you'll all have taken your place in history as the force that changed the destiny of the mining men for all time to come."

Isaac abstractedly shook his head in agreement and Michael, misinterpreting the assenting nod, smiled in appreciation as he wondered who, during the pre-speech conversations, had been able to sway the old man's thinking. Grateful, he returned his attention to Mr. Walton.

"I'd first like to bring your attention to the fact that our demands have been presented at meeting after meeting since July 9th, in one city after the other. The leadership of this union has left no stone unturned trying to make the very best settlement for all you lads, with the hard headed operators balking at every turn. They're unwilling to submit to a wage hike or the check off system claiming they will cause an increase in the cost of their production, but they find no fault with paying a man by the car load instead of the ton, decreasing his income while they increase their own." Small rivulets of perspiration dampened his fiery sideburns, but not his enthusiasm as he continued. "And now, what about that grand hospital being built by you men, and subsidized by your state. Do you know what that means, lads?" His neck jutted forward, punctuating the question, while the bright green eyes scanned their faces as though expecting a reply. Then lowering his voice to a pitch the assembly strained to hear, he answered himself. "It means, lads, that you gave as originally agreed, but the company let you down again and did not. You, who have already given your fathers, your sons and your brothers, are giving still, while the company fills it's own coffers and allows you the right to die in it's behalf. Allows you to work more than an eight hour day without a thought to overtime. Allows you to spend a lifetime bending your back without a thought to your old age. And what of your fine new hospital, lads?" His brows rose even higher. "Have any of you ever considered that you may not be able to afford being a patient in it?" The men started as he again smashed his fist against the lectern, bellowing. "We need, and must have a 10% wage increase, we need, and must have time and a half for overtime, we need and must have double time for Sundays and holidays. We need and demand a plan where a man is paid on a ton basis of 2,240 pounds, and not the consideration rate. Now the company says this will make a man lazy and feel hisself not havin' to pull his own weight." His laugh of derision sounded more like a gurgle. "I say if a man has to plough through rock to get to coal, and his output is curtailed, he's still worked as hard as the lucky bloke on the piecework basis."

A few shouts of agreement rose from the men now suffering under the consideration rate, which, like their production, was considerably less than the earnings of the contract miners.

Jeb Walton allowed himself a condescending smile. "Men, I know many of you feel you're better off now than you've ever been, and well you may be, but I'm here to tell you tonight, that of all the great industries in this land, you're still on the bottom rung." The smile became sardonic. "Be ye men enough to change it?" His frightening eyes poured over the thoughtful faces in the crowd as he clenched his fist before them. "We're asking for a two year contract this time lads, and we're asking for the good life too. In your hands lies the commodity that turns the work wheels in this country, and warms the world in winter. It makes men rich and nations powerful, and it's controlled by you, lads, as it has been since Abijah and John Smith first shipped their ark-load of stone coal down the Susquehanna River in 1807. These were enterprising young men who could see ahead of the normal march of events, and we earnestly try following their incredible examples of foresightedness by planning ahead for your future, lads. Read the propositions handed to you as you entered, and may the good earth spew from her very bowels any man who would vote against them. We lay down our picks on the morrow, lads because the company has not seen fit to meet our fair demands. Mr. Lewis refuses arbitration, standing firm on the issues at hand as befits any strong leader."

Isaac's head automatically nodded again. A strong and powerful leader, he thought, whose begun to live by the motto of rule or ruin. Feeling a sense of depression, he watched as Jeb Walton's eyes flashed around the room with satanical fire, his face almost a contradiction as he whispered audibly, "God bless you all, and may the heavens protect our valiant leader, Mr. John Llewellyn Lewis!"

A cry of approval filled the auditorium as Michael, grateful for a cessation of pain, rose and congratulated Jeb Walton on his delivery, and then called for order. Looking amicably around the hall he announced, "Now men, I know you're all most anxious to get to the lunch, to say nothing of the liquid refreshments in the rear of the hall, so we'll take a moment for a quick aye vote, and get on with some socializing." There was a nodding of heads and a rumble of laughter as Michael reached for the gavel. "All those in favor of the aforementioned proposals answer by saying aye." The affirmative vote held the sound of a cheer as the men voiced their enthusiasm in unanimity.

"All those not in favor answer by saying nay." His tone intimated that any response would be deemed ludicrous, and yet a negative reverberation rose from a far corner of the room. Michael's jet black eyes strained to distinguish the faces of the dissenters and fell upon the unpleasant and offensive sneer on the face of Tom Quinlan.

"Sweet Mother, why does he plague me so?" he muttered. There's got to be a good reason for such devoted hatred, he thought, when I have done nothing but put up with his continued ire, trying to placate him in every way. I should march over and box his young ears in plain view of his rowdy cohorts, just to teach him a lesson. A sharp unexpected aching forced him to bow to prudence as the best policy for the moment. Hardening his smile, he soundly rapt the gavel soundly, as he proclaimed,

"The ayes have it, lads, so eat, drink, and be merry for tomorrow there's no work!"

Losing sight of Tom among the men rising from their chairs and stumbling over themselves and each other in their eagerness to reach the refreshments, he again thanked and congratulated Jeb on his eloquent rhetoric. Then assuring him that Miner's Haven stood solidly behind their leader, and recognized his tactics as the only possible means to an honorable end, he turned to Isaac for affirmation, only to discover his father-in-law had deserted him, and was already threading his way through the maze of empty chairs in the direction of the now cheerful miners. By nine o'clock the crowd had totally relaxed, speaking confidently of returning to work within the week, with more than likely, all of their demands met, by a company that could not survive without them, This errant bravado, and an ingrained fixation with striking, left them bereft of understanding that their own existence, in turn, was reliant of the company they had so determinedly set out to bring to it's knees. None would return to the mines for one hundred and seventy days, and then only to an industry that would never recover from the ego and obstinacy of their revered leader, and their own gullibility. All would suffer severely for this stroll down the primrose path of promises without having given any consideration to the possibility of the path's calamitous end. Trusting in all they were told by men they considered to be intelligent, and striving endlessly only to gain improvements for them, they had not felt the necessity of delving into the fact, that perhaps these noble men had, this time, demanded the impossible. Instead they reveled prematurely in the belief that right was on their side, and this thought, plus the intake of sufficient spirits, spurred more than a few of them to thinking perhaps their demands may have been inadequate, and needed some bolstering up. As Michael good naturedly listened to this nonsense, an impudent and familiar voice caught his attention.

"Yeah, well why should he worry what happens when he's living off the fat of his father-in-law? Sure I'd be up there telling you the same thing myself if I was him, but I hain't, so I'm telling you this, and you'd just better believe it. If we're out of work for a long time, he eats, we don't! You see, lads, it's easy to have the courage of a lion when the lioness is the one providing the food."

Michael, compressing his lips, felt the heat of anger flood through him as he looked about to determine who else had heard. Catching sight of Isaac's stricken face, he strode towards Tom in time to hear the older man questioning in harsh tones.

"Have you lost your mind or your manner, Tom Quinlan? Either way there's an apology due here, young feller, and it better be pretty fast in coming, believe you me!"

Isaac's voice trembled as he tried controlling his temper, the translucent blue eyes turning opaque, as they clouded over with resentment. Deference stifled an impetuous reply, as Tom answered in a subdued voice.

"Sir, I'm sorry, but I cannot apologize for what I believe to be the truth, and to me, truth were the only words I spoke." Looking down, he self consciously dug the empty toe of his boot into the worn floor boards.

"And who has given you the authority to judge what is truth in my house, pray tell. You're nothing but a boy, without any right to be putting your nose into things that are none of your business in the first place,"

Isaac's eyes had begun to glitter like fine steel, and his balled fists clenching and unclenching at his sides, caused Tom to waver slightly. The old man's words were almost identical to those his daughter had shouted that miserable Saturday afternoon, that now seemed so very long ago. Reluctant as he was to carry this confrontation further, pent up frustration did not allow him to remain silent for long.

"The truth be damned then!" he exclaimed bravely. Let's just look at and examine the plain facts." He took a step forward, buoyed by the overflowing river of his bitterness. "This braggart decides to force his way into the life of an innocent young girl, a girl as exquisite as any rose in your prized garden, and then despoils her like she was just another one of his disgusting conquests he so enjoys bragging about day and night." A look of unbearable pain creased his features, as a note of disbelief crept into his voice. "And you, Mr. Hobbs, have approved his act with your presence here tonight. Standing behind him in another union proposal that will be of no benefit to your old friends and neighbors. I say this stamp of your approval can only add to her disgrace."

It has surfaced at last, thought Michael. The lad truly loves, and longs to be with her, while I, who have only to reach out, can find not even the smallest moment of contentment because of her. He could feel the augmenting pressures slowly returning, or was it grief that lay like a pall across his throbbing chest? How cruel and complicated was the road of life, with it's twisting and tantalizing thoroughfares, that forced unsagious men to choose only one path, a path that so very often led to woeful lanes of no return. Perspiration oozed from his every pore, as he wistfully imagined the happiness that rightfully should have belonged to Tom. A man who would gladly have given Jessica the unconditional love she so ardently longed for. A man who could gain pleasure from his own steadfast devotion, and bask in the luxury of her nearness. His latent ear once more heard the whisperings of the parish priest through the grating of the confessional.

"Man is the only animal with free will, my son. Strange, is it not, how he continues to choose sin over the teachings of our Lord?"

Had he not freely willed his own immorality, with no real intent to change it? After dutifully performing his penance, attending Mass and receiving Holy Communion as piously as the innocent nun kneeling beside him, his attempts to remain free of mortal sin had always been feeble, at most. His complacency laying in the knowledge that his endless iniquities would be forever forgiven through the intervention of the faithful priest. But now his willfulness was making him the destroyer of men, and this was beyond his own forgiveness. A valiant effort forced his attention back to the room, only to find Isaac's face livid with rage, as Tom, reaching out, tried to restrain his threatening fists.

Michael's remorse for any wrong he had perpetrated against the young man vanished in the immediate light of the need for Isaac's rescue. Springing to his side, he released Tom's gripe with a less than passive wrench, and Tom in his turn, swung free with a violence that threw Michael into the wooden crates that had served to hold the refreshment table. Momentarily leaning against them, he tried to regain his equilibrium in a world entirely out of focus. A wild roaring filled his head as he felt, rather than heard, the scuffling of feet around him, and then suddenly, a pressure on his shoulder was forcing him around to once more meet his tormentor. Raising both arms defensively, he again lost his balance, and heard, like some distant drum, the thud of his own body as it hit the dusty floor.

Sticky, nauseating fluid filled his mouth and throat as he stared blindly into the splintered boards beneath him. He lay docile in a sudden void of silence, remotely aware of the gentle hands that strove to turn him over. Isaac's beard mingled with the dripping blood on Michael's chin, as he supported the younger man against his breast. Soundlessly he cursed the mines, the companies, the union, and even God himself, for allowing a human being to suffer the indignity of spilling his life's blood on some drab and dirty floor in front of an inebriated and curious crowd. Almost crooning the question, he asked.

"Can you sit up, poor lad?" Remember we promised to be home early."

He rocked Michael tenderly, as a woman does her ailing child, unmindful of the torrent of tears unashamedly washing over his frosty beard.

Tom, turning to the stunned watchful mass encircling the distasteful scene, shrugged his shoulders and spread his arms out in denial.

"I swear I never touched him, lads. I swear I never even touched Him."

Chapter Four

The grandfather's clock tolled the hour of ten as the two exhausted men reached home. Neither had spoken till now, conserving their small remaining strength for the arduous walk up the hill. Michael, staggering, fell gratefully into a kitchen chair as Isaac, opening the stove's damper, began raking and stirring the banked coals into a frenzy of heat that soon had the coffee pot humming. Carefully placing a steaming cup on the table before Michael, the old man spoke at last.

"How long have you known, lad?"

Michael's impulse to repudiate melted under the scrutiny of those icy glacier-like eyes, which dictated to him that the old man would accept nothing, save what was the truth. Rigidly poising his clenched fists on the table's top, he listlessly stared into them and mumbled.

"It's been almost a year now, but I must say that tonight was by far the worst. It's never been quite this bad before, never so much pain and light headedness." He looked at Isaac sadly. "That young lad, Tom, he was right, you know, he never did touch me." Eyeing his knotted fists more intently he examined the why of it all. "I must have just passed out from the exertion of the scuffle, or maybe the terrible spasms of pain I'd been having all night just took their toll. Who will ever know the real reason for it?" Try as he might he had not been able to disguise his tone of depression, and fell silent, bombarded by a barrage of dismal and sorrowful speculations that served only to increase his despondency.

Isaac, trying to control his sympathy, drew the back of his hand across his moustache, whisking away a few beads of excess fluid and shaking them unto the kitchen floor. Then tapping his now empty cup with one heavily veined finger, he spoke in a voice that betrayed his commiseration.

"I think it's time that maybe we think of going into this hardware business before the main partner even gets here." Holding up his hand at Michaels' first sign of protest, he pressed on. "Just hear me out now, lad, because I've given it a lot of thought all the way home. As a matter of true fact, I've given it a lot of thought over most of my lifetime, but just never quite had the courage, or maybe the need to put it to the test." He gazed heavenward theatrically. "Maybe God himself has intervened, in his own way, to correct the error of a young man's illness that should never have existed. What do you think, lad?"

He watched as Michael, having fingered many a rosary in his own behalf during the past few months, sat stupidly bowing his head in totally amazed agreement. Pausing to digest his own thoughts, and satisfying himself that all he said was perfectly logical, Isaac pushed on.

"Anyway, the way I figure it we'll have to take a mortgage on the house to get enough money to lay in our stock, and then try to rent that empty building next to the Majestic if the landlord is amiable, and the price is right. That way we could stay open evenings and try to cash in on the theatre crowds by making ourselves available both before and after every showing." His voice became more animated as he continued. "By God, the very thought of it is enough to make an old man feel young again."

Michael, blinking to rid his vision of the excess moisture rapidly satiating his eyes, placed a trembling hand on his father in law's shoulder.

"I've never known goodness like yours, sir, but there's no way I could agree to a venture like this. What if--?"

Brushing the quaking hand aside, Isaac walked to the cupboard and withdrew a dust covered sheaf of papers, whose tattered corners had curled and yellowed with the passage of time. A tremor now passed through his own fingers as he held onto his treasure. With the trepidation of an author presenting his first manuscript, he spoke almost shyly.

"Long ago I compiled this list of essentials necessary to the success of a business, editing and adding to it over the years, until I felt it was perfected into a sure fire manual, insuring anyone's prosperity in the world of hardware." His beard parted in a self conscious grin. "So now you can see I've really have given a lot of thought to this project long before I made your acquaintance, lad, but it's all remained speculation, day dreams used to satisfy an old man's musings and soften the rigid monotony of a routine and more or less regimented life. Let's just say it's been half a hobby and half a dream that now, might well become an actuality."

Whisking his arm across the top sheet, he swiftly removed the dirt with his shirt sleeve and thrust the deteriorating catalog in front of Michael. "If we're going to be partners, you, of course, would have to agree with my basic ideas, and I'm hoping you're not too tired to look them over with me now."

Leaning over the table in an anticipatory pose, eyes twinkling with delighted excitement, he nervously spread the papers about the table and waited, like an impatient child, as Michael reluctantly began to rummage through the multiple, in depth entries.

Every sheet contained heading representing necessary stock items, extraneous stock, and the expense and possibility of broadening into durable household goods, such as skillets, cutlery and pewter. There were complete compiling of expected expenditures, such as insurance, advertising, improved methods of display, salaries and possible rent increases. All forecasts and projections had been painfully handwritten in clear and distinct script, belying any careless or hurried resolution, and had obviously taken much time and concentrated effort to bring it to it's meticulous completion. Michael's eyes poured over the worn musty papers, scrutinizing every entry with intensified interest and disbelief. The old man had painstakingly thought out every contingency right down to earned interest on extended credit accounts, the allowable number of such accounts, and the limit of their extensions, if the company were to survive. Such methodical planning and astute foresightedness, surely could not fail, he told himself, as he thumbed through the pages, his excitement growing with the turning of every page. Besides he owed a debt here, and if it was really what Isaac wanted it was most certainly not his place to put a damper on the old man's dreams, but rather, his obligation to prompt whatever would insure his happiness, and enable him, at last, to bring to fruition his long longed for ambition. Conveniently failing to consider his father-in-law's obvious contentment until now, without this supposed benefit of consummation, allowed him to think of himself as the tool the requisite needed for the final honing of a cherished vision, rather than the implement that was digging into, and forever altering, an established and satisfactory way of life.

His anxiety to escape or side step issues that may prompt feelings of guilt, prevented any further soul searching, while his all too optimistic nature easily eradicated all small doubts struggling to enter his subconscious mind. Feeling almost pontifical about his decision to assist Isaac in the fulfillment of his dream, he lapsed into silent, eager rhapsodizing about a rosy future, contemplating only the promise of success and the security it would provide for his beloved Maggie.

Like all dreamers since man's inception, his happy projections were all far into the future, and negated any concern for the problems of the present. Their business would be well established by the time for proper schooling had arrived, and he would, of course, have become a man of importance in the community by then, heading up committees, volunteering his spare time to worthwhile causes, and quite possibly entering local politics. He was, after all, a natural leader of men, and many the man at Slope number 2 that would gladly attest to it. He envisioned Maggie, elegantly garbed in the latest fashions, being introduced into the society of genteel people, attending the holiday parties and teas given each year by the affluent families in the park section. Yes indeed, every head would turn at the sight of her, including, more than likely, some suitable young men, all of whom would have to pass his severe scrutiny. No ragamuffin type lad would ever get the chance to tamper with the daughter of Michael McClellan. Smiling to himself, he dragged his eyes away from the sheets to find Isaac impatiently waiting, his brows raised quizzically in expectation. Without a thought to his own reprehensible misconduct against this man's daughter, he slapped his large hand vigorously on the table top.

"By the Saints!" he roared. "I've finally met a man smarter than myself."

Laughing and filled with congeniality, the two men fell into heated discussion, unable to control their enthusiasm, carried away by waves of eagerness and fervor. Each man's ardor had became an involuntary propellant for the other, and only until after the clock had tolled twelve did they finally reach across the table, committing one to the other in partnership. Climbing the stairs, arms flung about each other's shoulders, they were elated by their newly discovered camaraderie of purpose and it's inevitable accomplishment. Isaac began singing softly.

"My sweetheart's the mule in the mines,
I drive her without reins or lines.
On the bumper I sit. I chew and I spit
All over my sweetheart's behind."

The men roared with delight, as though hearing this ditty for the very first time. Then suddenly remembering his sleeping wife, Michael gently pressed two fingers against his father-in-law's lips.

"Perhaps we'd best save some of the celebrating until we can share it with our Jess."

Isaac's eyes softened at the sound of what he considered an endearment. "You're right, of course, lad. And what a time we'll have with our little surprise for her. I can barely wait to see her face when she hears of it." Pumping Michael's hand he whispered, "Sleep well, son, sleep well."

Michael watched the old man as he almost pranced down the hall to his own room, filled with the same light hearted vigor he himself was experiencing.

Michael undressed quietly, tossing his discarded garments into a small heap in the corner of the bedroom then stealthily slid beneath the whispering sheets, his mind exploding with the tremendous prospects of the future. Unnoticed, the form beside him moved irritably, tugging at the covers while emitting a sigh of extreme disgust.

Her heart had pumped wildly when at ten o'clock she had heard the men's voices in the kitchen below her room. On tiptoe she had dashed nervously to the bureau to dab her wrists and earlobes with rose water, Michael's favorite scent. Once again in her bed, a shiver of anticipation passed over her as she lay straining to hear his footsteps on the stairs. Her breathing quickened with excitement, forcing her to throw back the coverlet in a vain attempt to escape the heat of desire pervading her feverish body. Unable to contain her conjecture, all manner of wild fantasies danced before her mind's eye, and she soon found herself reliving their first night together on Raspberry Hill, every minute detail magnified to magnificence by the urgency of lust. In retrospect she remembered it only as the magical culmination of two souls who had longed for nothing but each other, both consumed by undeniable desire, and beyond resisting it's demands, when, at last, sweet destiny played it's part by bringing them together. Her lips involuntarily moved in prayer for his immediate presence, stopping at every sound that may have been the announcement of his coming. However, as the hours ticked wearily away, her ferverant ardor turned to vengeful wrath, and her pleading prayers to ruthless curses as she realized that she lay as completely forgotten as his promise.

When finally Michael entered the room, her body had become rigid with hatred, the only desire left in her now, to humiliate him by her flat refusal of his attentions. She would nevermore be the pursuer, she vowed, making him beg and grovel for her slightest recognition, basking in his misery and enjoying his abasement until her own pride had been appeased. What a fool she had been to agree to waiting up for him! Her very first condescension in months had been abused, relegated to a sphere of unimportance by his obvious show of mindless indifference. Prepared to do battle, she sat upright in bed and turned to look at her husband. His recently longed for lips had parted in complete repose as the sonorous sounds of deep sleep escaped from between them. The bastard had not remembered even after he lay down beside her! She stared at him disbelievingly; her eyes distended with loathing and detestation, then drew back from the sight of him, saturated with repugnance. Beads of frustration dotted her furrowed brow as she cursed, within herself, this vile abomination sleeping peacefully beside her. Her eyes glinted in the dark, her mouth becoming hard, settling into an odious line of absolute aversion. Her jaw muscles tightened as, between clenched teeth, she vowed his destruction through the only thing that had ever mattered to him, the thing she knew had destroyed them both, Maggie.

The coffee pot hummed cheerily atop the coals as Michael entered the bright, sunny kitchen on Sunday morning. The shabbiness of his Sabbath outfit had never distressed him before, but now he picked self-consciously at the frayed cuffs, dreaming of the pretentious suit he would soon be able to purchase the moment the expected profits began pouring in. He brushed Jessica's cheek with a mechanical morning kiss, insensitive to the unusually loud clamor rising from the pans she suddenly put into motion. Within the space of a few minutes, Isaac entered the room, and joined Michael at the laid table. Both men wore smiles of conspiracy as they waited impatiently for Jessica, who, performing with a perfunctory air, almost slammed their breakfast before them, falling into her chair with complete disdain.

Unmindful of her display of frustration, Isaac satisfied himself that he could now command her full attention, and stealing a last knowing look at Michael, cleared his throat in the magnanimous manner people usually employ when they are about to make an important announcement.

Intrepidly he began to impart the plans and hopes for the future that he and her husband had decided upon the previous evening. Spasmodically Michael found it necessary to interrupt, insuring that Isaac did not delete one single thought or promise of what was certain to be. Their total enrapture with the subject obscured her reaction, with neither one of them noticing how she sat, immobile in her chair, unwilling to seriously consider any of this idiotic prattle falling about her ears.

"So that, my lass, is the sum and substance of it," concluded Isaac, with satisfaction. "And Michael and I will be going to the bank the very first thing in the morning to get this thing rolling. Yes ma'am, there's no way we're going to let any grass grow under our feet on this project. We're going to step right out there in the arena, prepared to do battle on the boards of business." Leaning back comfortably in his chair, he stretched and snapped his red suspenders with two crooked thumbs in the further affirmation of his confidence. Nodding in unison, the two men smiled smugly as they waited for Jessica's astonishment, and unqualified approval of such an industrious undertaking.

Compressing her lips momentarily, she delayed a reply to this idiocy while she struggled for self control. The agitated beating of her heart had forced an unhealthy color to her cheeks, and the moisture of exasperation to her brow. Most assuredly her father had lost his senses to be, even vaguely, considering a move as prodigious as this. These were the ramblings of irresponsible little boys, who seemed willing to play the game of chance and gamble away all of the security each of them were dependent upon on some concocted, unnecessary and fanciful whim. Many a year had passed since Isaac lay down his pick, and never once had they known wanting. The whole idea was ridiculous, impossible and without feasibility. It's entire conception must have been devised by Michael, a man so infused with his own personal need for success he could only briefly be content with his lot in life, forever pursuing something beyond himself, relentless and disregardful of the harm his untamed ambition eventually inflicted upon others. The true reason for his activity in the union was his nagging dissatisfaction with mere worker's status, and his plaguing desire to be, just a cut above everyone else. All of his railing protestations against injustice and the company's failure to acquiesce to the needs of the men had never fooled her for a moment. Each and every outburst only served to personify the planned, attention getting stratagem, designed to garner even the smallest amounts of power. The power needed to rule the nondescript world of darkness beneath the earth's crust.

Well, let him play his little game to his heart's content with his poor unsuspecting cohorts, but she was not about to have any of it in this house. Shooting a scathing look in Michael's direction, she rose on trembling knees, and spoke in a deadly whisper.

"I'll not have it. Do you both hear me and understand what I'm saying? I'm saying that I will not put up with one more silly thought from either one of you, because it's quite obvious to me that you have both lost your minds, and I am the only sane person in this room, the only one who can save you from you from your own stupidity."

Her mouth was set and uncompromising as she stared down at them, watching the smiles freeze on their lips as they stared dumbly at the distraught girl they had expected to be jubilant. Isaac, accustomed to his daughter's stubbornness and mulish obstinacy, tried to be fore-bearing, asking gently,

"What possible objection could there be to a better future for you and your child? Come now Jessica, I don't think you're looking at this properly. Let me just remind you that the mines have been struck, with the possibility of no work for a time, and you stand here objecting to plans that will make money outside of them. I am really hard pressed to fathom this kind of thinking."

Jessica threw her hands over her eyes, needing desperately to escape the sight of her gullible parent, and sucked in a deep breath.

"What a fool you are! You both Are!" Lowering her arms slowly, she spoke as she would to small children, patiently and condescending. "Don't you two see that if there's no work there's bound to be no money, so how will anyone be able to buy your wares, even if they wanted to, or are you planning to live off the credit you're going to have to extend to others?"

Her over tolerant tone irritated Isaac, and he slapped his knee loudly. "Listen, my girl, this strike has to be looked at as a temporary thing and a chance for Michael and I to get started. By the time the men get back to work and have their first pay check in hand, we'll be set up and ready for business, and they'll be well out of supplies and needing to replenish them. Yes sir, there's no doubt about the fact that there's going to be money to be made, providing we get started now." Noting that her expression had remained unchanged, he dismissed her with a wave of his hand, exclaiming, "Ah, your just a girl and not expected to understand these things anyway. We probably never should have told you about it in the first place."

Expectantly he looked to Michael for support of his assessment, but Jessica's cold voice was his only response.

"I understand perfectly well that you're acting like a damned old fool, letting himself be led down a path of destruction by an irresponsible young fool whose got no stake in it. Since when have either of you been able to predict the future, or do you have some crystal ball that I don't know about that's already foreseen the strike's end? Can't you see that this is a showdown between the union and the mines, and believe me, the mines hold all the aces, just as they always have. Your grand Mr. Lewis is about to make an all out stand on his bull-headed insistence that his precious union be fully recognized by the company, and the company is not going to bend to his demand this time any more than they did last time. This strike could go on indefinitely because this time the union is prepared to settle only on their own terms." She sighed deeply. "Papa, you read the paper every day. You know what's going on and I heard you say yourself that the union will never want to maintain peace as long as their paid officials thrive on petty grievances, and the holding out of false hopes."

Michael rose slightly out of his chair to protest this blasphemy, but his wife's blazing eyes silenced him. "You have no say in this, Michael, you have nothing to lose but my father's money." Turning to Isaac, she continued more patiently.

"Papa, some wise man once said, choice, not chance rules the destiny of men. I beg you, Papa, please don't make this foolish choice. For God's sake, be guided by some reason and not some pie in the sky foolishness you'll live to regret." Her voice had risen in a crescendo of anguish as Isaac jumped to his feet in anger.

"You'll not speak to your father and husband in that manner again! Not under my roof, young woman. I demand a little more respect and a lot more manners, starting right this minute!"

Jessica moved toward her father, the fire in her eyes matching his own. "I would like to remind you that this is now my roof, Papa. Your generosity to me and your devoted son-in-law has made it so, and I will have my say about what happens to be my property."

Breathing heavily, she faced Michael who had returned to his chair and sat stone faced, staring blindly into the flowered table-cloth. His illness had been the real cause of all of this upheaval, and by simply agreeing with his wife, he could put an end to it. Her irritatingly petulant voice stayed his own as she continued her insolence.

"Let me assure you both that I will never sign away all your hard earned security, Papa, to satisfy the needs of a selfish young man, and the folly of an old man's fantasies."

Her eyes bore into the back of Michael's head, willing him to face her she shouted loudly.

"Never, never, never!"

She literally ran from the house, smashing the screen door behind her ferociously, and falling unto the fading grass with abandonment. Faintly the two men heard her plaintive cry heavenward.

"Dear God, have you ever created two more foolish men?"

Neither man dared face the other in this yawning gap of silence that penetrated their very souls. Michael, betrayed by his own guilt, could only wallow in his supposed deep remorse for having allowed the continued acceleration of a confrontation that could, and should have been terminated with only a few words from him. He was, like most men, incapable of viewing himself with honesty, and so, conveniently side stepped both his egotism, and long standing desire for retribution against Jessica as the logical reasons for his chronic silence. Instead, he allowed himself the full enjoyment of true repentance, regret, and self reproach by wondering why he had not intervened, and chastised himself with the suffering of contrition.

] Isaac, sinking wearily into his rocker beside the stove, felt his eyes glaze over with the unrecognized parental pain inflicted by a rebellious child. How had she dared to call him a damned old fool! He, whose every act for the past seventeen years had been dictated by his desire to accommodate her every pleasure and comfort. A man who had put up with her childish willfulness, and admittedly had allowed it to grow, channeling itself into floodgates of temper and titanic outbursts, which until now, had never been leveled at him. Yes, indeed, he had been a fool! He should have taken the strap to her long before this, and curbed all these vile tendencies, instantly loathing the very consideration of it; he tasted the bile of self disgust rising rapidly to his tongue. If only her mother had lived, all would have been so different, he told himself. I did my very best, but dear Mary would have done so much better. A soft wind whispered in his ears, interlaced with the sweet remembered voice from long ago.

"Come to me, Isaac, and find the peace I have found. I wait for you my love, I wait for you."

Nodding in silent acquiescence, he rose out of his chair, both arms reaching forward, futilely searching the space before him. One hand reached out for support as he turned to Michael, whose stricken face had become a blur.

"Go, fetch the child," he mumbled, then closed his eyes and allowed the darkness to overtake him as his son-in-law dashed to the garden, sobbing for his wife to quickly come and help them.

Chapter Five

Although the calendar proclaimed the arrival of spring, a gusty wind howled a baleful song, it's icy breath clouding every window of the old house with unseasonably heavy frost. Despite it's size, the huge grate in the center of the hallway never allowed quite enough rising heat to seep through it's filigree from the rooms below, leaving the upstairs as damp and chilly as an empty tomb. Jessica's shivering fingers rummaged through the dresser in search of the cashmere sweater her extravagant husband had presented her with at Christmas time.

As she pulled the garment about her shoulders a tremor passed over her, not owing only to the icy room, but to her cold recollection of the holiday past, and all of it's dire portents as well. Isaac had lain in his bed, uncooperative, and seemingly oblivious to the bustle of the preparations for Christmas. He had neither spoken, nor given any signs of recognition to anyone since their confrontation, lying totally inert, in a pool of what Jessica considered, self pity. Doctor Salters had assured her weekly that her father suffered from no physical ailment he could discern, intimating the possible beginnings of senility, or any one of a number of other mental disorders. She had not agreed for a single moment with the good doctor's laughable diagnosis, knowing full well that Isaac had deliberately set about to punish her defiance, and would never be satisfied until she had complied to his wishes in every respect.

On several occasions Maggie, in her childish wanderings, had crept into the sick man's room, pulling herself up on the side of the bed, and addressing him in the gibberish understandable only to herself. The old man would respond by softly crooning a lullaby, remembered from Jessica's childhood. His voice, crackling like old parchment paper, always delighted the baby. Clapping her hands together with glee, and forgetting the needed support of the bed, she would soon fall to the floor with a resounding smack, which set both she and her grandfather into peels of laughter. Jessica's arrival on the scene to investigate the commotion, would always find Isaac wearing his usual stoical expression, apparently still lost in indifference.

The strike had dragged on just as she had predicted it would, but there was no solace to be gained by the fulfillment of her prophecy, nor from the fact that her father's increasing good health did nothing to erode the wall of discord between them. On several occasions she had been encouraged by an almost undetectable loving glance, or a response to a pressure, as she held his limp hand, however these small, and possibly imagined gestures, were soon forgotten by his prolonged, and punishing silences. His resignation from life.

Unable to stand up any longer under the subjection of this charade, two days before Christmas, and against her better judgment, she and Michael had presented themselves at the City Bank to take out a mortgage loan against a home that had been passed down through four generations without encumbrance.

The bank's manager had smiled congenially, and well aware of the property's worth, had taken pains to assure both of them that there would be absolutely no problem in securing the necessary funds. Then proclaiming his envy and his ambition to also one day be his own boss, he intently pushed the application in front of them, indicating with tiny red check marks where their signatures needed to be placed. The paper blurred before her eyes, as she nervously searched the page for the space that was about to alter all of their lives, then grudgingly scrawled her name. This time as they made their way homeward, it had been Michael who spoke of the future, and she, who marched in stony silence. Her actions, however, had ended in futility, doing nothing to deter her father's uncommunicativeness, and Michael, although appearing outwardly pleased, was not able to display the enthusiasm or appreciation she felt her sacrificing act had merited.

The holidays had passed with an aura of apathy that only served to heighten her feelings of resentment and indignation. Had she not acquiesced enough by allowing them to have their little toy, despite the incongruous timing and her own deep, and deserved apprehension? Why in God's name were they both now acting like they were no longer interested in the game. Michael had half heartedly set about implementing Isaac's original plan by leasing a suitable store site, and laying in all of the previously discussed inventory. Adhering precisely to the old man's basic concept, he had tried to do everything exactly as the design demanded, but his optimistic zest for the operation had visibly ebbed, and the force of his spirit had decidedly waned with the passage of time. It was as though her compliance had been too long in coming, and she had somehow desecrated their dream by her tardiness.

Each night she had listened with mounting anger as Michael, pausing at the door to the sick room, stood flaccidly reciting his monotonous accounting of each day's happenings, always embellishing the facts with false figures when it came to the reporting of the daily receipts, in a hopeless effort to resurrect his father in law's interest. Depressed by his need to lie and the failure of Isaac to respond, he would slink down the back stairwell to the cozy warmth of the fading embers in the kitchen coal stove, and console himself with a few long pulls from his, now always handy, bottle.

Jessica, ever alert to Michael's moods, had watched both men with a wary eye, and for the first time in her life, her heart was pierced with a splinter of hate for her father. On her return from the bank she had knelt beside his bed, pleading for his attention, and groveling like some beggar for the smallest hint of approval. Isaac's demeanor had remained impassive throughout her long and enthusiastic narration concerning the successful bank transaction she and Michael had concluded that afternoon. Describing in detail the wonderful courtesy that had been extended to them by the bank's manager, and his knowledgeable appreciation for the value of their property, she had feigned eagerness for the great venture they were all about to embark on, ending on a joyful note, but without apology for her past transgressions, she had waited expectantly for her father's reply. As she finished, the pale blue eyes had rested on her momentarily with an unreadable expression, then slowly the wrinkled lids lowered over them, shutting in unmistakable dismissal.

By this time many plans for settlement had been submitted and rejected by both sides. Governor Pinchot, after familiarizing himself with both sides of the situation, had announced in mid September that he was not about to intervene in the controversy, but by the end of November, had submitted his own plan to end the stalemate that was now affecting his entire state. His proposal to guarantee the miners the same pay rate for the next five years, and denying the companies the opportunity to increase the price of anthracite for that same period was, understandably, rejected by the companies. By January, a desperate Governor had called a special session of the legislature, for the sole purpose of declaring the mining industry a public utility, and thereby subject to control by the Public Service Commission. No legislation was ever enacted, primarily because it was felt by many, that the proposal gave to Mr. Lewis unwarranted support. Undeserved because of his initial withdrawal from the preliminary meeting in Atlantic City, and his continued refusal to arbitrate with any view to softening his original demands. It was to be a theme repeated over and over before becoming finally heard. When forces continue to reject arbitration which is reasonable, one must begin to wonder if any justness in their position truly exists, or do they employ power to secure what cannot be gained through plausible equity.

The entire nation soon became familiar with those scowling shaggy eyebrows, and determinedly sagging jowls appearing defiantly in the middle of the Pathe News in every movie house in America. School children living through this part of history were taught to honor or castigate his name, depending on the region in which they lived, and their teacher's personal analysis of a highly controversial subject in current events. He was now looked upon as the long awaited for savior of the down trodden or the unneeded perpetrator of superfluous problems, but either way, there could be no doubt that he had gained the public's attention in his relentless quest for the union's dominance over the operators. Eventually the American people wearied of Mr. Lewis's constant and ever increasing demands, along with what had begun to appear as sheer bull headedness. An article in the New York Herald flatly stated that "sooner or later Mr. Lewis must bow to public opinion, or to the opinion of the workers whom he represents. When he does, his first step will have been taken toward a resumption of the administering of coal, which is the important thing." These and other pressures spurred both the union and operator negotiators back to the bargaining table briefly, only to end, once again, with both factions making charges and counter charges. The operators were forced to stand idly by and fearfully watch their markets being invaded by substitute fuels, while the workers grubbed their way through the long winter months without compensation.

When negotiations were again broken off on February 2, 1926, it was commonly felt, and often printed, that Mr. Lewis had given up fighting for the miners, but continued the contest for his own power, and the right to remain on the payroll of The United Mine Workers of America. It was said that he had entered every meeting with a flare of trumpets, declaring each conference to be entirely different from the last, and yet each time, both he and his associates, were willing to agree to only that peace proposal that best suited their own particular needs. It had by now begun to dawn on the American public, and the mining men affected, that if, in fact, Mr. Lewis had genuinely wanted to settle the anthracite strike, he would have listened, long ago, to propositions that put the miners back to work, pending negotiations.

These sentiments, along with personal pressure from R.F. Grant who, although identified with an anthracite company, was personally acquainted with Mr. Lewis, brought about a final agreement, signed in Scranton, Pennsylvania on February 16, 1926. After one hundred and seventy idle days, work resumed on February 18, with absolutely no victory gained by either side. Ironically, never again in any future negotiations, would the union ever press for a wage increase. Unfortunately, the point had been driven home all too late, that the survival of the industry now depended on cost cutting and the ability to be competitive in the supply and demand market.

The strike had been prolonged until all had come to know the meaning of a growling stomach, and the discontentment spawned by the need for entertainment and the lack of funds to provide for it. The hardware store had been a dismal failure from the start. As Jessica had sagely foreseen, no one had any money left for extras, spending only for the table, and an occasional bottle to buoy the sagging spirits and forget, if only for a little while, what had become all too apparent. All their suffering had been for naught, and the impossibility of ever regaining lost wages, secretly haunted every man, but this bitter thought must remain unspoken. They had all made their choices, and must now pay for them with the shame of having to deprive their families.

As a small crowd gathered outside of the store as it prepared for it's grand opening, Tom Quinlan had pushed his way to the front, and quickly attempted to drive home his point.

"There shouldn't be a man among us patronizing this place. Sure, and wasn't he the one up there on that stage egging ya all on to vote for the strike, when he knew full well there was no way it was ever gonna affect him. I tried to warn ya then, but nobody wanted to listen to a kid, so ya just up and followed his lead. Well hain't it something that now you don't have barely enough money for food, but he's got enough to open a whole damned store, and expects ya all to be his customers besides!"

Reaching down, and grabbing a loose brick from the sidewalk beneath his half empty boot, he had pulled back his arm preparing to throw it through the store's front window, but just as quickly Jim Bolen had grabbed hold of him, whispering."Don't go behaving like a fool, Tom. If you've not enough money for eats, you've not enough money for broken windows either. Use your head, lad, or you'll end up in the hoosegow."

He smiled weakly. "Course, maybe that wouldn't be all bad either, cause the city would have to see to it that you got plenty to eat while you were in there."

Patting Tom's shoulder, he moved away, as did most of the men, shuffling their feet and grumbling about some men's luck, especially if they were Irish. They desperately needed a scapegoat, and Michael was, without question, the most convenient. Dismissing their own involvement by choice, they were easily able to channel their feelings of guilt into agitated demonstrations of blame.

When the mines finally reopened in February, it had become quite evident that Michael would have to return to them if there was to be any hope for their meeting the loan installment, and other mounting monthly obligations. Rent on the shop had fallen behind, and although the landlord, a retired miner himself, had been most sympathetic, the electric company clamored relentlessly for payment, threatening to shut off the power to both the house and the business if the bill was not brought up to date and remained current. But the nation had learned in six months that coal was not only undependable, but dirty and unsafe as well. Rapid conversions to other commodities had drastically reduced the demands on the mines, and the men were called back slowly, and subjected to shorter and shorter work weeks.

Michael found himself once again resented by the men who vied daily for a few hours of work to support their complaining families and considered him an unnecessary invasion into their already sparsely scheduled days. The many friends that once were his quickly deserted him now, whispering behind his back about his excessive greed and unequaled conceit. His once entertaining stories were now looked upon as braggadocio, and there seemed to be no end in sight to his connivance for the begetting of money. Wondering now what price he had extracted from the union for his help in seducing them with his grand talk about the good times they could expect, they recalled how craftily he had swept poor Jessica into a liaison with him in his attempt to marry into a well to do family, and how, once he had gained their confidence, had been cagey enough to grab off enough to open up his very own business. Well, that was not skin off their noses, and more power to him, but now the rascal was trying to infringe on their meager incomes by denying one of them a chance to earn a few extra dollars every time he set foot in the mine, and this, they considered unforgivable. They should have known better, they told themselves, and stayed away from that slippery tongued Irishman, who always seemed to have all the answers. Well they'd learned their lesson now and never again would they be taken in by any mick, dago or pollack who happened down the pike and so they allowed their animosity to become flagrant, without pretense, or attempt at concealment, directed toward him contemptuously at every opportunity, a denying of their own confusion and desperation that was unjustified.

Misinterpreting their disdain at first, as understandable disappointment with the union's handling of the strike negotiations, and it's dismal outcome, he good naturedly accepted their scorn as his just punishment for his heavy involvement and unflagging support of it's officials which, to this date, he had not withdrawn. Relying on the fickleness of men he had at first set about mending his fences by refreshing their memories with the many benefits they had already gained over the years, and stating flatly that the best was yet to come, inviting every man within ear shot to join him in a free cup at Dougal's and a chance to discuss it. But his optimistic forecasts and persistent amiability, this time, gained him no favor in their eyes.

Their flat refusal to partake of an offered cup in these times soon made him realize that the rift between himself and the men had been caused by something that ran much deeper than mere disillusionment, and his innate pride soon disallowed any further pursuance of their companionship, leaving him melancholy and crushed beneath their hurtful rejection. He had been hoping to find a haven in this underground world, free from the accusing eyes of his wife, and unseeing star of his father in law. Instead he had had to face baffling silence and chaotic astonishment as his fellow workers progressively displayed their distaste for him. Saint Augustine had wisely observed that habit, if not restrained, soon becomes necessity, and a man whose life had been habitually consumed by the dependence of approval and commendation of others, could not long endure repudiation and continuing hostility. Michael, after vainly using every known ploy to re-ensconse himself in the good graces of his one time friends, was finally forced to label their antagonism irrevocable, and retreat into a more satisfactory, though solitary existence, more compatible to his nature. Like most human beings, he heartily approved of himself.

Jessica buttoned the cashmere sweater to the neck, wincing as the wind rattled the rain gutters with it's frigid fury. It was almost senseless to open that damned store today, she told herself, only a fool would venture out on a day such as this. Catching her reflection in the mirror as she passed by, she smirked, and thought, well you're one fool that's going to go out in it, if only to be able to pat your back and congratulate yourself on being a devoted daughter, wife and mother. She stood motionless, staring at the face before her. Were those two lines beside her mouth always there? She had never noticed them before and in the dim cold-light, they appeared to make her look older than her years. Sticking her tongue out in a futile childish gesture, she spoke aloud to the tired image miming her.

"It's both of them that makes you look like this, you know. That sick old man and his hateful eyes following you every time you're in his room, as if it was your fault that he won't get out of bed, when all the while you both know he could speak or even walk if it wasn't for his cussed vengefulness. He does it just trying to make you feel guilty, but don't you dare give in! You did what he wanted and it's him that should feel guilty for all that's happened to us now, not you."

Turning away from the mirror angrily, her thoughts continued in silence. Besides all of this I have to put up with my dear so called husband, who hasn't an ounce of manhood left in him. He's not even able to look square at me anymore, spending all of his days working, and all of his nights drinking himself into a stupor once he's finished coddling an old man, and a small child who could care less if he does or doesn't. A child whose affection he's managed to steal from her own mother with his constant pampering and unwillingness to discipline. Pausing to look at herself again, she asked aloud.

"I wander if it's me he hates or if it could be himself he hates for things turning out the way they have. No, I'm sure it must be me, self love would not allow him to honestly face any of the blame for this miserable alliance of ours, with all of it's incredibly wretched outcomes. No, he will always see the blame as mine, me, who have given all my love and am despised for it, jeopardized my every possession, and he considers it merely his due, and who now work my very fingers to the bone to save his precious pride, despite all the havoc his wild schemes have wrought, and still the sight of me sickens him. God, how I hate him!"

Her twitching fingers frantically pulled at the neck of the sweater, popping buttons everywhere as she tore it from her body, kicking it violently into a corner of the room.

"I hate you all, every last living one of you!"

She screamed the words and they echoed softly about the chilly walls of the room. She was still staring spitefully at the crumpled, discarded sweater when Annie Benfield's voice called to her from down stairs.

Chapter Six

Annie had been caring for Isaac and Maggie since it had become necessary for Jessica to tend to the store. The strike had forced Jim and Molly to give up thoughts of moving into their own home, and extra mouths called for extra money. Burying her detestation in the wake of expediency, Annie had catalogued Jessica's unforgivable behavior at Molly's wedding in a corner of her mind best reserved for days when animosity was a luxury she could afford. Her voice was cheery as she asked.

"How's your Papa, and my little darlin' this morning?"

Jessica stiffened. Maggie had taken to calling Annie, Mama after spending so much time with the old lady, and Annie had done nothing to staunch this flow of childish error, for she knew intuitively that it infuriated her niece.

"Papa's, of course, still the same, and your little darling is still sleeping," Jessica snapped, unable to control her anger.

Annie, taking due note of the hostility, smiled with satisfaction, and immediately changed the subject.

"I've a bit of news for ya, although I haven't yet decided if it's good or bad. These days weddings aren't always good tidings, even though they say two can live as cheaply as one and all that malarkey, I can't say that I believe it. No, not the way things are today, with every single penny having to be counted before and after you go to the grocer, so's you're sure ya got enough to go again tomorrow."

Jessica plopped a knitted cap upon her head as the woman spoke, tugging irritably as she forced the wiry auburn curls beneath it. Each time she secured one side, a ringlet would spring from the other, until her frustration found release at Annie's expense. Interrupting rudely, she almost shouted her words.

"Good Lord, if you've news, just spit it out and get it over with. I haven't got all day to gossip, I'm late already as well you know."

What a piece of baggage she is, without a mite of manners, thought Annie, aghast at such unseemly behavior. Beauty she has I must admit, but the social graces and tact are total strangers to this one. My poor sister would twirl in her grave to see a daughter of hers mean mouthing her own Aunt, but such is the pity when you're left with no mother to guide you properly, as I have been able to do with Clara and Molly. Donning a patient smile in tribute to her long departed relative, she forced her voice to be tolerant, despite it's sounding condescending.

"Well, I'm so sorry to detain you, missus, but I just thought you might be interested to know that Tom Quinlan has spoken for my Clara. Can you believe that, now, and here I was always thinking he had such a spark for you that he'd turn into an old bachelor. But that's an old lady's fancy for ya and just goes to prove you never know what a young feller's really up to, when you feel sure of one thing, he up and shows his real bent. Well, Tom's a fine young man from a good old family, and it's proud I'm gonna be to call him son. Just imagine, getting two son-in-laws in such a short space of time. I swear, if someone had told me this was gonna happen last year, I never would have believed it. No ma'am, it's just like I said to Tom's mother, you never know what the fates have in store for ya, wouldn't you agree missus?"

Hurriedly mumbling a few words of congratulations to a smug and gratified Annie, Jessica flung her muffler about her face and stumbled out into the dim grayness of the morning. The wind howled about her ears echoing pitiful sounds that served to deepen her depression. Pulling the wayward cap tighter about her head, she scolded herself. She was being ridiculous, of course, after all, she was a married woman and could not expect Tom to sit around for the rest of his life feeding his ardor with futile yearnings. Every good man needed the pleasures and comforts of a good woman, and sweet Tom, above all, was most certainly deserving of both of these, but how in the world could he have chosen Clara Benfield, with her faded yellow hair, and homely painted face? Perhaps he had succumbed to her leaning over the banister trick. The very thought of it disgusted her, for most assuredly Tom Quinlan was not a shallow man, but, she decided, he was a man nevertheless, and easily persuaded by womanly wiles. Completely dismissing the fact that not too very long ago she had longed to emulate the very person she now decried she thought about the other eligible, and quite pretty young women in Miners' Haven, and found his preference offensive, almost a disparagement to herself, and no matter how she tried, she could not erase her feelings of deception and inner misgivings because of it.

They're all alike, she told herself pensively. Michael had lied about loving her, Tom had deceived even himself, if his affections were so easily transferrable, and Isaac's attachment weakened whenever she was less than his expectations. Not one had had the courage of their convictions, and not one was worthy of the consternation and upheaval she was now forced to endure because of all of them. Somehow she must mentally free herself and become impregnable to this unending infliction of pain.

Reaching the store she prepared herself for another day of waiting for customers who would never arrive, leaving her alone with her maudlin thoughts of love and it's many disappointments. Even the elements were against her, she decided, as she turned slowly in the doorway and smiled, watching the dark foreboding clouds, whipped by fierce winds, race across the heavy gray skies. I guess I must credit Mother Nature with this day, but how typical of God and man to place the blame for all unpleasantness at the feet of women, beginning with the dawn of the world and it's very first scapegoat, Eve.

Torrents of rain continued to fall for seven days. The small sulpher creek that ran through the center of town, right behind Main Street, was almost level with it's banks, causing every store owner to cast a wary eye through his back windows several times a day. Many of the men were forced to remain home from the mines, as flooding water made certain sections inaccessible. Six weeks of work had not begun to refurbish their larders, and now, being a superstitious lot, they foresaw ill omens in every situation, from the ominously overcast sky, to the midnight baying of a mongrel hound. The plaintive patter of daily rain had washed away their temporary respite from idleness and frayed their already jangled nerves, leaving them discontent and quarrelsome. Like the ever wakeful insomniac, who is plagued by the incessant dripping of his faucet, and then lays the blame for a sleepless night at the feet of his landlord, they, too, needed to find fault with someone other than themselves, and soon resorted to nit picking and innuendo. Tempers grew short and more than one customer was lost to Dougal's, not only for the need of tight closed purses, but rather for the need of occasional tight fisted brawling.

The hour was late, but Jessica and Michael remained in the store, piling their small inventory into every available inch above ground level. Sand bags already lined one side of the creek, brought in that very day by other distraught businessmen who likewise struggled to save their stock from deluge and destruction.

Michael, stretching to reach the corner of one shelf, endured a sudden spasm of chest pain that forced him to crumble limply onto the nearest stool. His daily distress and heavy achings had diminished considerably upon his departure from the mines, but his return to their dank and dust laden caverns had soon stimulated his sufferings to even greater heights than had plagued him before. Touching a shaking hand to his forehead, where the dampness already clung to his furrowed brow, he felt the now familiar finger of fear etching it's hateful pattern about his heart as total fatigue conquered him. Gingerly tilting his head against the stucco wall, he tried to breathe in short, shallow gasps, for even the rhythmic rise and fall of his breast was beginning to produce unbearable pain. In his torment the sweet lament of the Confiteor sprang to his arid lips as they moved in silent intonation.

"I detest all my sins because I dread the loss of heaven and the pains of hell, but most of all because they offend thee, my God."

His offenses were multiple, and he prayed his God would not extract every ounce of retribution. "I have already paid in so many ways," he cried within his heart. "How can I be asked to desert life now, and be denied the chance to watch my own dear Maggie become a woman?"

Agonizing guilt overwhelmed him. Perhaps the greatest sin he had committed was to have been so narrow of mind and heart, that in an entire lifetime, only one soul had ever entered his consciousness and forced his awareness away from himself.

"Oh God, surely you are not going to punish me for only loving once, as selfish as that must seem to you in Your Goodness. I beg you not to take me from her, but let me live and show her how to be the obverse of me. I will teach her how to love profusely, without meanness or the need of compensation for each and every comfort she has afforded someone else, with a purity of mind and heart that had been alien to me. I will explain to her how great is the gift of love when it is not tarnished by the compulsion of needing gain from it, and I can teach her all these things only because I have learned them well from my love of her. Above all, dear God, please allow that she will love deeply and be loved in return....."

He knew he had been loved totally, without reservation, with total abandon, with devotion marred only by his own inability to reciprocate. It seemed almost impossible for this sobering thought to, indeed, be the truth, he told himself gloomily. All of his life he had struggled with his greatest need, which, of course, had been to be loved, and when, at last, it had finally been given, he had found it stifling and burdensome, wishing with all his heart to escape it's tentacles of caring, consideration, devotion, and fidelity.

In his wretched anguish he did not notice Jessica's hard stare as she stopped momentarily to catch her breath. The electricity had gone off hours before, with the threat of yet another impending storm, and the flickering candle light cast eerie shadows about Michael's face, causing his sunken eyes, and now gaunt features, to assume an almost skeletal appearance.

So this was the man she had spent her life hopelessly loving, and futilely longing for, her once gallant knight, who now sat slouching meekly beneath his rusted corroding armor, shielded from the world only because of her own ambivalence. The irreplaceable Michael McClellan, who would be forced, at last, into some semblance of humility by his own, still unspoken, recognition of the fact that he had failed. A touch of pity stroked her emotions as she looked down at the frail face of her still handsome husband. Struggling to control a tender impulse, she frowned, stepping closer to him.

"Michael, you're not at the mines now where you can lean on a pick whenever the fancy suites you. Let's get this thing over and ourselves home. I'm exhausted from dragging this junk, around all afternoon, and I need my bed."

The depression of his thoughts had trapped his mind in an endless web of morbidity, his entire being longing for the solace of communication. Without opening his eyes he asked brokenly.

"Do you believe in God Jessica?"

The desolation of his voice cautioned her against flippancy, while her reason totally rejected entering into this, or any serious conversation with him. A sigh of self disapproval escaped her as she succumbed to the pressures of pity, and reluctantly began to answer.

"I would have to admit that I don't believe I've ever really thought about it, not even all the while I went to Father Reagen for instructions. I guess it was just sort of doing what had to be done to get you to marry me."

She lowered her eyes for only a moment and allowed her humiliation to erase her tenderheartedness. "Besides why would you asked about God at a moment like this, when here we are trying to salvage what's left of our lives on these tiny little shelves? It's so typical of you Michael to have absolutely no priorities at all." Her tone was now sharp and depreciative.

His weary lids opened slowly. "Would you just humor me for one moment and think about it now, please, and then try to give me your honest answer?"

His eyes held a pleading she did not understand, Was he deliberately trying to aggravate her with this religious prattle? What possible difference could it make what she thought, anyway? He believed, and it was important to him, while she had never found the necessity of it, nor the necessity of discussing it, but the glistening black orbs held her captive, and she knew she could not deny him his answer. Why was it she could never resist giving in to him, she asked herself angrily, and immediately began her reply.

"I guess I just believe there is something Godlike in everyone, including you and me. If I look for and find good in you, I have found a part of what God intended you to be. Love between a man and woman is a part of God, and he blesses their love with his creation of a new life and allows them to share in one of his many miracles." She looked closely at his face for some response, and finding none, she continued. "But I can't see him on a throne somewhere in the clouds waiting to pass judgment or deciding on whether or not you're worthy of going to heaven the way you do. He has given it all to us here and now, what we make out of it is our own heaven or hell, and He's wise enough to know we all manage to punish ourselves quite thoroughly and there's certainly no reason or need for fire and brimstone. But I think he asks too much when he expects all of us to love one another, and see only the good in others, folks seem to thrive better on hate bitterness and superstition, wouldn't you agree?"

Michael's voice held a note of sadness. "I want you to promise me, Jess, that if anything ever happens to me, you will see to it that Maggie receives her First Holy Communion, and faithfully attends the Mass. I want you to swear it to me on the love you have for her."

He had leaned forward in his chair, reaching out eagerly to touch her hand and hear her vow of commitment. At his words, every muscle in Jessica's body tightened, and a slight tingling raced across her scalp as his fingers forced their way between her own. He had rejected her every thought merely because it had turned out to be less than what he wanted to hear, and then had not cared enough to comment, even moderately on a response that had appeared almost crucial only moments before. A response that she, with her customary compliance, had foolishly supplied, and he, with his customary indifference, had conveniently ignored. His only concern, as usual, had been Maggie. Maggie, the bane of her life, her competitor, her constant reminder that Michael's love lay elsewhere. Maggie, her flesh, her daughter, her downfall! Here they sat with their lives crumbling about them, and the most important thing to him was the exacting of a promise for regular church attendance.

For one flicker of an instant she felt the need to reach out to him, to explain how impossible it had become to live in the shadow of a child, her child as well as his. To tell him how much she still felt the need of him, and always would, how she could forget all things if only he would love her or just accept her love for him, and respect it by honoring their marriage, and attaching some importance to it's immediate survival and less to an irrelevant religious education somewhere in the future. Their eyes held, his still pleading for her promise, as she released her hand and slowly turned away from him. Fearing he had detected her temporary weakness, her back stiffened in an unnecessary show of pride as she discarded all thoughts of any solicitous petition. She had already played the fool today by kneeling to his insistence for a reply which he then chose to ignore.

With jerky rapidity she moved across the room and quickly donned her coat and hat. Without a backward glance she sailed to the door, then turning on her heels, made an almost stage-like exit through it, and onto the sidewalk.

Michael's eyes closed once more as he vowed to himself that he would never understand this woman. The most simple conversation habitually ended in either ill-tempered outpourings or prolonged sullen silence. There could no longer be any doubt that they had reached the end of whatever small amount of communication that had been left to them. Each could depend on the other for only misery and inevitable indifference. Dragging himself out of the chair, he fell into a fit of coughing that drenched his body with perspiration, and his mind with renewed thoughts of death.

When finally he had regained enough strength to open the shop door, the rain had subsided somewhat, and the few drops splattering against his fevered face were most refreshing, restoring some of his lost vitality and vigor. The walk home turned out to be just long enough for his optimistic nature to reaffirm itself, leading him to believe that, somehow all would be right with his world. By the time he entered the kitchen he was whistling softly, but confidently. A sound that turned his wife to secret thoughts of murder.

Chapter Seven

The ultimate demise of his ill-fated business venture forced Isaac's reversion to a more normal existence. All manner of papers now necessitated his signature and, considering himself an astute, though failing businessman, he regarded his assessment of each and every word as essential. Another mistake would not only compound the original, it would destroy them. An appraisal of their position after the sale of remaining stock and fixtures found them owing their creditors $5,000., a formidable figure. Determination to set to rights what had gone awry, drove the old man from his bed, turning his lethargic apathy into frantic concern.

Discouraging meetings with creditors and unsympathetic bankers became his daily routine until it became painfully apparent that total extraction from debt would be all but impossible. With most of his assets depleted and the family home so heavily mortgaged, it would take a miracle just to accommodate their everyday living needs and still meet the payments on their outstanding loans that remained. He had attended to business in a stoic and solitary manner because of Michael's return to the mines, and his own inability to endure even the slightest hint of smugness on the part of Jessica. She would have to content herself with silent "I told you sos," he determined, as he wrangled his way alone through another bleak day of chaos and bitter disappointment. The bank manager, originally so eager to fund this venture, now considered item a poor risk, and would allow for no leniency regarding the repayment of his debt, looking only with an avarice eye to the foreclosure on this very valuable property, and it's final acquisition by his bank.

Meanwhile, the adult family of three, as was their want, worked independently of one another, each knowing it was necessary to contribute but remain voiceless if any kind of order were to prevail. Michael's return to the mines was hindered by his chronic cold and influenza, compelling him to remain at home every few weeks. Jessica, feeling degraded and base, nevertheless, hired herself out to do any menial tasks for the few affluent families left in Miner's Haven, and Isaac and Maggie trudged each day up the hill, packaging and bagging as much coal as one so young, and one so old could possibly carry. Jessica had fashioned around the neck slings from discarded canvas potato sacks that readily adapted to the weight that each was equal to and lessened the burden of their lowly task. Actually, going to the waste bank was, for Maggie, almost a social occasion. Women and children gleaned the pile each and every day, gathering up it's abundance of refuse that supplied them amply with sufficient fuel for the winter months. The children, once their bags were filled, were allowed a short respite for a game of tag or ring around the rosy, depending on age. Maggie's shyness prevented her joining in the activities, but not from the enjoyment of watching them. Clapping her tiny hands together, she would squeal with glee as the excitement swirled about her, but all too soon the mothers would rescind this short dispensation from labor and oblige their children to help cram the larger bags with even the puniest bits of the precious anthracite.

Despite these valiant efforts, the end of summer found empty spaces on the once over laden tables in the parlor. Many of the Dresden figurines had found their way to collectors and antique dealers in order to meet the ever pressing need for cash, and the family avoided entering the once prized room, as though it's very existence was the cause of their plight, rather than their respite from it.

Isaac could not help but wonder what his dearest Mary would think, were she here to witness this bitter trade off, and the loss of the things they had held so dear. Would she be pummeling him with recriminations, and looking at him with contemptuous eyes, or scorning him in silence as her daughter had chosen to do. Sitting by the kitchen stove on the creaking, well worn rocker, he moved slowly back and forth forcing his mind to conjure up his sweet wife's face, but time and forget-fullness had somewhat worn away the clarity of her features, and they remained distorted and distant, escaping his every effort to recapture them. Suddenly rising out of the chair, he hurried out of the room, walking quickly toward the great oak doors of the sitting room. Roughly sliding open one great panel, his eyes frantically scanned the wall to find the portrait hanging just above the organ. The afternoon sun drenched the once grand room, and he was immediately filled with an air of felicity and well being as he passed through it's portals and strolled tentatively across the fading carpet to better view the elusive face upon the wall. A single sliver of light seemed to magically add a twinkle to his darling's eye, and blessedly widen the smile on her dimpled cheek. Looking up the old man sighed with relief.

"Ah, just as I thought," he whispered gratefully, "she would have forgiven me."

Isaac's hand, inside his coat pocket, lovingly fingered one of his favorite pieces as he walked unhappily past the home of Annie Benfield, once again on his way to Mr. Solomon's antique shop. Annie, rushing from the, now seldom used porch, tugged at his sleeve with agitation.

"Good heavens, man, I've been calling your name over and over again, has your sickness dimmed your hearing or what?" Not waiting for his reply, she continued. "I guess Jessica's told ya about Tom and Clara, and you know the wedding's only a few weeks away now, and as you can easily imagine I'm wanting to get them something extry special. You know, something they'll have all their lives to remember their special day by."

She stopped momentarily to gulp a breath of air while trying to pat her straggly hair back into it's proper place, then deciding to ignore it's immediate return to it's original position, she rattled on.

"Anyways, I heard you're selling off some of those fine China pieces that belonged to your mother, and I just know that Clara would be thrilled to death to have one of them. I've managed to put away a few extry dollars, Isaac, just for a day such as this, and I'd be able to pay you right away, just like Mr. Solomon does. Besides this would like keeping in the family, don't you agree?" She smiled widely up at him in anticipation.

Tense fingers wound more tightly around the cherished piece in his pocket as he looked down at his disheveled, untidy relative. How could such a contemptible old hag ever have been kin to his beloved, he asked himself, searching the greedy eyes and gaping mouth on the face before him. How cruel God was in his supposed infinite wisdom, to have created from the very same loins, one so beautiful of form and spirit, and another so plain of face and void of vivacity, selfishly taking back all the radiance and charm, and leaving only the nondescript. Being deceitful was alien to him and he detested himself almost as much as Annie when he answered lamely.

"I've no need to sell this day, perhaps next week." Turning, he began to walk away, but Annie jumped in front of him, her bulky frame blocking his path.

"But you know I can't rely on a maybe, Isaac, not for something as important as this. No siree, I've got to have your promise now. I can't wait for the very last minute to go rummaging for a gift as special as this one. Come now, man, surely you remember how it was when Jessica got married."

Malicious lights danced in her eyes, as she quizzically raised her brows in an air of innocence. The indispensible need to inflict this barb over rode her common sense. Being unforgiving and vindictive at heart, she would find it forever necessary to compensate for Isaac's ill treatment of both her and her daughters, despite their every effort to assist him.

"I remember it well, madame," answered Isaac, stiffening. "And trust you'll fair as well with your son-in-law as I have with mine." Grinding his teeth down on the stem of the unlit pipe, he again attempted to continue on his way.

"You've not answered me, Isaac Hobbs," she called after him persistently. "I already told ya, I need a definite yes or no."

With measured steps Isaac continued to move away from her in utter disgust, wishing only to escape those virulent eyes and harpy tongue, but Annie's insistence was not to be denied. In a single motion she had caught up with him, snatching at his sleeve with a demanding tug. Her unexpected strength and suddenness of movement was startling, catching him unaware, as she unknowingly yanked his hand from the safety of the pocket, dislodging his grip on the treasure. The delicate sound of splintering China shattered against his ears as his disbelieving eyes found the mutilated pieces scattered about his feet. Annie jumped back, sucking in her breath, and clasping both hands over her open mouth to stifle her cry of astonishment. The beady fearful eyes rose slowly from the debris on the cobbles, afraid to face the vehement fury she knew would be now waiting for her, but Isaac had remained motionless, staring down with alarmed incredulity at the glistening sidewalk, his mind incapable of accepting the hideous sight of the disconnected pieces, and their portent.

Studying him tentatively, Annie's racing heart was quick to subside after the first few seconds it had taken her to fully analyze the situation. Regaining her courage, and seizing upon his apparent inability to react to this dreadful scene, she grasped at the opportunity to turn the circumstance to her own advantage. Pulling herself up, she crossed her arms over the top-of her protruding stomach, and began to bellow indignantly.

"What a liar you are, Isaac Hobbs, deceiving your own kin like this, and all because of greed. Mind, I wasn't looking for no bargain, I already told you I was willing and able to pay whatever your Jewish friend was willing to give ya, but oh, no, you'd rather have traded with a stranger, and a Jew stranger at that! But then you always did set yourself apart, you and your fine daughter with her almighty airs, always looking down on my fair lasses like they wasn't good as her, when God himself knew, they was much better. Well all of your uppity ways didn't do either one of you any good in the end, now did they? Just see where you've managed to come to now, about as broke as that piece of junk at your feet, I'd say."

Stopping to catch her breath and tap her toe impatiently, she waited, unruffled, for a reply that would not be forthcoming. Instead Isaac languidly dropped to his knees and began dazedly trying to fit the fractured pieces together. The brilliant afternoon sun created dancing prisms among the irreparable fragments, causing him to whisper.

"Aye, you're beautiful still, even lying here in all of this devastation." His sigh was the sound of pain. "You are all like the pieces of my life, unbendable, without further purpose, and of no possible use to anyone, but somehow, beautiful still."

He toppled to one side with what seemed to Annie a slow deliberate motion, then rolling slightly on his back, his now faded eyes gazed up at her, until gradually, their shaft of light, like the sputtering candle, extinguished itself forever. Without hesitation Annie scooped the particles from the sidewalk, then carefully concealing them in her carry all apron, raced the short distance up the hill to tell Jessica that her father was dead.

The odious funeral odors remained as evening shadows slowly filled each corner of the once resplendent parlor with eerie and frightening fantasies. Long before the departure of the last mourner, Michael had taken to his bed; his grief heightened by the alcohol he had hoped would bring forgetfulness. Young and old had turned out to pay the old man honor, but no voice was more opulent in it's praise than that of the dead man's sister-in-law, Annie Benfield. Eyes brimming, she tearfully recounted how Isaac, the very soul of generosity, had tried to force her into accepting one of his treasures as a wedding gift to his favorite niece, Clara, then, just as she had convinced him that his own need must outweigh his unselfishness, the final seizure had struck, destroying their object of discussion as he toppled to the ground. Truly a man to be admired, who, to the very end, thought only of the happiness of other's. With pious eyes turned heavenward, she implored God's favor on this recently departed soul, with occupancy in the mansions reserved for the magnificently selfless, whose rewards must certainly exceed the normal mortal.

The oration, designed to goad Jessica into committing for the fulfillment of her father's final wish had been heeded even less than Annie's futile supplications to the dead man. Jessica, stunned by the events of the last few days, could only think that this was the final desertion. At last her father had joined his one true love. The one who had never disappointed him, or angered him, never deceived or disrespected him, who waited patiently, even in death, only to be again with him. The thought of it had lessened her sorrow at Isaac's passing, for she intuitively felt he had welcomed it's release, but the pains of guilt still moved steadily against her conscience as, mentally, she aligned her list of transgressions against her poor dead father. Everything they had once been, each to the other, had somehow dissipated into nothingness, and now his escape from this life left her with the enormity of her offenses, and no possible way to amend them.

If only she had never seen the face of Michael McClellan, their entire lives would have turned out much differently. Michael had been the cause of the very first dissention in their happiness, which was then nurtured and grew because of him, and his ability to turn her own father against her. Isaac had been in agreement with Michael almost from the very beginning, starting with the nursing of Maggie and it's benefits, and ending with the unnecessary risking of their fortunes. Her opinions no longer mattered once Michael had gained her father's ear, but it was all over now, and he would hear no more, save perhaps, the endlessly longed for voice of her mother. Shrugging, she dismissed this inane thought, unable to picture an afterlife where her parents now stood, happy and reunited after all these years. It was almost like believing in Santa Claus, and she had never even done that.

Alone now, in the dusky living room, she sat dry eyed, distractedly tugging on the fine hairs of the sofa, her tired mind trying to focus on their dire financial situation. Isaac's small insurance policies would help some, but Michael's failing health and endless doctor's bills were a constant drain on their now meager income. What in God's world would happen to them?

"God's world," she repeated aloud, tilting her head and scanning the ceiling. "At least a thousand times I must have denied you, both silently and aloud, and I don't think I accept you even now, but if you do exist, show yourself to me with just one small comfort, just one answer to my many problems. God, show yourself to me in just one way, so that I can go on living. Show me the reason for all of this and all of the other things that will happen that I am not able to understand. I have never really called on you before, but if you can hear me now, I am pleading with you for an answer, a sign. If you exist, dear God, please let me know it I beg you!"

Softly, and from a distance, she heard a voice calling her name. Disbelieving, she bolted erect, listening intently as the voice repeated her name. With wildly beating heart she bounded from the sofa and faced the direction of the sound, only to find Tom Quinlan's sympathetic face pressed against the window screen.

"I thought I'd best check to see if you needed anything now that the crowds gone," he said shyly. "It's a poor time for being alone so I'll sit with ya if you're feeling the need of any company."

Relief and disappointment simultaneously flooded through her as she lifted the front door latch. Reaching for his hand she almost yanked him into the room and over to the sofa, where she plopped down beside him in resignation.

"I was really expecting God," she said, smiling sadly into his eyes. "But I guess you're just going to have to do, Tom."

He wondered at her words, but, as always, was so mystified by her presence that nothing in this world was as important at this moment as the nearness of her, and the buzzing in his brain that had been set off by the pressure of her thigh against his. His entire body felt the vibration of her vocal chords, as lightly, she lay her head on his shoulder and began to murmur her protests against an unfair deity, the cause of her perplexities, and the frugality of her life. Deaf to everything except the immediate roaring through his brain, he sat abstractedly patting her small hand that lay docilely next to his on the worn mohair. As her head rose from his shoulder, his better judgment rose in unison, dictating the time had come for his departure, but the doe like eyes held him captive as they implored him for an answer.

"What is to become of me, Tom? I am so alone in this world now, with the terrible responsibility of a child, and as is plain to see, with none to rely on, save myself." With lowered eyes, she continued. "In truth I feel I'm still a child myself so how can I possibly be expected to make the right decisions for both us? Good God, I am in a valley of despair, with not a soul to help me. I would give anything to have just one person who cared what happens to us, just someone who would help us." Unheeded tears slid slowly down her pale cheek as she strained to suppress a sob.

Gently Tom touched her chin, forcing her to face him as he smiled brightly. "But Jessie, of course you have me! Did you think for even one minute that your old friend Tom wouldn't rise to the occasion? Your worries are all over, my pet; as long as Tom Quinlan breathes you'll not want for help and advice at any time. Whenever you feel the need of me, you've but to say the word, and I'll be there for the both of you, and you know it's the truth. Haven't you always been able to depend on me ever since we were both children? Of course you have, and nothing will ever change that, I promise ya."

All of her cunning sprang to the surface, and like welcome water in the desert, she relied upon it for her salvation. Pressing the palms of her hands against her bodice to remove the tense moisture, she patted her hair into place, hoping she was not too disheveled after this harrowing day, and then smiled poignantly up at her companion.

"Tom, Tom, how truly wonderful and sweet you are."

Both hands clasped his cheeks as her lips fleetingly touched his in gratitude. Searching his face with admiration, she repeated.

"You are truly sweet, you know. Just caring enough to be here on this horrible night tells me how truly sweet you are." She lowered her voice to almost a whisper. "No wonder I have missed you so, my dearest Tom."

Reeling from the impact of their first kiss, he eagerly placed his hand on her waist, pulling her back with uncontrolled zeal. Then, as their lips melted together in a swirl of ecstasy, he allowed his hand to slide slowly up her side, resting only when it had reached the beginning swell of her breast. His breathing became labored as his blood, surging vigorously through every vessel, swelled him with unrestrained excitement. Every pore in his body responded to this exquisite stimulation by releasing small beads of perspiration that soon covered his face, causing it to glisten passionately in the rapidly dimming room. A warning bell clanged distantly in his brain as Clara's scowling face swam through the red hot blur beneath his closed lids, and forced him to slowly and reluctantly lessen the pressure on the sweet lips beneath his, but Jessica, sensing his failing ardor, immediately drew slightly away, deftly maneuvering her bosom to the very brink of his palm. Deploying all the sincerity she could muster she clutched at his shirt front and spoke almost urgently.

"I need you in so many ways, Tom. Many, many ways."

The spark in her eyes soon reignited the flame of his desire, and his wayward hand inched forward to fondle her breast and disregard his promise to Clara or Jessica's commitment to the man he had hated for so long because of it. She was beautiful beyond his most fanciful imaginings, and he sobbed out his vows of fidelity and love, while he drowned with pleasure in the sea of rapturous sensation.

By the time they finally stood at the door saying goodnight, the room had darkened completely, except for the delicate design cast upon the carpeting by the arc light's rays dancing merrily through the disintegrating lace curtain.

Tom, pressing her hand to his mouth, reaffirmed his love and protection, his eyes still bright with the intoxication of his new found happiness, and the pressing desire to spend the rest of his life pleasing her.

"You'll want for nothing ever again, my love, Tom Quinlan will see to that. For the rest of your sweet life you'll not have to worry again, never again do ya hear? I swear it on our love, Jess."

"I hear Tom, and I'm sure I'll always be able to depend on you." Her eyes were inordinately sad. "I think now maybe you have always been the only one I could ever really depend on all of my life, and I thank you, Tom, with all of my heart for your loyalty."

Exhausted, she rose on tiptoe to lightly brush his lips with hers while her hands pressed against his chest, gently forcing him through the door. Bitter tears stung her eyelids as she leaned against the closed portal and tried to swallow down the huge ball of sadness that was about to strangle her. How different was the passing of Tom through this door than the passing of Michael had been. How she had yearned for the return of one, but now merely needed the return of the other. For the first time she vaguely understood Michael's complacency towards her. Indeed, it was almost as difficult to feign love, as it was to discover yours could not be reciprocated. Her thoughts evoked a resurgence of tears and she shook her head fiercely. This was not the time to be maudlin or dream of what might have been, it was now the time to face what was and what had to be done about it. Twirling about she scanned the ceiling for the second time that night, speaking belligerently.

"Well, God, I gave you your chance and up jumped the devil with a ready answer. You're no better business man than my father was, you never give any breaks or bargains, yet you demand constant payment in prayers and penance. No wonder half of the world turns to your competitor."

Angrily squeezing the gathering moisture from her eyes, she groped her way through the parlor and up the unlit stairway. Pausing by Michael's door she listened soberly as his fitful sleep was interrupted once more by the relentless and savage need to clear his lungs.

"There's another thing you should take care of God, but I'm sure you won't, at least not until you have extracted your pound of flesh from both of us."

Fumbling her way down the narrow hall she entered Isaac's room and fell across the large double bed in despair.

"OH, Daddy, Daddy," she cried into the counterpane. "How I wish you were here with me again. How will I ever face all of this without you to pick me up every time I stumble over my own stupid mistakes?" Her quivering lips settled into a sad smile. "Well, I guess it's plain to see I'm as selfish as ever, Daddy, wishing you back to this unhappy place that I, myself, would give almost anything to escape. Remember when you told me that death is supposedly our punishment for the sins of Adam and

Eve? Well life is sure as hell no great gift either, is it Papa? The bible tells us the dead know not anything, which sounds like very little suffering to me compared to a life filled with the knowledge of things you'd rather not know about, and the brutal human compulsion that leaves you with the inability to forget them."

Her shoulders shook slightly as she stood up and tried to restrain another emotional outburst. Forcing herself to undress slowly in the darkness, she carefully slid between the cool sheets of her father's bed, again gazing at the ceiling in dismay.

"I hope you're not able to look down and pass judgment on what's going to happen now, Papa, but if you can, please try to remember that I do what I do for my own survival and the preservation of your and Mama's home."

Her brows knotted together in a dubious frown, knowing her conduct this night would never be condoned by Isaac for any reason she would be able to conjure up in this lifetime. Rolling quickly toward the wall, she shook her head back and forth briskly, ridding her mind of all infiltrating doubt or any misgivings that may tempt her to weaken in her resolve and turn away from her decision. Clamping her lids shut determinedly she rolled to the other side and whispered decidedly to herself.

"Better that he be dead than to have to live through another disappointment from me. I'll leave all my disappointments now to my husband, who will really never know or care about them anyway."

BOOK THREE

Chapter One

Maggie McClellan was Miraha Wingate's favorite student. The child's deep humility despite her uncommon beauty and evident scholastic achievements at first interested and then attracted Miss Miraha to her. Enchanted by the bright blue eyes, so anxiously awaiting approval, and watching them dim with veils of doubt and disbelief whenever the long sought after admiration finally came, she found in the pathetic child, an almost mystical quality, and one easily related to her own youthful insecurities. She too had been the result of an unhappy union between two incompatible and unyielding people who had spent their entire lives bickering nonsensically; attributing their child's every flaw to those they daily sought out in each other. This unhappy childhood had played heavily in her decision to remain single, a resolve she had never once regretted. Helping to mold other people's children had been gratification enough for her, and when now and again a favored youngster turned sour, she unblinkingly lay the fault at the feet of the parents who, quite obviously, had not carried through with her dictums of dire discipline and only well deserved praise on occasion.

Peering over the rims of her crooked wire framed glasses, Miss Miraha watched as Maggie's wagging raven head studiously scanned the primer, oblivious to the antics of the lad behind her as he impishly knotted her black, shimmering braids together in an attempt to entertain the nearby students. Finally aware of Miss Miraha's hard stare he quickly abandoned his desire to amuse and returned to his studies grateful for the answered prayer that had kept the teacher in her chair and away from the cat O nine tails. Miss Miraha's attention remained riveted on Maggie. Poor lass, she thought, all they do is try to torment her for lack of their understanding why she is different, and how she came to be that way. The old lady repressed a sigh as her dismal conjecture continued. I can at least be thankful that my mother remained respectable, never needing to gain the attentions of any man save her husband, content to embroil herself in every day conflict with him and the thrill of an occasional vanquishing of her worthy advisory. Poor lass has no advantages at all except wanting to learn.

Maggie had shyly submitted a few short poems which had delighted the teacher with their unexpected ring of humor, a trait almost alien to the young girl's timid and cautious personality. Miss Miraha had enthusiastically insisted they be published in the school's monthly magazine, despite Maggie's protests and subsequent humiliation at the sight of her own words staring back at her in bold print.

After five years attendance at Franklin School, Maggie still had not earned the friendship of one other student. The girls, immediately suspicious of anyone so quiet and comely, chose to ridicule her shyness rather than befriend her, while the boys, attracted as they may be, found her wall of reticence too difficult to scale. In typical boy fashion they tried frightening her with live spiders and dead mice and when these dismal efforts to gain her attention failed they resorted to calling her stuck-up and hoity toity, deciding she was one girl no longer deserving of their torment. All of this ostracizing did nothing to deter the young girl's application to her studies and she easily excelled in every subject, much to the chagrin of her classmates who considered her a boring bookworm.

When the dismissal bell sounded, Maggie, as usual, hurried to the first grade room where she was expected to see to it that no mischief befell her little cousin, Mary Bolen, as she walked her safely home each school day. The younger child would run in circles around her as they moved up the street, her whining voice repeating the many taunts she had heard from the older children, without really understanding any of them, Maggie tried hurrying her little cousin along as the blonde curls, bouncing about the small sallow face, reminded her that Molly Bolen would be waiting on the front porch, readily showing her disapproval for their tardiness, and holding Maggie solely responsible. Molly seemed forever taciturn, displaying only a faint grimace whenever her eyes fell upon her pale replica. Showing the small child into the house, she would silently drop a penny in Maggie's reluctant hand in resentful payment for the duty, Mary felt, should have performed gratis, but Jessica had insisted was Maggie's due for such great responsibility. Turning immediately, Molly would follow the child into the house without so much as a good day or thank you, leaving Maggie wishing for a way to overcome this uncomfortable situation. She had tried to make herself like cousin Molly, despite the woman's obvious animosity, mainly because she and Aunt Annie were the only relation she had, but the woman's hostility had only increased with her every endeavor until she finally accepted the fact that her cousin found no favor in her and probably never would, so she would have to content herself with Aunt Annie's spasmodic showerings of affection as her only link to her relatives. She could barely remember Cousin Clara who had moved away some years ago, evidently in the midst of some unspeakable scandal that she had never been privy to. Of the two cousins, she had always favored Clara who, unlike her sister, although not overly friendly, had portrayed a sympathy for Maggie, the girl could not quite understand. Sometimes while visiting with Aunt Annie and sampling her delicious, fresh from the oven, pastries, the child would look up to discover Clara's eyes quickly averted away from her, but not before Maggie had been able to detect their mysterious look of pity. Not long before she left Miners' Haven Clara had pulled her aside, whispering secretly to the young girl.

"I'm only your old spinster cousin, but I wish we could have gotten to know each other just a little bit better now that I'm going away and probably won't see you again. The fault of it all lies with me, child, and not with you, and maybe someday when you're all grown up we'll meet again and be able to be friends." She pressed Maggie's hand against her jaundiced cheek. "I would very much like to be your friend, Maggie."

Blinking rapidly she turned abruptly away to continue her tasks, without ever speaking directly to the girl again before she left.

Once or twice Maggie had questioned her whereabouts only to receive a rebuke which ended with having to suffer through Mama's disfavor for days. Pleasing Mama was difficult enough without occasioning additional problems. Of course heaven knows Mama had reason enough to be irritable saddled with so much responsibility since poor, dear Papa had taken to his bed six months ago.

An involuntary smile brightened Maggie's features at the thought of Michael. Dear Papa, always smiling bravely through his pain, while spinning his sea stories, of improvising on the old Irish ballads, the years and medication had stolen from his mind. His once strong voice was little more than a whisper now, punctuated by fits of coughing and the constant rattle of phlegm, all of which he valiantly ignored in his determination to entertain her whenever she entered his room. Raising himself up on his crimpled pillow, he would reach out to her, his face radiant with the pleasure of her presence, and she would mirror his happiness, knowing him to be the most courageous man in all this world. Even Uncle Tom, who wasn't really related to her at all, could never measure up to Michael, despite his many kindnesses to both Papa and herself, and his constant concern for Mama that had somehow entitled him to a place in the family. Mama would spend every Saturday primping until she heard the honk of Uncle Tom's shiny black roadster, then fastening a large straw hat over her unruly curls, she would dash gaily from the house in a flurry of ribbons and bows, to do the weekly marketing or whatever other business demanded her attention. Maggie had begged to participate in these shopping excursions, but Jessica berated her selfishness with the admonishment that Michael would then be left alone. Every curious request had ended with Jessica shrieking.

"So, you would rather leave your father, the one you supposedly love so well, here alone in his condition. I pray to heaven and all that's holy the poor man never discovers the clay feet of his idol. The very saints themselves must be protecting him from the knowledge that his precious darling cares so little for him that she would prefer tagging along on some tiresome shopping trip in preference to an afternoon of being companion to her ailing father."

Maggie had to admit to herself that only the saints could protect Michael from this knowledge, as Jessica's voice sounded through the house as loud as the colliery fire horn. Plodding up the stairs, and once again filled with disappointment, she would stand by the bedroom window closest to Michael, watching while Jessica, smiling happily, climbed in beside Tom and turned to carelessly flutter her kerchief in their general direction. Michael, seeing her frustration at being left behind again, tried to quell his own pangs of disappointment, knowing his daughter would have preferred spending this day with her mother and her, not so secret lover, to a dull afternoon with a dying man. His eyes glistened with moisture as he patted the small raven head beside him.

"Always remember, lass, it was your Uncle Tom took over when I was no longer man enough to care for my own family, and I hope that you'll always respect him, and be grateful to him, even when you grow up and maybe understand things better." He spoke more to himself than to the child. "God only knows he didn't owe it to me, and now I owe him everything, especially for the things he's done for you, pet."

"Why does he help us so much, Papa?" the innocent mouth entreated

Michael's eyes remained two pools of sadness, despite the smile playing about the corners of his mouth. "Because he has learned the secret of how to love well, that's why, little Maggie."

The clear blue eyes searched his face like two questioning beacons scanning a midnight sky. "What is it you have to do to love well, Papa, buy people things they want and can't afford themselves, is that it, Papa?"

Stretching out on the bed, he motioned her in beside him. "Seldom does money ever have anything to do with love, pet. NO, it's learning how to love another better than you love yourself, which some day you'll discover, is most certainly not the easiest thing to do. It's when not being with someone makes you feel hollow, and being happy for their successes, and sad for their failures. It's like two people being one person, completed by each other."

After a long silence, Maggie questioned again. "Do you remember when I read Oscar Wilde's ballad to you which says "All men kill the thing they love, the coward with a kiss, the brave man with a sword?"

"Aye, I remember, Maggie, and it's the way of it. We kill even ourselves with pretenses cause we haven't the courage to look at the blunt edge of the sword of reality."

"Miss Miraha says that ignorance is bliss and if one were never to think they would always be happy but the alternative is to be able to think intelligently enough to be happy despite the face of adversities." She raised herself on one elbow. "If the choice were yours, Papa would you choose blissful ignorance or destructive knowledge?"

Was she in her childish wisdom able to discern what had happened between he and Jess? He shuddered with fatigue, drawing her head against his chest. "I would always choose to be aware. There is nothing in God's beautiful world I want to pass me by. If some of it is short of the finest, I know that shortcoming is somewhere within myself, and only I can make my life what He intended it to be. One long glorious road to home."

After another long silence the child's breathing told him she had drifted into sleep. He sighed with relief. Her prodding and probing had become more and more difficult and by thunder, why wouldn't she be curious? How many mothers went off every week for a day of shopping and heaven knows what with some male benefactor? Soon enough her suspicious would be confirmed by a snide remark from a classmate. Surely all of Miner's Haven knew Tom's generosity was thoroughly compensated for by Jessica. His mind grudgingly tried pinpointing the beginnings of this wretched triangle.

Remorse for Isaac's death had forced him to retreat from the world around him, finding release only in the endless tankards devoured at Dougal's. Even this old sanctuary offered no solace. The few men able to afford this luxury cliqued together discussing the new electric lamp they could attach to their caps and by means of a slim wire leading to a belt battery, have more illumination than ever thought possible.

Most had known the carbide head lamps which were activated by water flowing from one compartment onto carbide pellets in another, generating a gas easily ignited by a spark producing flint. The resulting bright light was most certainly an improvement over the old oil lamp whose smoky, flickering illumination caused many an accident in the black world beneath the surface. But now, thanks to the genius of Mr. Edison, the old fears of naked flame and explosion were expurgated forever. In addition, the mechanical coal loader was being utilized broadly, saving the men's backs and the company's money. Like all things mechanical it served to lessen the need for so many workers. So while the miners either griped or gloried, Michael only wallowed. Weeks slipped into months before time finally assuaged his soul, permitting the end of his penitence and the return to his wife, who had learned by now how to manage very well without him.

Before the long strike forever changed their lives Jessica faithfully entertained both husband and father by playing the organ every Sunday afternoon. The still beautiful sitting room swelled with the popular music of the day, and Isaac, without fail, would request the melancholy "Baggage

Coach Ahead." The song told of a young father deserted, through death, by his beloved spouse, and his valiant efforts to return her body home despite the protestations of the other train passengers, annoyed by the wailings of the now motherless babe. The final verse

> Oh where is it's mother, go take it to her
> One kind woman softly them said
> I wish that I could was the man's sad reply
> But she's dead in the coach ahead,
> As the train rolled onward
> A husband sat in tears
> Thinking of the happiness
> Of just a few short years
> Baby's face brings pictures of
> A faded hope that's dead,
> But baby's cries can't waken her

In the baggage coach ahead, always found Isaac in teary eyed contemplation of Mary's portrait,

Once this ritual was behind them Jessica always tried something light and cheerful like "Ain't She Sweet?" which forcibly turned both men's mind to the living, now slumbering Maggie.

Jessica had continued her Sunday afternoon recitals long after her captive audience had both deserted her. The haunting strains of "Who Is Sylvia?" floated mysteriously up the stairwell, enticing Michael to again participate in this stabilizing family setting.

The sour after taste of Saturday night lay dormant on his spongy tongue. His bleary eyes watched as the water dripped from his stubbly chin, as he tried uselessly to revive himself at the wash stand. Gingerly patting his hair in place he struggled to the chiffon robe, rummaging through it's drawers with some effort to find something suitable for this Sunday's concert. His shaky fingers unexpectedly brushed against an old chambray shirt Jessica had spent a good part of their early marriage pouring over, striving bravely to redesign and style the stubborn material into a copy of something she had admired in the latest fashion catalog, Smiling confidently, he threw his arms into the rediscovered clothing, knowing the sight of it would surely please her.

His hands still trembled as he fumbled with every button suddenly realizing the garment was surprisingly looser than it's original fit. Peering closely into the mirror he had to admit he was not the comeliest of men this day, but his ability to optimize rushed to his rescue. Sauntering down the hall he resolved to, if not totally, at least substantially, limit his intemperance, thereby allowing more time and a even more importantly, the desire to see to his personal appearance. His mind gratefully accepted this solution and dismissed immediately any need to look beyond it.

Quietly he slid open the parlor doors as Jessica's fingers found the last chords. Tom stood directly behind her, his hands, resting lightly on her shoulders, turned her gently toward him. They kissed as only familiar lovers do, without hurry or hesitation. She rose from the bench pressing the length of her body against him, while his moan like sigh of ecstasy filled Michael's ears. This unexpected scenario transfixed him in a momentary limbo of indecision. Instinctively he began to withdraw, then vacillating uncertainly he deliberately rattled the doors against the gliders and stepped into the room, smiling fixedly. "Well I see we've company, for whom you played as beautifully as ever, my dear."

Jessica, completely unruffled, looked disdainfully in his direction, "Well if it isn't himself, Mr. McClellan., pronouncing his name with an affected Irish brogue, she continued, "I'm so happy you're able to hear again. I was beginning to think your loyalties to the living were all but forgotten, like most of your promises."

Tom made a sudden move, "Jessica---" She raised her hand to silence him, continuing to stare at Michael. "Tom's been good enough to take over for you during your, shall we say illness. His genuine caring has seen us through some very troublesome times, and his generosity has been beyond measuring. As a matter of true fact, he has been the answer to everything we've needed and more, right down to the very food on the table. Unhappily, it would seem Maggie and I can't live on Dougal's fare.

"Jessica, please," whispered Tom as he turned to the window unwilling to participate in this stripping of manhood. Completely ignoring her lover, Jessica walked toward her husband, her face filled with contempt. "For some reason unknown to me you have always thought Mr., Quinlan inferior to yourself, while he, being a gentleman of concern, has seen fit to become the benefactor of your family. Once again I'm afraid you'll find yourself owing a debt of gratitude to yet another man for having tried harder than yourself to relieve the privation of your family." Her lips parted in an unbecoming sneer. "You owe a lifetime of repayment, if only for the things he's done for your daughter."

The flow of words assaulted Michael's still dulled mind like the distant, yet ever persistent blare of the fire horn alerting everyone to disaster. How many times had he answered frantically relentless belching of sound? Now he was the endangered one, the one in need of rescue, the one about to lose his life and everything of importance in it. Woodenly he crossed the room to face Tom. How could he fault this man for making his wife happier than he had ever made her, for loving her as he had never been able to love her, for being everything he had never been man enough to be. Desolated by his seemingly never ending inadequateness he, clasped the young man's hand warmly.

"I do thank you, lad, if you've done all the things Jess says you have, and I'll do my very best to pay you back. I expect I'll be working steadily from herein, and I swear I'll make it up to you. Every red cent of it."

Another commitment! Another pledge! Michael bitterly searched for the answer to why he found himself once again having to correct wrongs that he was not responsible for. Jessica had pursued him like some wanton Jezebel, while his only sin was a weakness of the flesh. Isaac had all but begged him to fulfill a lifetime dream that failed through no fault of his. And now the malignancy of the endless strike spewed it's abomination at his door. Of course he had pressured for walk out, but most every man had cast his vote in favor of it also. Fretting over life's unfairness he barely felt Tom's strong hand covering his. The young man strained to steady his voice, "There's no need of it. You were sick and I helped, there's no more to it than that. His eyes studied the floor, while his crippled foot dug into the carpet pile. Tom had hated this man since he was a boy, but now felt only pity and that strange kind of regret that accompanies the realization you may have been wrong. He knew Michael had always been a cocky braggart, so full of himself and his accomplishments; it galled Tom whenever he had to give ear to it. A man who schemed his way through life at the expense of anyone, including his own family. A man who wished only to enjoy, without the burdensome responsibilities of daily existence, and the confinement that marriage brings. Tom also knew he was the man who had vilified that marriage.

Michael's pretense at joviality interrupted obscure thoughts. "Well maybe it was good experience for you, Tom. Now you'll know what it will be like when Clara gets the ball and chain on ya." His laugh sounded hollow in the tense room.

Jessica, toying with the fringed table cover answered icily. "We're going to have to bring you up to date, Michael. There'll be no wedding. Tom has found Clara to be tedious, tasteless and dull, just as I have always said she was."

Michael could not resist a taunt, "I must admit these words surely do sound more like yours than any I'd expect to hear from Tom."

Jessica bristled, "Some men are quite capable of making consequential resolves, strange as that may seem to you. After much consideration this was totally Tom's decision, and he's telling her tonight." Her eyes flew to Tom, whose pained expression added to her fury. Isn't it tonight you're telling her, Tom?" A demanding note accented the question.

"Yes, yes, tonight," Tom stammered, his face glowing with embarrassment. Unable to think of anything more to say he clumsily searched for his cap among the sofa cushions. "I must be going now, good day to you both." He made an almost comical half bow, then hurriedly began his retreat. In his urgency to leave he almost stumbled out of the room, without once glancing at either wife or husband.

He felt somehow demeaned, perhaps ashamed. Thoughts of the hatred he held so long for Michael raced across his brain, but somehow did not diminish his total disgust with himself. He had always been proud, not haughty or puffed up with his own importance, merely proud of his inherent compassion and tender benevolence, traits governing all the attitudes and actions of his life. Perhaps having his minor handicap had forced him to be more sympathetic, better able to understand or trade places, mentally with the unfortunate and troubled.

In a supreme effort for vindication he forced his mind to concentrate on Jessica, the torments of her life, and how only he had been her salvation. He had done the noble thing, the only thing the expediency of the moment allowed for. Even the most vindictive would be compelled to admit his actions were faultless when weighing all the evidence. If Jessica's loneliness and desperation had driven her into his arms she could not be held in contempt either, when her only sin was the need to survive, to protect her child and herself against the carnage left by an uncaring husband. His heart constricted at the thought of her vulnerability, her dependence on him, and the many wonderful ways she had altered his life. Like man inmemorium, he was able to justify everything within one block walking distance, and guiltily or not, found himself barely able to wait for his next encounter with his beloved Jessica.

As the door closed behind him, man and wife faced each other one with sorrow, the other with belligerence. "Would you be wanting a divorce, Jessica?" Michael asked with feigned nonchalance.

The doe eyes smoldered with hatred. "A divorce is what you'd like me to get isn't it? It's not enough you shamed me once, now I'm to let the whole world know you don't want me, that you never wanted me!' Fury and frustration raised the pitch of her voice to within a scream. Gasping for breath, she continued, "It's so typical of you to take the easy way. You get your one way ticket on the freedom express, and I get the unpaid bills and a child to raise alone."

"Keeping his voice calm, Michael interrupted, "I'm sure that situation would be temporary."

Ignoring his allegation, she tried without success to match his composure. "Oh no, mister, there'll be no divorce. I won't need one. All I have to do is outwait you. What the coal dust doesn't do to you, you do to yourself with your bouts with the bottle. Have you passed a mirror lately? Just stop and take a good look at yourself you're half dead already." She tugged at the slackness of his shirt. "It's only a matter of time, but for that time, my man, you're staying here," her hand slapped her thigh in emphasis, "with me in this Hell until you graduate to a more permanent one."

Unhurriedly she walked toward the stairs leading to the nursery where Maggie, having just awakened, gurgled happily, unaware of the turmoil.

The stinging words and his inner fears that they well may be true blinded him with rage. Following her he shouted, "Don't turn your back to me, you wanton little slut. As a woman, a disgrace is what you are, no better than the bimbos at Dougal's."

She stepped on the first riser, leveling their gaze. "What I am, dear husband, is all woman! she snarled. "My big disgrace is you. You who turn sodden with every misfortune, whose deceitful lips drool with promises all too soon forgotten, without even the pride to care when another man performs your husbandly duties."

His hand shot to her cheek with a muffled clap, and instantly she returned the blow with a resounding smack.

"Your turn, husband." The words hissed like venom, Michael saw the exited rise and fall of her beautiful breast, the flushed defiant expression as her pulse throbbed wildly in the hollow of her throat. Plunging his hand deep within the matted auburn curls, he wrenched her forward. Voraciously his lips sought hers while his free hand greedily clawed her body. The familiarness of her heightened his ardor as his hand found her still firm breast and the well remembered dainty curve of her waist. An all but forgotten longing embraced him as he felt the suffocating need of her. Abruptly he realized her mouth had remained wooden beneath his. Her arms hung limply at her sides in a position of resignation. Yanking her head away from him, he noticed the light of defiance had dissolved into a twinkle of amusement. Gradually he loosened his grip as a flush of embarrassment suffused his features,

"You're too late, Michael, just too late." Her broad smile flashed momentarily then faded away. "But if you ever touch me again I'll devote my life to turning Maggie against you, She's all you've ever wanted out of this so called marriage, and she's all you're ever going to get. I'll do nothing to alter your great love affair, as long as the same courtesy is extended to me. There's no need for her to know about your deficiencies or my attempt to correct them. Actually she deserves better than both of us. Think about it, Michael and I'm sure you'll find it's a better bargain than you're worthy of."

Jessica had kept her word, and although she was at times out of sorts and almost critical of the child, she spoke only with respect in regard to the father.

Looking down at the still white face beside him he was comforted by the knowledge that any humiliation he had suffered, diminished beneath the light of love now so firmly established between himself and Maggie. Neither time, growing up, or even death, he thought, would erode their bond of admiration. The thick black lashes fluttered against her cheek, protesting some childish dream as he cuddled her more closely.

"My wee lass," he whispered into her hair, "Remember always this time we've shared together and how well your father loved you. How very well indeed."

"Oh god, if only it could it had been different for me and Jess", he thought. "It's almost over and we've wasted it with our petty pride and anger, so severe, the inflicted pains have become unforgiveable. Just as the unforgiveable pages of life, once turned, are irretractable, and the words written on these pages, answerable only to a higher power."

His lids closed, releasing trickles of regret, which, sliding across his fevered cheek, fell silently into the child's raven hair.

His breathing deepened, and soon they both shared the peace that only the oblivion of sleep can bring.

CHAPTER TWO

As the roadster ground to a stop, Jessica bounded to her favorite spot beneath a massive willow. Lovingly she smoothed the folds from the car blanket, then lying on her back, gently patted the spot beside her in invitation to her lover. Tom remained by the car, pretending to check the tires on his prized possession. He had gone into the capitol two years before and begun work for the railroad, which proved more to his liking than the drudgery of mining. He was already assistant time keeper and although he had made only a few acquaintances, enjoyed the excitement of a big city and the apparent hustle and bustling of people all rushing to their destination. The car became a necessity if he were to spend any of his time in Miner's Haven. At first his commuting was almost daily, but had gradually lessened to the point of having become a week-end ritual. Disenchantment with his and Jessica's situation had begun about the same time as his new job, but the force of habit, and no other interest allowed his attention to lessen, but never completely falter. Jessica's constant complaining and pouting over his ever lengthening absences served to heighten only his desire to remain away.

He had been virtually driven out of the mines by an unacceptable disaster, which, even now, dogged his memory during his stays in Miner's Haven. He constantly wondered of his preoccupied self centered concern for his own situation had affected his judgment. If he had been more involved with his family and less involved with another man's wife, perhaps he could have averted the terrible tragedy. If he had spent more time with

Willie, reminding him of the job hazards, perhaps guiding him in other directions, or just cared enough to insist the young boy stay in school.

Times had been hard after the strike, and anyone able to get work grabbed at the opportunity without question. Tom's young brother, Willie, was no exception, and having heard the O'Leary family, like many others, were moving out of the area, decided he would plague the fire boss for Billy O'Leary's vacated job of door boy. With unfailing persistence he daily besieged Mr. Lewis, begging for his friend's soon to be available position, while assuring the man he was capable and above all dependable despite his young years. He was most certainly not the only lad vying for the job and knew full well only unrelenting persistence would ensure victory. Each evening found Willie just outside the wash up shack waiting to question whether or not any decision had been made regarding the replacement.

Mr. Lewis had been fire boss since the days when along with his title came the dubious duty of descending ahead of the men, giving the all clear as to fire damp, carbon dioxide, and all other dangerous pollutants. It was a grave task, calling for bravery and good luck. He had spent most of his life underground, and tried in vain to recall whether he had ever had Willie's enthusiasm for work at such a tender age. Finally worn down by the small boy's doggedness, he acquiesced against his better judgment, sealing the youngster's fate.

Since the advent of the giant steam fans which ventilated the mines, sweeping away harmful gases, smoke and dust, it had become necessary to build huge doors allowing air currents to freely flow through the chambers. At each door was posted the door boy whose job it was to be sure the giant doors were open for cars and miners to pass through, then closing them as swiftly as possible so the air currents were disrupted minimally. Each boy sat alone in the dark, with only the company of his own eerie shadow cast by the flickering light from his head lamp, as he waited eagerly for the sound of the oncoming mine motor to ease his loneliness.

Willie soon came to regret his impulsive eagerness and longed for the companionship of his classmates, along with his daily scolding from Miss Wingate. However, being stout hearted and proud he could not confide his misgivings to either mother or brother, and so resigned himself to his lot, knowing full well he had most certainly not been prodded into his situation. Both had fruitlessly pleaded with him to reconsider. Tom plying him with horror stories about a life of darkness beneath the earth's crust, and all the men who had never returned from it. His mother begging that she be relieved from the worry of yet another son in the mines. Finally, bending to his stubborn will, they complied, allowing him to make his own choice. His total dislike for schooling had been a major factor in this decision, and he found it strange to miss the very things he had so ardently wished to escape.

As weeks turned to months he was gradually able to conquer his fear of the dark by spending the endless obscure days making up songs about the many men daily passing through his portal. He tried adapting each description to the tune of Danny Boy, not only because it was a beautiful song, but because it was one of the few tunes he knew. The slight echo in the chamber added timbre to his weak voice, and he imagined himself on stage, performing for an appreciative audience. Applause flooded the compartment at the end of each performance in recognition of, not only his accomplished voice, but of the valued portraiture of his fellow workers. He bowed gratefully to the imaginary sound, while his bobbing head lamp sculpted clapping hands against the blackened walls.

It was during one of these fantasies that the mine car holding the end of the day workers came crashing through the unopened door. So enchanted was he with his new rendition, the clang of the approaching car went unheard until almost the last moment. With a cry of fear he leaped to the door, only to feel it begin to splinter beneath his hand. As the massive wall of wood crashed against him, his last thought was one of regret for not having done his job.

Tom always waited for the last car up so he and Willie could leave the mine together. It had given Willie a grown up feeling to walk home each day with his older brother, both swinging their empty lunch pails, laughing and joking about the days' happenings, and how glad they both were to be soon sitting down to a good supper. They had developed a new closeness, a comradeship of mutual respect and unfeigned enjoyment that made young Willie feel very close to manhood.

Before the last blare of the distress signal Tom was savagely pushing his way through the sprawled cursing men, shouting his brother's name. The certainty of disaster brought the surrgence of hot angry tears transforming his blackened features into a streaky half crazed expression. He never felt the wooden spears dig into his hands as he unyieldingly tore away at the splintered door, pleading with the deities for a miracle. Then in the slowly settling dust he found poor little Willie laying against the wall. His small slender body had been no match for the giant door's mammoth weight. A long wail of agony was the last thing he remembered, and to this day had never recalled how Willie's limp body had to be pried from his grip when, at last, they reached the surface. He did not remember the funeral, his mourning or their mother's horrendous heartbreak. Now he felt only numbness, which at times, became a searing pain of frustration when circumstances forced his memory alive.

The tire's shining rim reflected his consternation and he kicked it with a vengeance directed toward himself. His eyes squinted in the sunlight as they scanned the beautiful form on the blanket, so peacefully at rest. He knew that in just a few moments all this tranquility was going to erupt into wails of recrimination and accusations of betrayal. Jessica had raised herself up on one elbow, the other arm stretched along the length of her body, while impatient fingers drummed against her shapely leg. Her entire pose was one of expectation, and he knew he was going to disappoint her. Reaching her side he looked down with disbelief at the being that had, not so long ago, seemed unattainable, so desirable, so necessary to his life. The face, the form, the loveliness were there, as they had always been; only the desire to hold it fast was missing. Was there always so little left after passion withered? Was it's withering because of his guilt, the loss or lack of love, or possibly discovering your goddess was, in reality, an ordinary woman, with more than her share of pettiness, and less than her share of empathy, mere mortal, not a goddess at all.

He watched as her lids drooped, her lips parting as she awaited his embrace. Clumsily he pressed his mouth to her ear with affected tenderness.

"We must have a little talk first. There are some things need sayin', and can't wait much longer. It's so very hard to remember my life without loving you. I think I was born loving you." He smiled shyly as he slipped his hand atop hers. His face held the earnestness of the supplicant. "I always will love you, Jessica, you and Maggie. We've shared some really grand times together, "he hesitated, "and some pretty awful ones too." His downcast eyes closed in an effort to suppress any unwelcome thoughts of Willie.

Nervously kneading her fingers he continued, "I'll always love you because of the total happiness I've known, only because of you."

The sensually drooping lids narrowed into slits of suspicion. A bitter smile tugged at the corners of her mouth. Removing her hand from beneath his, she flippantly tossed her massive curls over one shoulder and sat upright.

"I know what it is you want to tell me and I'm going to spare you the embarrassment. You see Annie's already hinted to me long ago that you've seen Clara in the city, but of course I never cared, knowing that was over long ago. For some reason Aunt Annie enjoys saying thing's, and doing things she knows will upset me. It's almost disgraceful, her being my own dear dead Mama's sister. Anyhow, she didn't get her way this time, because I know my Tom,"

Realizing she was rattling on she stopped to catch her breath, studying his face for a flicker of denial. Concealing her rising panic she opted for appealing to reason rather than recriminations. Patting his hand affectionately, she afforded him her sweetest smile as she whispered, "Don't feel guilty, my love, over nothing at all. I know you would never intentionally hurt me. We'll both just forget it."

While Jessica spoke Tom's mind registered only his extreme anxiety and longing to be quit of this bitter scene. Disregarding her plea he shook his head back and forth slowly, "I can't forget it, Jessica, because-----,"

She pressed her fingers tightly over his lips, sealing off his reply. Her heart beat frantically as her mind searched desperately for some scheme to stay the remainder of this conversation.

"You must listen to me, Jessica, please," begged Tom as he pulled his mouth away. Clara and I have seen each other more than just once, and in the last few months we-----"

She jumped to her feet, clamping her hands tightly over her ears, shrieking, "I don't want to hear your silly confessions about some stupid woman who couldn't possibly mean anything to you." Her arms fell to her sides, her eyes glistening with some inner inspiration. Looking intently into his face, she almost whispered, "And if it did mean anything it will all be forgotten when our son is born."

The sudden dryness in his mouth made speaking difficult. The words fell from his lips in a monotone.

"What the hell do you mean our son?"

Enthusiastically she again sat down beside him, her eyes; sparkling with feigned delight. "Yes darling it's true. I was just waiting for the right moment---"

He no longer heard her words. This had been his right moment. The moment of extrication! The moment for starting the beginning of his own new life with a woman truly his, bereft of the need to be shared with someone else. A woman, he had to admit, who loved him far better and beyond any love he could ever possibly return, but having lived the other side of the spectrum, he openly welcomed the reversal of roles. The adulation so long given, and somehow yet to be received. Devotion bordering on heresy which, in truth, he did not need, but the freedom to be just Tom Quinlan, husband as well as provider, he needed to the point of frustration.

"You are incredible," he gasped. "How could there ever be a right moment to say you're pregnant to me while you're married to someone else? You always told me you never wanted any more children and knew how to prevent their conception, and what about Michael? How can you explain this to him when he hasn't been near you for years? And what about---? He stiffened in surprise as her open hand slammed into the side of his face.

"You dare call me incredible, you who panted after me since I was a child. You who took advantage of a woman's grief to satisfy his own lust, you who now decide to worry for the man whose wife you have bedded even under his own roof. You, who I must assume from your attitude, will incredibly now try acting unaccountable." She stood up; jerking the blanket from beneath him with such force he snatched it back to steady himself. Suddenly they were transformed into small children struggling for more than possession of the blanket, feeling it's ownership held the symbolic right to override the other's contention. In desperation he yanked it fiercely and both she and the cover fell across him with a dull thud. Exhausted they lay motionless, each with their own secret thoughts. As the pain of exertion subsided, Jessica slowly slid her hand along his thigh, raising herself only far enough to look at him. She watched as his closed eyes opened drowsily and an even deeper flush tinged his already florid cheeks. She snickered inwardly as she recognized the faintly flickering lights of desire. Holding his eyes with her own, she inched her hand even more slowly along his leg until she heard his sigh of submission.

They drove home in silence, one in doubt, one never doubting. One victorious, one defeated.

Chapter Three

Jessica stood before Michael's bed, arms firmly planted on hips that had noticeably widened. The fading rays of the afternoon sun barely entered the drab airless room making expressions difficult to decipher in the ever deepening gloom. Bundled in night shirt and sweater he lay toying with his dinner tray, while Maggie, squinting in the dimness, read the evening paper aloud.

Jessica crossed the room, lighting every available lamp on her way. "It's obvious" she snapped, "the fare is not to your father's liking. Take the tray downstairs, child, and clean up the kitchen while you're about it."

Maggie's eyes darted from one to the other with trepidation. Jessica's manner warned her an argument was about to ensue and she did not want to desert her father. His deep wracking cough and constant chill, regardless how pleasant the day, increased her formidable suspicion that his condition worsened daily.

"Do you hesitate, child, when your mother has given you an order?" Jessica's tone was sarcastic rather than quizzical, although her raised brows and cocked head suggested she anticipated some response. Maggie was about to object when she felt Michael's reassuring pat as he spoke in a voice audible only to her. "Do as Mama says, my love, please." Still hesitant to leave him she impulsively grabbed his pale hand, pressing it to her lips in a childish effort to console him. With a pleading look toward her mother she reluctantly started out of the room.

Walking behind the child, Jessica closed the door emphatically, saying, "We have to talk, dear husband." He struggled to sit upright and assume a more combative position, as it was unbearable for him to have her looking down at him, scrutinizing his indisposition. He sighed inwardly wondering if his last dying breath were to be used up in this never ending futile contest. One supreme final shove brought him to the bed's edge.

"That's become quite obvious, dear wife," trying not to reveal the suffering his maneuvering had erupted, he smiled indulgently, "I've been waiting patiently for your confession."

She threw back her head laughing cruelly. Damn you, if you're not a Catholic right down to your being cuckolded. So it's a confession you want is it? Well I have none to give, my man. I did what was necessary to care for my family, which includes the wreck you've become. That tidy piece of beef you turned your nose up at tonight was on the table because of me, like every other worthwhile thing we've had since Papa died. Don't sit in judgment of me, Michael McClellan, you haven't earned the right." She had advanced across the room as she spoke and once again stood directly before him.

"I would just like to know how you managed it." Michael's voice was conspiratal,

"For a time there I thought he was getting wise to you, but I should have known you would win in the end.

"You're a born winner, my dear Jess, by whatever means." His mouth twisted in a sardonic smile.

Unraveling balls of pain had begun threading their tenuous path across his tightening chest. Small beads of protest lined his upper lip where they lay unnoticed in a web of uncared for whiskers. Gratefully he fell back against the pillows as she momentarily turned away.

"And you're a born loser because you've never known when to act or even when you had the advantage of action. You just sit around and wait for everything to come to you like some deserving dynasty, but the worst part is that it always does come to you." Her hand slapped against her thigh in defeat. "But never through anything you do, oh no," her head wagged frantically from side to side, "It's the whole world doing for you. Or maybe it's that almighty God of yours, who spends all of his time looking out for all you deserving Catholics."

She paced up and down the room waiting for his reply. Noticing his eyes had closed along with his expression, she felt thwarted by the fact she could no longer bait him into a response. Her mind flashed back to the day of the picnic. God how lucky to have feigned something and then have it become reality; but if that hadn't worked something else would have, of that she was certain. Michael was right about her. Most assuredly she knew how to manage having her way with Tom, but only because, mercifully, his benign disposition was so easily directed. She always thought about him as a medium man. Medium height, medium weight, medium brown hair, with medium boned easily forgotten bland features. She prided herself for having taken this mass of mediocrity and molding it into a man of some significance, with a capacity for unbound less love and devotion to her. She soberly remembered how she and Tom had lain on the grass, docilely basking in the afterglow of subsiding love. A deep silence had fallen between them as he tried to take measure of their pathetic situation, his mind vacillating from spasms of insufferable guilt and incomprehensible regrets, to justifiable pathos and forgivable innocence not being a man of lengthy cogitation or analytical musings, he soon fell victim to what he considered to be his lot, and a determination not unlike Willie's to make the best of it. To further insure himself against erring judgment he allowed his male ego to convincingly persuade him that no other man could ever satisfy or care for her as assiduously as he.

Jessica nestled against him, timidly dreading any further conflagration. The distant mournful striking of a church bell had depressed her senses into a delirium of hopelessness which was quickly dispelled by Tom's tentatively searching hand. At last relieved of the tension and devastating fear of losing his solidity, she returned his ardor in a frenzied release unknown to them before.

Her thoughts turned back to the man who lay before her, the only one she had ever truly wanted. The only one whose single touch vibrated through her body, loosing torrential streams of passion that could be quelled only by his continuing embrace and the mad, magic moment of capitulation. Her now heavy breasts strained against the cheap material of her dress as she bent closer with an uncontrollable desire to be near him. Her heart started involuntarily as his eyes flew open.

"Regrets, my dear?" the malevolence on his features rocketed her back into reality with sudden unexpected propulsion. Her disquieted mind swelled with disbelief and ambiguity. Why was it every time she felt some small semblance of contrition, some pigment of caring he so aptly and rancorously was able to dissolve her intentions with only a few shattering words. She swallowed the bitter taste of hate. Malicious shards of detestation lighted fires in the once doe like eyes.

"Only one husband" she hissed, "you've lasted longer than we planned." Clamping a trembling hand across lips whitened by remorse she promptly regretted the impulsive insidious words, but once pronounced, found herself incapable of tempering their meaning. Her sad heart lurched, thudding achingly with self reproach and loathing. She longed desperately to touch that frail body once more, to breathe life back into those decaying lungs through the power of her love, to hold that raven head against her breast and purge them both from the sins they had committed, one against the other. Instead she sighed deeply and trudged wearily towards the door.

He felt rather than watched her leave the room. Waves of self pity and anger alternately buffeted his mind. "For the first time I see her clearly," he said aloud, "without the tainted vision I've had of wife and mother." His wretched voice filled the lonely room. "A woman who willingly stepped into a mire of self inflicted martyrdom, drowning all her sensibilities and genuine affections, then emerging with vindictive intolerance and cunning. She stalks me like some pitiful prey, waiting with impatience for the kill, and all the while knowing, in her shrewdness I cannot expose her for Maggie's sake alone." He sobbed despondently, "My poor Maggie, what is to become of you when I am gone, with yet another one to compete against for love and attention?" He turned his head into the pillow, biting his lip until the blood soaked through the bolster, coloring the down beneath.

Chapter Four

Jessica was eight months pregnant when Michael finally died. He spent the last three months closeted with Maggie, preparing her for his departure and the advent of the new arrival. Maggie's evident enthusiasm over the unborn infant never failed to sadden him for some inexplicable reason. It was natural for her to look forward to a new brother or sister, he reasoned, but nonetheless her eager anticipation was a constant depressant, so, as he felt the cloak of death slowly draping about him, he spoke only of Maggie's future and his hopes in her. He prepared many sealed envelopes for her, each to be opened at designated times. These he believed would be her guideposts through life and, selfishly, a way to insure his remembrance. He had neatly sealed the latest envelope when Maggie peeked through the slightly open door.

Her voice was edged with concern, "I heard you coughing Papa, are you warm enough?"

"Yes, lass, I'm quite warm enough, but maybe a mite lonely. Come sit with me a while.

Not entering the room, she answered in a whisper, "Mama has ordered me to bed. Uncle Tom's coming, and they have important business to discuss that Mama said is not for the ears of children."

Michael forced himself to sit up, disregarding the pain that cut across his chest like a saber. "Surely she didn't say which bed, so if you crawl in here with me you'll not have disobeyed."

Delighted, Maggie danced across the carpet to the bottom of the bed. They had spent so many delightful evenings together, Papa always eager to have her read to him and explain all the new things she had learned. Sometimes she knew intuitively he did not always understand the poetry or prose she chose, but afterwards they would discuss it at length, her constantly conveying its meaning, he, consistently agreeing with her assessment of it. Seeing her father more clearly in the light of the reading lamp, an unexplainable spasm tugged viciously at her heart.

"Are you afraid, child?" he asked, seeing the consternation envelop her sweet face.

"No, Papa," she lied, more loudly than intended.

"You must try to be courageous through life and certainly never fear death." Feeling almost hypocritical, he continued, "It does its damage only once, but unhappiness is repeated over and over in a million ways, a million times. Keenly feeling his own distinct suffocating fear, he crinkled his eyes under the onslaught of yet another tortuous twinge of agony.

Maggie, unwilling to witness his distress, averted her eyes, speaking with soft sincerity. "I love you, Papa, and I'm sorry if you're unhappy. May I read to you? Would that please you Papa?" She did not want to talk or even think of death.

"Come lie beside me, love. This room has a chill about it, we can warm each other." He shuddered slightly as he spoke.

Crawling over the foot of the bed she inched her way up, intently studying him. The strain of sitting up had drawn his brows together, fading white lips into an already ashen face. As he grasped her hand to help her, an unintended groan escaped him inundating the child with alarm.

"Are you alright, Papa?" she whispered with dismay.

Deep red fluid gushed from his mouth as he vainly tried to reply. Surprise suffused each face as they numbly watched the garish liquid spread over his night shirt and splatter on the counterpane.

"My dear God," he gurgled, slumping back into his pillows, automatically pulling her across the bed with him. Tearing wildly at the spread with her free hand she valiantly wiped away the horror, only to see another repulsive stream reappear at each corner of his mouth. Through her frantic desperation she felt the pressure lessen on her hand, until it lay loosely detached in his open palm. Excitedly she grabbed the thin slack shoulders shaking him as she screamed, "Papa, Papa, don't leave me, dear Papa, please, Papa.

For one sweet moment he showered her with a look of love that transcended all illness, all misfortunes and all the unresolved gravities, transforming him into the personable, handsome young fellow who had so totally captured her mother's heart.

"Never, my sweet, never," he promised, as the tired eyes fluttered closed. She remained on the bed watching the stilled breast as the fingers of death sketched their unmistakable mask across the beloved face. Transfixed in disbelief and sorrow, she gazed fixedly at her father, hoping to forever indelibly imprint her mind with his image. Being ignorant of religion she had no God to call upon for solace and surcease, nor one to blame for this merciless injustice.

Gently she tucked the cleanest part of the blanket about the once proud shoulders, then, slipping from the bed, pressed her lips against his cooling forehead. One small tear trembled precariously on the edge of her lashes. Whisking it away impatiently, she rose, walking on wooden legs towards the door. Papa had worked zealously to instill in her the need for bravery and strength when her time came to face adversity. She could not disappoint him now. Troubles and woes are an inescapable part of living, he had told her, otherwise life would be boring and flat, without ever any victories or need for striving, without the elation of having overcome or the intolerable suffering of having lost. It's really the bad times that make the good times so very good, you see.

She wondered if life could ever be good again without him. With difficulty she tried to stay her quivering chin as she paused in the hall asking herself. "How will I live without the sound of his voice, his exuberant exaggerated stories, his ready smile, despite the gnawing misery, his constant comfort and unconditional love? What will I do with the love left in me for him? Will it die now and be buried with him? Uncontrollable tears blinded her as she looked back once more, calling to him softly, "Good-bye, dear Papa, goodbye."

Jessica and Tom huddled near the kitchen coal stove, toasting their hands and feet on the last fading embers when Maggie appeared in the doorway.

"Whatever are you doing up at this hour?" questioned Jessica with impatience. "You're about to feel the strap if you don't march right back up those steps immediately."

The child remained motionless, staring past them into her own thoughts. Irritated for having to leave the soft comfort of the waning warmth, Jessica laboriously rose from the chair, emitting an oath. "How am I expected to put up with this outright impudence?" she bellowed, ambling clumsily across the room. "You're just a willful girl bent on having your own way with no respect for your elders or their wishes. I told your father just this morning we must begin applying some type of discipline here, before you're totally out of hand. I can't be expected to carry all the burden, your father has got to---"

The child's weak, tremoring voice could barely be heard, "Papa has gone away, Mama."

"What the devil are you talking about, child?" She reached out to shake her, but seeing the soiled gown, pulled her out of the shadowy doorway, examining her carefully. Daggers of dread sliced across her innards with a formidable sharpness, forcing her to grab her protruding stomach against the convulsive, piercing spasm of pain.

"What is that mess on your gown, Maggie?" Jessica felt herself begin to tremble as the unanswered question hung in the air like some ominous black cloud.

Maggie raised her still tearing eyes, trying to swallow the capacious lump of grief that rendered her speechless. "Papa---Papa was so sick," she managed to murmur.

Without waiting to hear another word, Jessica mounted the stairs as quickly as she was able. Rushing to the bed she unconsciously slapped the bottom of his feet. "Get up, get up, you faker!" she screamed. The hideous brown stains were everywhere as she yanked the covers to his waist.

"Oh, dear God," she moaned, pressing her nails into the still clenched coverings. Her shoulders heaved with suppressed sobs, as suddenly she threw herself across the fragile, still body, crying aloud, "Michael, Michael, you've left me again. Dear God, why did it have to be so? My own dear Michael, what will I do now? There's nothing left for me, you see, you've taken all my hopes with you."

All the bitterness ebbed from her body, as she allowed herself at last to be honest with the unhearing body beneath her.

"I have not, nor never will again, love as I have loved you, my darling lad. All I have done you have driven me to because you could never return my devotion. God, what happiness could have been ours. A life of tender admiration, instead of endless rebukes, a life of limitless affinity, rather than limited tolerance, if only you could have loved me---" Her tears splattered everywhere, but she was beyond caring. "Why couldn't you have loved me just a little more, Michael, God, I only wanted such a very small part of you, why, why couldn't you give it to me?" She threw her head on his sunken chest with total abandon, sobbing. "How will I be able to live without your forgiveness, knowing now there will never again be any means to gain it, never again a time to say I love you, a time to tell you I will miss you all the days of my life, reliving over and over the sweet pleasures we shared not so long ago." Her sobs subsided somewhat as she tried regaining her composure. Speaking almost resolutely, she concluded, "My well deserved punishment will be to live with all the unspoken words that bitterness prevented, wondering if ever you had longed to hear them, and the deepest sorrow for never having spoken them."

Entering the room Tom watched her with suspicious wonderment. Surely this display had to be for the child's sake, but the child was not with them. Gently he touched her elbow, whispering, "Maggie's not here, Jessica, she stayed downstairs."

Her bewildered eyes searched his face, "What has she got to do with this? She took him away from me in life," she protested loudly, be damned to her. I'll have my own moment with him now." Burying her face into the blankets, she allowed her weeping to fill the room until, distantly; she felt the persistent aching which foretold this night would yield up a new life to replace the one death had stolen from her.

Chapter Five

She lay nuzzling the infant against her bosom, as he dozed contentedly, his tiny clenched fists snuggling beside each cheek.

"You didn't give me a moment's trouble, my darling. The good old doctor barely got here in time for your grand arrival, and I think you and I could have handled it all by ourselves anyway." She cuddled him even closer. "Oh what a fine life you're going to have my little Michael," she whispered against the small pink ear. "I'm going to raise you to be a real man, fearless and brave, but mostly filled with love, and not ashamed to show it. Yes sir, you'll be the man in this house from now on, and a pure pleasure to your mother."

Looking down at the still ruddy face she felt a delight she had never known before, and began studying every finger and toe, marveling at the perfection of her creation.

"How I love my little man already, and him only a few hours old.

The child wriggled under the tightness of her grasp and she giggled aloud. "You don't have to worry, lad, I don't plan to hold you down, I've learned that lesson well enough to know better. No, you'll have your own lead, but we'll understand each other and nobody or nothing will ever come between us. This I promise you on your very first day."

Kissing the auburn down covering the tiny head she rose slowly from her bed and placed her prize in the small cradle that had once held Maggie She felt compelled to watch and marvel over him as Michael had marveled over the cradle's contents all those years ago.

"Tom's left us, you know," her one sided dialog continued. "And I'm sure he's not coming back, and you know what, my precious," her relaxed smile widened, "I really don't care anymore. We'll make it alright on our own." Her thoughts drifted, "He was right to accuse me of still loving Michael." Her brows drew together and an obtrusive sickness grabbed her at the thought of her dead husband. Forcing this ugliness from her she stumbled back into the luxury of her warm bed. "From now on," she called across the short distance between them, "You're my number one fellow. Just you and me, my new little Michael."

The door creaked softly as Maggie's small anxious face peered tentatively into the room. "Are you alright, Mama? Is everything alright? Isaac's crystal blue eyes danced quizzically in the small frightened face.

"How like you to interrupt our very first conversation. The repellant thought remained unspoken. "Of course I'm alright," snapped Jessica. Who told you could come up here anyway, there must be at least a dozen things you could be doing to help Aunt Annie."

Maggie began meekly, "Uncle Tom said you'd probably want to see me to talk about everything, and," the sweet face brightened somewhat, "and I wanted to see my baby brother."

The words stung Jessica's ears, driving her to unreasonable rancor. Staring at the girl with unmasked hostility she answered tightly, "I'm not well enough to talk; besides talk never changed anything I've ever heard of. Papa's gone and that's that." Once again the detestable waves of sorrow assailed her. In a voice filled with tension she said, "Uncle Tom and Aunt Annie will be making all the arrangements. I have to remain here, in bed." A fact she was most grateful for. "So you will take my place." Maggie's downcast look prompted her mother to continue. "Don't worry it won't be hard for you, you've done it very well to now." Turning on her side, practically obliterating her head under a mass of covers, she dismissed her daughter. "Now away with you, I'm very tired."

A familiar lump of grief constricted the child's throat as she struggled to comprehend her mother's meaning, but she could not bring herself to leave the room. The entire house seemed empty without Papa. An almost frenzied need to be with someone drove her to persist.

"May I come in and see the baby, Mama?" she pleaded.

Jessica, sighing propped herself on one elbow, her eyes squinting with loathing. Does she really expect to hang on me as she did her father?

The small dejected figure caused her to relent somewhat as she answered without enthusiasm, "Alright, come and see what a beautiful baby brother you have, but you must be very quiet."

Maggie, in her eagerness, tripped on the corner of the worn carpet, falling to her knees with a resounding thud, evoking a startled howl from young Michael.

"You wretched child," screamed Jessica, "You've deliberately frightened the life out of him, after my just asking you to be quiet.

Get out of this room and don't come back until I call for you."

Maggie, still on her knees, began whimpering, I'm sorry Mama, I didn't mean to scare him, honest I didn't. Oh please don't send me away, Mama. There's no one else in the house. I don't want to be alone, please, Mama,"

"It would appear you are just as disobedient as ever. I want you to go to your room this very moment and not come out again till Tom or Annie comes for you. Do you understand me?" Mother and child stared into each other's eyes, both aware of Jessica's bitterness.

"Why do you hate me, Mama?" Maggie questioned pitifully, as her tears poured forth. "Whatever I've done wrong or harmful to you, Mama, I'm truly sorry." Despite her innocence, child like intuition dictated the pressing need to resolve this ambiguity between them.

Stunned by her perceptive insight, Jessica began shouting, "Hate, you, hate you! Is that what you think, you stupid little girl. Don't you realize I'm your mother, the one who gave you the gift of life, the one who has cared for you and will continue to care for you as long as God gives me breath, despite your ungratefulness?" Her bosom heaved under the pressure of secretly acknowledged negligence and dereliction. Her transgressions cried out for vindication as she continued her verbal attack. "All I have ever asked of you is a reasonable amount of obedience and dutiful respect, certainly not more than a mother should expect from her child. But you, you're exactly like your father, always wanting something from me, always draining me away and never able to give anything in return

Maggie's head moved slowly from side to side, unable to fully comprehend her mother's words. "I don't understand, Mama. I just want to be with you, not drain you away. Why can't I just be here with you?"

Inflamed by her own guilt and the girl's persistence, her resentment became boundless. "Get up off that floor and be gone with your idiot questions," she answered, screaming and violently slapping the counterpane. "Get out! Get out of this room!

The outburst set the infant to crying in earnest. Jumping from her bed she snatched him from the cradle, soothing him with soft words and kisses, consoling and composing herself simultaneously. She did not notice Maggie's slow retreat from the bedroom, nor did she remember to call her when Annie came to prepare the lunch.

Maggie inched along the gloomy hallway until she came to Michael's door. Opening it slowly she stole inside and leaned against the wall. Annie had tidied up the room, removing the soiled sheets and coverlets. A small indentation in the worn mattress was the only visible reminder of the man who had died there. She allowed her body to slide down the wall and sat gazing at the bed. "I remember everything you told me, Papa," she whispered to the lonely room "It's better to experience everything in life, but, Papa, it's so hard to be aware of and experience hatred. So hard even for me to understand it. Mama says she doesn't hate me, but I displease her with my willfulness. I guess I don't know when I'm being willful so I don't know how to stop it. I do so wish you were here to help me." Emitting a long sigh of resignation she squared her shoulders, her voice becoming somewhat stronger.

"I will have to grow up a little now, and learn to care for myself. Mama will have so much to do without you, Papa, caring for the house and little Michael, worrying about paying all the bills. Yes, it's the very least I can do to help. Do you think she won't feel drained by me then, Papa?" The thought brightened her. "Then she'll know I have something to give her, won't she Papa"

She stared around the room, willing some sort of assurance, waiting for an answer that could never come. With one last sigh she dragged herself to her feet and slowly plodded down the hall, to her own lonely room

BOOK FOUR

Chapter One

Miraha Wingate, newly appointed principal, and Jessica McClellan faced each other across the teacher's littered desk. Miss Wingate's dull grey hair remained motionless inside its net covering despite the rapid shaking of her head. Her thick grey brows knotted in disbelief, her voice filled with disapproval.

"I find it impossible to believe you would remove an A student from school and deny her the education she is not only eager for, but deserving of. The child has a talent for words and expression. A talent not to be denied for any reason. She's a born writer, a conveyor of thoughts, thoughts worthy of consideration, even at her young age. I know she can make something of herself if given the chance."

"Right now I'm interested in her making a living," snapped Jessica. "I've carried the burden alone long enough. She has a brother to be considered, you know, whose educational needs will surpass hers if he's to make a living. I was only slightly older than she is when I left school, and never found I missed too much."

"But, my dear, how can you determine what's been missed without having had the opportunity to explore it?" Miss Miraha smiled pleasantly, "Women are taking on a new status in this country and educating them is very important, and someday will be important all over the world. Women are ready to make their mark. Just examine our own community, with so many of the men idle because of mine closings, one after the other, a woman would do well to be educated and self supporting. Don't you agree?"

Jessica stood up. "I did not come here to discuss the local economic situation, but rather for you to sign the necessary papers." Extending her hand in a demanding manner, she added, "If you please!"

Leaning back in her swivel chair, the teacher persevered, "Since it would seem I cannot sway your determination to commit this travesty, would you be willing to have her tutored evenings or weekends?"

Dropping her hand in disgust Jessica answered, "You're a fool Miss Wingate. I'm taking me daughter from school to make money not to spend it. Tutoring indeed! I've always thought that was for the very wealthy."

Miss Wingate's ample bosom heaved a heavy sigh, "I don't believe you understood my intent, I will do it without charge, Mrs. McClellan I have a deep feeling for your daughter, and an even deeper respect for her capabilities."

"That's not surprising, it would seem almost everyone has deep feelings for my daughter, but unfortunately this time our consideration must include the entire family. I'm afraid her evenings and week-ends will be filled with caring for Michael while I work at the Down Town Diner. I will not have him be alone or with a stranger. He's a very delicate boy, demanding much attention. Unhappily he seems to have inherited his father's poor health."

Miss Miraha allowed her glasses to slide to the very tip of her nose. Peering over the rim in owl like fashion she answered, "That's surprising news, Mrs. McClellan, it was my understanding his father's health is excellent."

Jessica leaned over the desk, all of her senses alerted to danger. "Would you care to explain that remark, Miss Wingate?" Lowering her voice to a conspiratal type whisper she continued slowly, "I understand you have only a few years till your retirement and full benefits of tenure, I would hate to see you dismissed because of a gossipy tongue."

Pressing her glasses against her nose, Miss Wingate smiled coyly. "And I understand you already secure a miner's pension for yourself and Mr. McClellan's two children. I would hate to see that already meager amount be diminished for the same reason."

Jessica's hand flew to her throat, fingers fluttering like the wings of a small sparrow. Was it possible, she wondered, for anyone to prove or disprove the fathering of her child? An article in the Daily concerning new blood testing sprung to her mind, but try as she may, she could not recall whether or not the test had been considered conclusive. This constant seeker of knowledge sitting before her must know something or she wouldn't be casting innuendos. She paled as the teacher stood up and came around the desk toward her. Miss Miraha placed her ink splattered fingers on the younger woman's arm, leading her slowly to the door. "I'm so glad you dropped so we could have a little chat. Whatever evening next week is convenient, please contact me and I will make myself available." Miss Miraha smiled charitably in her direction, "And by the way, my dear, perhaps having missed your schooling you would like to sit in on the sessions. We're never too old to learn you know." Her huge frame blocked the doorway, trapping her adversary in the classroom.

Jessica, repulsed by the aphorism, drew away from the mottled fingers. "I think not," she answered icily," and moreover it will not be necessary for you to come to my home, I will send dear Maggie to you. I don't feel we have enough in common to share more than this one conversation together. If you'll stand aside, I'll say good day to you, teacher."

The old woman smiled as she watched Jessica tramp indignantly down the hall. "A little more education, and she might have known how to call my bluff, how not to be intimidated, how to be a worthy opponent. A little more understanding of human nature and she would have wisely perceived that even her obstinacy could not have driven me to perform a detrimental act where Maggie is concerned." She closed the classroom door, wearily shaking her head, speaking softly to the fleeing figure, "How very wrong you are, my dear. We have something very important in common. Each of us has become accustomed to getting our own way."

Jessica's curls bobbed irritatingly about her face as she jammed still shaking fingers into the pockets of her jacket. Once outside the building she slowed her pace in an effort to regain her composure. That old prune had actually blackmailed her with her damned insinuations, looking down her puritanical nose, which obviously sniffed out the town gossip. Of course it was easy to understand an old spinster's curiosity and the possibility of resentfulness as well. How boring her life must be having no one to devote herself to, save other people's children, who grew up, moved on, and probably gave not one backward glance to this dedication. The dried up old weasel was actually jealous of me now that I think it over.

She sighed contentedly. The things people will stoop to through envy never ceased to amaze me. Jessica was totally relaxed now, and smiling to herself, allowed perhaps the old woman was right. Maggie had reached the brink of womanhood, strikingly beautiful of face, with a body that merely hinted at maturity, being painfully thin and delicate, which no manner of dress seemed to improve. "The child is pleasant enough, but totally without personality," Jessica told herself. She may very well need to be self supporting, as few men are going to be attracted by her lack of charm.

In truth, Maggie's inner beauty was her greatest asset. The promise of a smile forever hovered in the corners of her perfect pink lips. Thick black lashes surrounded the translucent blue eyes, soft, yet sometimes sad, almost belying the contented half smile. She was, a tall girl, her lean frame adding to the illusion of height. Only her graceful flowing movements helped disguise an otherwise over thin somewhat gangly body. Her clear ivory skin was almost too pale against the long jet black hair pulled severely from her face and fastened behind each ear with large mother of pearl combs. One of her grandfather's last treasures. Everything about her was subdued and gentle. Her hair, unlike her mother's unruly tresses, lay in place, waving softly over her back and shoulders. Her fingers were thin and delicate, the nails barely pink. Her voice, hauntingly soft, was reticent and reserved, emitting only profound serenity, reflecting inner peace. Her demeanor was exemplary, leaving nothing to be desired, and most certainly nothing to be criticized. She had long ago evolved into the perfect child, obedient, respectful and above all, totally giving.

The result of this evolution was a well disciplined woman, careful never to display emotion of any kind, or draw unwelcomed attention to herself by voicing contrary opinions. No one, especially not her mother, could have suspected that she filled her dull life with unadmittable fantasies, dreaming only of the day she would be able, at last, to leave Miners' Haven, no longer in need of a refuge. Standing alone because of her strength and confidence, a woman, invincible by virtue of her own tenacity, with none to lean on, and none to lean on her.

Chapter Two

Maggie and Jessica sat in the small employment office of the Eagle Silk Mill. There were several other girls waiting for interviews, each eying Maggie with disgust and suspicion for evidently having had to be accompanied by her mother. Maggie looked up only when Mr. Flynn finally called her name, then blushed furiously as she walked past the other applicants. Once inside, Jessica took the initiative, inquiring politely concerning Mr. Flynn's health and volunteering information concerning hers and Maggie's. Smiling pleasantly, she turned to her daughter.

"Did I ever tell you, my dear, that your Grandfather was responsible for Mr. Flynn's important position here in the factory? I can't recall the details; it was all so very long ago. Perhaps Mr. Flynn would enlighten us." Preening, she looked expectantly at the uncomfortable foreman.

"Mama, breathed Maggie, in confusion, "We are here to discuss my position, not Mr. Flynn's."

Turning her radiance upon the unhappy man Jessica conceded, "She's quite right I suppose. I hope you'll forgive my remembering someone who was always doing good for other people. We all miss Papa so." Her smile had saddened somewhat, and Mr. Flynn, fearful of a woman's tears, began immediately questioning Maggie as to her qualifications. The girl sat fidgeting with her purse strings, unable to admit she knew not the slightest thing about sewing, or the machinery involved in it. Feeling the man's eyes on her, she looked up, about to confess her complete ignorance when Jessica interrupted.

"Her qualifications, I would say, are similar to your own when you started here, Mr. Flynn. She is eager to learn, ambitious, and above all, and I'm sure you'll remember this, Mr. Flynn, most needful of money to assist her family, who must rely on the charity of old, true friends and family."

"Well," he stammered, "We are not in the habit of hiring girls who do not have even some home sewing training, We--"

"I'm sure you're not, Mr. Flynn, and that's why we so much appreciate your kindness to us. Rest assured you'll not have one regret regarding Maggie's performance, and, in addition, you'll at long last be able to repay your debt to dear dead, Papa." Rising quickly she dabbed daintily at the corner of one eye with her kerchief. "I must leave before my gratitude causes my loss of self control."

Grabbing the foreman's grimy hand between hers she whispered, "May God bless you, Mr. Flynn. I will pray to Papa to intercede with the Blessed Mother for you." She almost laughed aloud at the foreman's grateful expression. By God, these Catholics would do almost anything to get to their heaven. Leaving nothing to chance she called down the blessings of all the Saints on her benefactor, then grabbing Maggie by the wrist, scurried from the office.

The befuddled foreman shook his head with doubt, and disbelief. His recollection of Mr. Hobbs was vague and clouded by the passage of time. He could recall him only as a friend of his fathers', who had influenced both his parents by insisting the mines, was not the place for their lad to be employed. Joe Flynn had been an A student, excelling mathematically, which, according to Mr. Hobbs, automatically entitled him to an occupation above the ground, and one worthy of his proficiencies. His continual badgering and protestations gradually influenced the family to seek out alternative employment for their son. After much supplication and perseverance, on the part of his family he was finally accepted by the factory, which meant spending his days lugging huge bolts of cloth from the warehouse area to the ever humming machine tables. His then young body responded to this labor by becoming broad of chest with massive muscular shoulders atop a small tight waist. Known as the Charlie Atlas of Miners' Haven he was admired by the lasses and envied by the lads. The sweet remembrance brought a grin of pleasure to his wrinkling cheek. Scratching his now balding head did not help resurrect any notable intervention on the part of Mr. Hobbs. His insistence, however, he would have to admit had most certainly made his life an improvement over his poor father's who had long ago perished from the dreaded black lung. Perhaps there was some distant obscure obligation, but only Issac Hobbs daughter's retrospection could have caused it to surface.

Once on the sidewalk Jessica faced her daughter with wary repulsion. "I hope you realize now why it was so very necessary for me to come along today. Your drivel would have never landed the job. You're afraid to speak up, girl."

Maggie's undiluted eyes stared directly into Jessica's, "There was no reason for me to speak, mother. You, as usual, were able to take care of everything."

Jessica's brow shot upwards in surprise. "Are you about to be in some kind of a snit because you are finally, and at last employed?" Had she detected some sarcasm in Maggie's tone?

"The manner in which I became employed offends me. I am not qualified like those other girls. I am--"

"You are dreary! You are qualified for whatever becomes necessary and don't forget it!" Laying a solid whack on the girl's buttocks she continued, you're finished resting on that, my dear, you're going to move it." Then suddenly she giggled, throwing her arms about her daughter. Taken back, Maggie automatically responded to this unexpected show of affection, stifling a gasp of surprise against her mother's neck. A current of tenderness flooded through her as Jessica gently pushed her away, holding her at arm's length. "My little girl's becoming a woman with opinions of her own it would seem, and certainly not afraid to declare them." A bewildered expression suffused her features as she spoke. "A woman a mother could get puffed up over if she keeps going in the same direction..." Then, like coming out of a dream, she again slapped Maggie's backside, throwing her head back with a laugh of unadulterated enjoyment. "A woman with a behind that's not all that bad either." They leisurely walked home, arms about each other, giggling over some secret never spoken. A bystander would have immediately recognized two carefree young girls, possibly testing out a new found friendship.

The silhouette of the steel breaker was barely visible through the heavily falling snow. Like some heaving monster it emitted great clouds of steam, pulsating steadily, as it roared with the effort of its bull shakers to separate and size the anthracite, assiduously retaining only the useable, relegating the impurities to a refuse chamber below. Not too many years ago this arduous task had been per formed, in part, by men using sledge hammers and picks to break up the huge hunks of coal, they, being the original human breakers.

Maggie starred through the grimy factory window, watching the belching vapor evaporate into the cheerless sky. Hunching over her sewing machine she prayed for the sound of the four o'clock whistle, indicating the end of yet another endless day. Even in summer, when all the factory windows were flung open wide to combat the oppressive heat, the song of a bird or the children's' laughter from the playground below never filtered through the monotonous drone surrounding her.

Her back ached as it had ached every working day for the past two years. Miss Miraha's badgering had convinced her it was not a physical pain, but a mental resistance to work she detested because; in fact she was above such a menial job. A job requiring dexterity, but not one wit, of imagination or extensive thought. "The mind, like any precision instrument," Miss Miraha scolded, "corrodes with rust when allowed to remain idle, but constant and proper use improves its function, allowing it to accelerate beyond what was originally conceived as its maximum capabilities.

She smiled wryly, wondering what her maximum capabilities might be. She had certainly not been a success at the factory where everyone's output exceeded hers, try as she may. She found herself constantly daydreaming and even now as she tried looking through windows almost totally blurred, she was able to picture in her mind's eye the bleak culm bank behind the breaker, its half dead trees struggling for life in the mine sludge, the once white company houses fading into the grayness of the day.

"Imagination", Miss Miraha had extolled. "Stretch and exercise that wonderful mind of your. Look for beauty in ugliness, listen for the music in grating noises, feel for the softness inside the petrified shell. Imagination, you will find, makes all things bearable."

Maggie's foot paused on the treadle as she scrambled through her purse for the pad and pencil she always carried with her, allowing her to capture fleeting impressions, or someone else's profound thought. Hiding the pad beneath the table she began jotting,

Dense is the forest, lonely are the trees,

The flowers are all faded, the blossoms, and the leaves.
The snow falls down in flurries, neath a sky both blue and pale
Forming diamonds on the rooftops, midst a lovely crystal veil.

Pleased, she smiled to herself; Miss Miraha would have to admit that was somewhat imaginative, under the circumstances. The scrap of paper was snatched from her hand as Joe Flynn's raucous voice boomed mockingly into her ear.

"This is the very reason you never make your quota like the other girls. We took you out of the sorting room when your dainty little nose and eyes couldn't tolerate the lint. Now evidently your feet and fingers tire from the machinery and you must have time out to scribble nonsense. I've kept you on here because my father greatly admired Issac Hobbs, but you've taxed my patience with your laziness and I've reached my limit. Do you understand, girl?" Maggie's stricken face did not deter him. "This factory's been bought out and my job depends on pleasing the new owners." As did his impending retirement and pension. "Production is what they want, not dilly dallying." "You young people today can't hold a candle to your elders." "You totally lack ambition and dedication, content to be labeled wastrels, frittering away time on nonsense and pleasure, without any thought to obligation." "He seemed unable to staunch his tirade. The whirr of machines noticeably slackened as the line of workers strained to listen. "Remember the day your mother promised me I would never regret hiring you?" "Well please tell her for me I've not had one satisfying day out of you yet, and I can't run a business on sentiment, no sir, only on results, and you, young lady, show me none." "I'm going to ask you to turn in your time card at the whistle, and pick up whatever it is you've got coming."

The foreman turned on his heels, walking rapidly down the aisle between machines accelerated to top speed by fear of further reprisals. Maggie raced after him, catching his arm as they reached the office. On the verge of tears she pleaded.

"Please, Mr. Flynn, I know everything you said is true, but I'm ready to devote myself to doing better. I really will, you'll just be amazed at how hard I'll work if given one more chance." Appealing to his compassion, she asked, "Whatever will happen to Mama and little Michael without my income?"

The man angrily removed her hand from his arm. "The only thing amazing to me is why you haven't thought about all this long ago. This is certainly not your first infringement of the rules and you well know it. Stop living in a world of self deceit and accept the fact that this untimely incident was brought about by you, not me." He walked into the office slamming the door behind him.

Bewildered she looked back into the shop where every head was bowed with diligence over it's machine. Almost prostrate with self reproach she knew facing her mother with these tidings was a devastation she could not endure. Jessica, as she grew older, always seemed to have some aphorism befitting each and every occasion. Maggie, cowering, could already hear the dreaded words. "Like I've said at least a hundred times before, the apple never falls far from the tree." Actually mother and daughter had found a fragile but comfortable equanimity that Maggie was unwilling to jeopardize. Fearing this loss more poignantly than the grim ire of Mr. Flynn, she frantically pushed open the office door, sobbing,

"You can't do this, Mr. Flynn. I beg you don't do it."

Joe Flynn stood holding a sheaf of papers, while a young man seated at the desk was carefully examining each sheet, one at a time. Both men started as the door banged against the jam, revealing the desperate, somewhat disheveled young woman. Recovering swiftly, the foreman placed the papers on the desk, then walked towards Maggie speaking in a conciliatory voice.

"Now, now, Maggie, we'll talk about this later. Mr. Jennings can't be disturbed right now. I'll talk to you later." His eyes begged her acquiescence as he tried gently turning her around. The quitting whistle shrilled it's normally welcomed blare ending another day. An inhuman sound escaped her as she struggled against his persistent pressure on her slender arm.

"But that's the whistle," she cried, "We won't have time later; we must talk now, Mr. Flynn." Garnering all her courage she blurted,

"You owe it to my grandfather."

Joe Flynn's voice had become stern. "You must leave this office now." Her face reflected the pain of his renewed pressure.

Rising from behind the desk the young man asked very quietly, "What's the problem here, Joe?"

"It's no problem I can't handle, Mr. Jennings, his voice rang with confidence. "Maggie here is a fine girl, but not cut out for production work, so we'll maybe have to fit her into something else."

"But you said I was fired, Mr. Flynn, Maggie blubbered, turning to the younger man. "Mr. Jennings, I can't be fired even though I know what I did was wrong. I need the work desperately, as Mr. Flynn well knows.

The young man studied her consternation, captivated by the crystal blue eyes, sparkling with tears. His fingers longed to touch the crown of raven hair framing the pale drawn features, cascading about the narrow shoulders like a shimmering silk mantle. He asked very softly, "And what is it you have done exactly, Maggie?"

"I've wasted company time, sir," she murmured, lowering her exquisite eyes. A suffocating need to look into them again disturbed him.

"Look at me and tell me exactly what you did." An unexplainable excitement gripped him as she obeyed, answering contritely.

"I scribbled nonsense when I should have been working to reach my quota," Boldly walking to his desk, she smiled apologetically, disquieting his composure. "But I've learned my lesson, sir, and I'll never do it again, I swear." His delight increased at the serene; almost chime like sound of her now calm voice.

"And where is this nonsense now?"

Maggie turned to Joe Flynn who immediately fumbled to retrieve the crumpled scrap of paper from his pocket. Smiling sheepishly he handed over the bone of contention. "It's like I said before, sir, Maggie's a fine girl, but as you can see her mind's not on her work as it ought to be, and she sets a poor example for the other lasses who don't want favoritism shown on the line. Distinctly feeling Mr. Jennings was no longer listening, he added lamely, "I'm just trying to do my job, is all, sir."

Scanning the few lines the young man again sat down, his brows drawn together in concentration.

"Well it would seem that nothing on this sheet of paper will contribute anything worthwhile to production." The foreman registered instant, welcome relief. "I do believe Mr. Flynn is correct, you are definitely a detriment to the shop in your present position." Maggie's color deepened with shame. Feeling briefly giddy she steadied herself against the desk's edge.

"I don't suppose you know a thing about office procedure, bookkeeping, typing, etcetera?" His scrutinizing eyes caused her to fidget, mumbling, "No, sir."

"Well fortunately for you, Mrs. Bean, my office clerk, not unlike so many others, is literally fleeing the area to find work for her husband elsewhere. You will train under her for two weeks, at which time you will show some aptitude and ability to learn or you will continue writing poetry on your own time, at your own expense. Agreed?"

Interpreting her hesitancy as refusal, resentful disappointment assailed him. Perhaps he had been too blunt or harsh for her timid nature, but he expected her to accept any challenge if her situation was, indeed, as dire as she had portrayed. But Maggie, flooded with relief, stood mute before him, her mind racing to assess this sudden good fortune, while shades of doubt dimmed her already nebulous confidence, knowing her self esteem could not survive another dismal failure.

Shuffling his feet in embarrassment, Joe Flynn groaned inwardly wondering if he could be held responsible, in any way, for this girl's ill mannered stupidity. Silently cursing her and her entire family, he coughed nervously into his hand, inadvertently and abruptly penetrating Maggie's stupor. With supreme effort she overcame her uneasiness, extending a trembling hand.

"Agreed." The commitment was little more than a sigh.

They clasped hands across the desk, he drowning in the two bottomless sapphire pools, she noting how his hands held not one blue coal vein, how his manicured nails were immaculately spotless, his grip warm and strong.

Later that evening, in the privacy of her small room she vividly recalled every mark on Michael's hands where falling bits of coal had caused unsightly veins to rise to the skin's surface. She was able to clearly recount the battered nails, everlastingly embedded with irremovable sooty black dust. Those dear hands whose warm, strong touch she had all but forgotten. In some obscure way she felt comforted for the first time since Papa had gone away.

Miss Miraha, upon learning of Maggie's promotion, resurrected a somewhat antiquated, but serviceable typewriter and immediately set about instructing on the keyboard and correct letter writing procedures. Even Jessica insisted upon participating, conducting nightly spelling bees, and a word a day dictionary study, which she relished more than did Maggie. Her pride in her daughter was boundless as she stopped to tell anyone willing to listen how the young girl had advanced her position through hard work and diligence. Maggie's promotion was accepted by all as just reward and part of her due, for she, feeling not one grain of guilt, had failed to confide in anyone the particulars surrounding her advancement, choosing instead to enjoy this long awaited admiration from her mother.

The learning process was painfully slow, and only the encouragement of both teacher and mother, along with limitless patience on the part of her employer, spurred her on. The ultimatum of two weeks grace had long since come and gone when, at last, much to Mr. Flynn's chagrin, she began to show signs of increasing competency, and a promise of future efficiency.

Bob Jennings, totally aware of her ineptitude, and Joe Flynn's increasing annoyment, chose the road of forebearance, knowing full well someone already skilled could greatly lighten his daily work load. He excused his tolerance by convincing himself she would eventually be an attribute to the company because of her unending will to learn, and denying his need to feel her presence or his continual listening for the soothing resonance of her voice. His father, an astute Philadelphia businessman, had purchased this mill and immediately ordained he would be responsible for it's prospering.

"I know it won't exactly be the style you're accustomed to, but consider it an adventure into the simple life, where people work hard making a living, and sometimes die while they're trying to make it." His father's pronouncement, relegating him to this never before heard of, and evidently God forsaken area had stunned him. The older man, always a fair and loving parent, had heretofore a tendency to over protect his only son. "You'll be met by an abundance of inexpensive labor which, of course, should ease the profit making burden, and you'll find those workers loyal and reliable, traits bred into them by the fear of unemployment."

It was obvious the old man, as usual, had made an in depth study, before committing to this latest purchase. "Your two greatest obstacles," he continued, "will be your vigilant persistence in quality work, this being of the utmost importance in today's ever increasing competition with the foreign markets." The older man lowered his eyes, "And then there is your own adaptation, which will play a major role if you are to succeed."

His adaptation to the squalor of the landscape with it's unsightly barren black hills and sooty dust laden cobblestone streets had been as sluggish as Maggie's apprenticeship. The belching breakers daily obliteration of the sun depressed him, and the unfamiliar shrill whistles shrieking without warning all hours of the day and night had unnerved him immeasurably. Up to this time Maggie had been his only deliverance from what he felt was becoming a stagnating apathy of existence. Only compliance to his father's wishes forced him to endure these intolerable conditions, and he was not about to sacrifice his one pleasure in all of Miners' Haven.

Working with Mr. Jennings quickly became the most important thing in Maggie's life. Their desks were positioned opposite each other in the small office, separated only by a glass partition, allowing her to watch his perfectly manicured fingers as they opened the mail, or drummed impatiently through some tedious phone call. At times she found herself entranced with his profile, as he turned to consult with the foreman, ceasing to stare only when the pressure of her eyes caused him to look in her direction. She also found herself continually reminded of Michael by some familiar movement or expression, although the two men were totally different in appearance, her employer being sandy haired with gray green eyes, where, in her imagination, she managed to find Michael's identical twinkle of kindness. Unlike her father he sported a grand moustache whose abundant threads of gray set it glistening beneath a fine slightly pointed nose. His rather stern mouth seldom, smiled, yet his every action appeared gentle, deliberately directed not to intimidate or cause concern.

Her days raced by, gripped in the frantic fervor of learning and ever present longing to please this man whose mannerisms increasingly reinforced the ever sweet memory of her father.

Each day at noon Bob left the building for lunch, while Maggie remained at her desk, munching whatever Jessica had hurriedly popped into her bag in the morning. Once again as the mill whistle sounded it's respite, Bob pushed his chair back, while Maggie automatically unraveled her sandwich. Nearing the door he hesitated, then turned asking, "Wouldn't you rather leave the office once in a while, just for a change of atmosphere?"

She felt herself blush because, in fact, although she really would have enjoyed leaving, the truth of the matter was she had no one to go with. The shop girls who had never been overly friendly totally shunned her since her promotion, speculating in whispers what sacrifice had to be made for someone obliviously unsuited for mill work to suddenly rise to office assistant. Snickering behind their hands they unanimously agreed she had to be dispensing favors, This assumption, however, did nothing to alter their resentment, and all remained coolly aloof, devoting entire lunch periods to lewd suppositions and ribald conversation, almost grateful for some diversion.

Bob, seeing Maggie's embarrassment, and sensing the reason for it, picked her coat from the brass clothes tree, holding it out to her as though the query had, in fact, been an invitation. Walking self consciously beside him through the idle shop, she wondered whatever had prompted her to accept his invitation. Nervously expectant, she automatically raised her head slightly as they passed the gaping workers gathered in the lunch room. She had vindicated their malicious gossip and they would resent her even more for having forced them to find something new on which to speculate. Moreover she obviously could contribute nothing engrossing, conversationally, to such a well educated and worldly gentleman as Mr. Jennings. Swiftly stealing a side glance at him, she was warmed instantly by the thought of Michael. At least she had followed his advice when she had not let this luncheon pass her by.

Once seated across from him in the tiny neighborhood restaurant her mind searched fruitlessly trying to conjure up some interesting topic of conversation. All eyes in the eatery seemed focused on her and her unlikely companion, as the inexperienced waitress banged their order down before them, apologizing excitedly. Her trembling fingers found it difficult to stop fidgeting while the sandwich she ordered lay untouched on her plate. Bob, pretending not to notice, addressed her kindly.

"You know you remind me of someone who was very dear to me when I was a young man, and perhaps is even dearer to me now, even if she doesn't have your beautiful blue eyes."

He studied his luncheon of beef stew as the color rose in her cheeks, causing her to squirm uncomfortably in her seat. "She too was very shy," he continued, "But managed to instill in me every ounce of self confidence

I have by her constant approval and unflagging support in every decision I have ever made. Even when some of these decisions proved to be more than unwise and sometimes even a disservice to others, she chose never to criticize or reproach me, merely pointing out the wisdom of more seriously considering the alternatives when other judgments became necessary." His kind eyes smiled, his lips parting in a grin beneath the glistening moustache.

Maggie, still flustered, began munching on her food, creating an excuse not to respond. Undaunted by her silence he went on.

"Unfortunately she lives quite a distance away now, but I miss her still, and all the wonderful talks and intimate secrets we shared. Having a close friend is a magnificent experience, Maggie. Someone to trust, someone who trusts you, another person to partake with you in the tasting of life." Again he waited vainly for her response.

Her tea slurped onto the saucer as she tried picking up the over full cup. Why was he telling her this anyway? What did she care for his old love affairs, or friend affairs, or whatever. Could he be deliberately trying to hamper her self control? God if only she had not come. Food seemed to stick in her throat like dried out oatmeal, and when it didn't she still could not think of one intelligent thing to say. How very dismal this encounter was becoming. Just retribution for trying to rise above ones proper place in the scheme of things, her mother would say. She, a coal miner's daughter should not expect to be appreciated by this main line Philadelphian.

The kindly voice came to her again. "Do you have any brothers or sisters, Maggie?"

"I have a brother," she answered gloomily, "some few years younger than I." The sparkling blue eyes flew to his face. "Were you talking about your sister?" she asked with obvious surprise.

"Yes," his answer was almost a whisper; his eyes held hers and she did not care to look away.

"And I remind you of her?" she asked disbelieving.

A suppressed smile played about the corners of his mouth, "Except that you talk more than she does." She felt herself relax as they both gave way to peals of laughter.

Dabbing at her eyes she mumbled through her napkin, "You're right

I'm just a fountain of babblings, aren't I? Oh well, at least you won't be able to complain about my boring chit chat."

He reached across the table, touching her hand lightly. "I find nothing boring about you, Maggie." He felt her fingers tense beneath his tangent contact. "Now wasn't this better than spending your lunch hour in the factory?" He continued, saving her the necessity to reply. "We'll have to do it more often if only to discover if you're as much like my Jeanette as I think you are." He gave her fingers a slight squeeze which she pretended not to notice.

"I'll try not to talk so much next time," she giggled. She felt happier than ever she could remember. He was so right! It was wonderful having a friend. Her brain bubbled with a multitude of thoughts she had long ago forgotten, for the need of sharing. Only with Papa had she acquired the sublime gift of two people's participation in a single idea, the exploring of each other's perception of that idea, and the thorough enjoyment of retrospection and reflection. So filled was she with the pleasurableness and gratification for these resurrected moments she would have willingly trusted this man with her very life. In the space of one hour she had become resolute, boldly confident, and totally undaunted. After all there were surely many women he could have lunched with, but he had chosen her.

Now oblivious to the other patrons, they left the restaurant holding hands. It seemed the natural thing to do.

Chapter Three

Jessica stood in the stifling heat of the once grand parlour straining to see through the curtains without detection. Bending lower she found a convenient hole in the disintegrating lace, providing a clear view of the abhorrent scene before her.

Maggie and Bob Jennings sat comfortably close together on the front seat of his new, beautifully shimmering black Buick. Jessica sucked in her breath as Bob carelessly flung his arm around Maggie's shoulder, pulling her towards him. The windshield, refracting the rays of the scorching August sun, momentarily concealed them, but intuition told her they had kissed. Was she to be subjected to a re-enactment of her own foolish youth? The possibility was too staggering to contemplate. An irritating trickle of sweat slithered uncomfortably between her ample breasts, igniting a flame of perfidious thought. Vowing not to be duped by lies and protestations of innocence, she watched her daughter bounce gaily out of the car and head toward the rusted garden gate. Turning gracefully, the young girl waved, touching fingertips to her lips in final show of affection before disappearing into the garden.

Breathless, Jessica slammed the sliding parlor doors together, hurrying to the kitchen in time to meet her daughter as she entered. Puffing heavily her questions became punctuated with short gasps for air. "How dare you disgrace me with your trashy public display of sentiment? I'll bet half the neighborhood watched your carryings on and right in front of your own home in broad daylight. Have you no shame or morals left at all?"

Maggie, still immersed in her own world of euphoria, glided toward the ice box, unmindful of the oppressive heat still discharging through the banked fires of the coal stove. Expertly stabbing the corner of the freshly delivered block of ice, then popping the few loosened chips into her mouth, she faced her mother nonchalantly shaking her head.

"Mama, mama, why would I feel shame about Bob for having kissed me? We're both adult responsible people, and one peck on the cheek does not constitute an immoral act, even in Miners' Haven."

"Even in Miners' Haven," mimicked Jessica. "I guess you're too good for it now that a big city boy's taking to romancing you. But, of course, he's hardly a boy by any standard, is he? "I'd venture he's a lot closer to my age than he is to yours, young lady. With a shrewd cleverness your naivety denies you privy to, he has taken advantage of you, cheapening you in the eyes of your friends and family."

Maggie, accustomed to her mother's rantings, chose to retire from the kitchen until Jessica regained her calm. Perceiving her intent, the older woman raised her voice in protest.

"Just because I was a damned fool doesn't mean I'll allow you to be one."

Maggie, turning from the doorway, discerned her mother's need for assurance, and took both Jessica's hands in hers. "Mama, you were no fool and you know it. Papa just told me in my last birthday letter how he had honored you above all women, how very much you had loved each other when you were young, and how that love was strengthened by reciprocal need and being needed."

Jessica smiled sadly at the thought of her once handsome young hero. God, how could just the notion of him still inflict so much pain and longing? Mulling over his words she pulled her hands away with a vehement gesture, answering angrily, "Your father always was a glib tongued scoundrel, and what he didn't fancy, he downright lied about, so I wouldn't be putting so much store in the scribblings of a dying man."

Maggie's slight fingers combed through her perfect black tresses, "Are you saying, Mama, that all those letters Papa left for me are wishful ramblings or just presumptions on his part because he wanted it to be so?" Nervously twirling one ebony curl about her index finger, she watched Jessica press her apron against her dripping brow.

"Some things are better left unresolved, particularly the exploiting of a dead man's thoughts." Sighing with exasperation, she continued, "I'm merely trying to suggest that life is by far the greatest teacher of all, and should not be wasted pouring over some pointless delusion, or what you consider exalted opinions that no longer have any meaning. I would like to add that writings considered profound are best left to scholars, people of education, whose thoughts might merit consideration." Looking at Maggie pointedly, she hoped the girl had grasped her meaning.

She certainly has taken her word a day dictionary study seriously thought Maggie, somewhat amused. "I know, Mama, how you think my writing is a waste of time, but just today a small check arrived at my office for that piece I wrote about American Sweat Shops. The one you so disapproved of, remember? It certainly isn't going to make us rich, but to use one of your own phrases; every journey begins with the first step." She was enjoying her small victory.

"At the office you say," screeched Jessica, "why didn't it come to the house like the rest of them?" Suddenly sick and shaken by her unwelcome admission, she moved rapidly to the stove, rustling the dormant coals to life, refusing to look at her daughter, Maggie sat motionless, overcome by the unexpected portent of this revelation. Appalled by her mother's disclosure she felt the kitchen's heat swirl about her, dragging her into an inferno of disbelief.

"When were there others, Mama?" she asked calmly, unable to accept this treachery.

Jessica, perspiring profusely now, continued poking about the fire with unnecessary vengeance. "There were just two, the amounts too insignificant to mention." She spoke in an offhand manner, trying to minimize their importance. "I didn't tell you because I didn't want your flitty tendencies encouraged." She spoke more to the stove than to Maggie. "You know the old adage, 'Fool me once shame on you, fool me twice, shame on me.' I don't think Joe Flynn or Bob Jennings would put up with your didos again, regardless of your obviously close relationship." Startled by her own confused and continued stupidity she clamped a quivering hand over colorless lips, turning to face her daughter with fear and trepidation. What in God's name had instigated her babbling on, with one indiscretion leading to yet another?

Unable to contain her incredulity, Maggie had risen stiffly, her gray face reflecting the emptiness within her. "Are you saying that all this time, while you pretended to be so proud and appreciative, you actually knew every detestable detail of how I came to be promoted?" Her face seemed to shrink with grief.

"Of course I didn't, Maggie, I swear I only found out after Molly's daughter Mary started at the factory a few months ago, and what did it matter by then, you had already more than proved yourself worthy of the job." The girl's open suffering and pathetically distressed features plagued her. Reaching out she patted Maggie's slender arm, smiling warmly, "Oh come on, you know the way young girls gossip, especially when they're filled with envy, probably wish-they were in your shoes. Even cousin Molly was delighted by every spiteful word she could repeat to me."

Maggie drew away outraged, "And you, like all the rest, I'm sure, viewed the situation with your usual moralistic glint, rather than seeing the truth by crediting me or my accomplishments, you assumed you'd heard the truth and were ready to brow beat me over an innocent kiss because of it." Her devastation appeared complete as she plopped back into her chair despondently.

Averting her head, Jessica was silent a moment. She could not deny her own suspicions, nor trust her wayward, wagging tongue to give voice to any further conjecture. Perhaps a bit of wielding was called for here, she thought. A tactful shifting of the onus to another, and younger pair of shoulders.

"I don't think you're being quite fair, Maggie," she began. "I know very well how hard you've worked and how deserving you are."

"Deserving!" the word was almost a shout. "If I'm so damned deserving why would you ever have considered cheating me out of my well deserved recognition, to say nothing of my well deserved money you had no qualms about pocketing for yourself." The blazing blue eyes challenged Jessica.

"Am I to blame because you persist in your life of illusion, where you constantly set unrealistic goals for yourself, never considering their results or how your family could end up deprived because of your unquenchable need for personal fulfillment? You make it necessary for me, my dear, to try and protect you from the concealed evils life holds out, taunting and testing the unsuspecting innocents, such as yourself." Her tone was virtuous. "Pride is one of those evils Maggie, and you have been blessed with an overabundance, always placing yourself above others, acting superior, and now believing yourself to have literary talent because of the acceptance of a few small works." She glared at her daughter with stern condemnation, wringing her hands in frustration. "You have no idea how dark the human soul can be, the depth of cruelty it can reach, the meaness---"

"Don't forget greed, Mama. It surely must be evil. And what about stealing, Mama?"

The two women scowled at each other, eyes distended with grudging bitterness. Both hearts aching from pains so cruelly inflicted by one to the other. Jessica, blinded by unshed tears, turned slowly back to the stove, barely hearing Maggie's almost reluctant admonition, "It just wasn't right for you to keep them from me, Mama, you know it wasn't right."

As night fell both mother and daughter lay alone in their solitary beds, reliving the unpleasantness of the afternoon, each in her own way. Maggie, suffering a strange type of bereavement, knew she had lost her fragile, but amiable relationship with Jessica. The trust and intrinsic reliance, so long sought for, and so well nurtured had been destroyed by a single blast of deception. Her melancholy magnified itself through the knowledge she did not have the stamina or dedication required to resurrect it, because in fact, she no longer cared. Her only solace lay in that fact.

Jessica lay wide eyed in her totally darkened room, mentally probing the reasons her daughter had been able to force her, once again, into apologetic feelings of fault, when her only sin had been to regress into protectiveness. Squeezing her eyes tightly together she tried to erase any retrospective thought or remembrance that would vilify their relationship. Slowly relaxing, her eyes opened gradually, then at last pierced the murkiness only to see that she had lost yet another battle.

Chapter Four

Miners' Haven lay nestled among the blackened mountains and coal spewn culm banks of Central Pennsylvania, totally unperturbed, an enigma in the passage of time. It's city limits had remained virtually unchanged since the inception of it's colliery, void of expansion or improvement, suspended in a vivication of it's own. The well to do or their heirs still inhabited the western fringe of the city where a smattering of pretentious homes sat elegantly on the banks of the manmade lake overlooking the public park.

The townspeople, a contented lot, usually resided in the same home for their entire lifetime, changing little, save the plumbing when funds allowed. They had learned to expect little from life and satisfied themselves with the basic pleasures of home and family; able to live complacently with parents, grandparents, or whomever presented an existing need.

The arrival of the Great Depression was probably felt less in the coal regions than anywhere else in the country. Miners, already accustomed to deprivation, and most certainly not prone to stock market dabbling, found themselves by 1931 making ten per cent more than they had earned in 1920, despite the fact that the cost of living in the anthracite area had declined by over twenty eight per cent. This unrealistic insistence by the union of an abnormally high wage scale only served to eventually limit and finally obliterate the opportunity to work. Most miners, all under educated men, were staunchly loyal to the United Mine Workers, remaining blinded by bounty as they remained blinded by bigotry. The invisible cleaver of intolerance had not lost it's hone, glistening sharply through the years, while it continued to divide Papist from Protestant with the identical and absolute severance of segregation.

The small borough endured socially and geographically as two separate entities. True congeniality exited only deep beneath the earth's surface, where danger and death, showing no favoritism, forced a banding together that became superfluous and alien in the light of day. Few men questioned the hypocrisy of these conditions, and none ventured to change them.

The advent of World War II briefly strengthened the region's economic and national position. So great a demand for coal had not been required from the operators for more than fifteen years, but now, steel companies, pushing to their maximum productive capacity, commanded an ever increasing amount of coal necessary for the twenty four hour a day, continuous functioning of forge and blast furnace. Indirectly, mining became essential to the production of the weapons of war, and an integral part of the national defense. Mine workers found themselves being offered deferment from induction into the armed services based upon the government's decision that remaining on their jobs was now considered vital to the war effort. Only those who had chosen not to follow their father's perilous footsteps into the mines, now marched, without benefit of election, into the field of battle.

Everyone, drinking deeply from the well of patriotism, and having been assured by their sterling leader, Franklin Roosevelt, that there was nothing to fear but fear itself, endeavored to become involved, if only in the most limited manner, to aid in the preservation of freedom and the protection of their country. The women had graduated from knittin' for Britain to candy and cookie baking for G.I. Joe. The older men, forming air raid warden groups, good naturedly admonished each other with the fact that should the enemy fly over this terrain; one look down would assure them a bomb had already landed.

Even the mill joined the war effort, having been acquisitioned by the Army to produce nothing but regulation uniform khaki shirts. Prosperity was no longer something to be wished for, it had arrived. Maggie's earnings were now well over $40.00 a week, an unimaginable sum a few short years ago. A sum of such magnitude, that Jessica had opted to remain at home, devoting herself full time to the prodigious task of rearing her son.

Michael, at eight, was a child to be reckoned with, his brilliant red hair calling attention to a broad flat face, crusted, regardless of season, to large dark brown freckles. Born void of childish innocence, his illusion less cat green eyes brimmed with secret inner knowledge, brilliantly assessing his world, divining with complete accuracy every situation that may later prove to be advantageous.

The family had just finished Sunday breakfast when Jessica began taking Michael to task concerning his recent, less than satisfactory report card. Not unlike most parents, Jessica habitually extolled Maggie's academic performances, drawing unsuitable lines of comparison, which served only to further enhance an already negative attitude toward schooling. Wise enough not to be combatant and risk spending a beautiful Sunday afternoon in his room, the boy faced her with a mechanical smile and a placatory promise to try and do better. Jessica, relieved at having successfully performed her duty to chastise without the usual doleful conflict and contention, patted his arm affectionately as she left the table to freshen her coffee. Michael promptly bent forward, and with contorted features, repeatedly thumbed his nose in her direction, his vitriolic eyes daring Maggie to expose him. Shocked by this unbecoming display and even more fearful of Jessica's catching sight of it, Maggie instinctively grappled with the obscene arm, causing the sugar bowl and it's contents to roll across the kitchen table, spewing it's sparkling mounds in all directions.

Michael instantly leaped out of his chair and away from the soiled table. "You sure are clumsy for a girl." He said with distaste, then walking deliberately to Jessica, he fondly embraced her thighs, as small children habitually do. Then looking up with adoration, he smiled sweetly. "If only you could teach her to be as graceful as you Mama."

Jessica, flushing with pleasure, patted the fiery head pressing into her skirt, then bent to bestow a kiss of appreciation on his freckled cheek. "You may run along with your friends now, sweet-heart, but just remember dinner will be at five, and then we must have study time, and Mama will help you, alright?" Answering by throwing his robust arms about his mother's neck, he winked mischievously at his sister, then skipped out of the house midst a flurry of hand waving and cheery good byes.

Watching the small bouncy figure disappear through the kitchen screen door, Maggie began tentatively, "Mama, I think we should have a little talk about Michael."

"And I think you should begin cleaning up that mess you've made rather than to begin again with your tiresome berating of your brother."

"Mama, I don't mean to berate him. I'm honestly worried about him, and what's going to happen to him if you don't soon begin to discipline him in some manner or somehow control his increasing insolence and lack of respect for authority."

Jessica banged and rattled the breakfast dishes against the porcelain sink as a warning that her patience with this repetitious conversation had already reached it's limits.

Maggie, undaunted by the excessive clatter, slowly raked the errant sugar into one large gleaming mound as she persisted. "I don't think you realize, Mama, that Michael has been spoiled to death by your catering to him, giving him things his friends with fathers don't even have, superfluous things that we can ill afford, and he shows his gratitude by being hateful and mean to you, laughing behind your back every time he gets his own way. Mama, you're making a monster out of him by bending to his every whim and forcing me to do the same just to escape your tirades." Her cheek muscles flexed rapidly, and her voice, so tightened with anxiety, increased in volume with every accusation. Vaguely she felt a moustache of perspiration sprout upon her upper lip, yet she could not staunch the rampant issue of her words. "He has absolutely no respect for either of us, and even less for his teachers or anyone else who tries to help him."

Jessica whirled about to face her. "And I suppose you're talking to me in this tone is being a sweet and dutiful daughter," she sniffed. "You seem to forget your brother's delicate condition, and refuse to admit that even from infancy his tantrums have all stemmed from ill health. He's always been a frail, sickly child. Why is it so hard for you to see that and try to have a little compassion for him?"

"Frail as a freight train," snapped Maggie. Where is the sickly one now? I'll tell you where, out running the neighborhood with his friends getting into God only knows what kind of mischief, and by the time he gets home he'll plop down, eat a man sized dinner and spend the evening lounging in his room, pretending to study, while he plots out his next bout with trouble. You're blind to him, MAMA."

Jessica's lip curled, "Well I'm not blind to your running around with a mill owner twice your age. I can see right through both of you, and particularly him, always flaunting his fancy manners wearing those high hat clothes like he was some kind of matinee idol. I'm sure with all those impressive trappings he's able to charm the pants off almost anyone," she smiled wickedly. "Let me warn you about being led down the primrose path, my dear, a path I trod once myself and know what I'm talking about. Just don't let him try being convincing by suggesting he'd ever consider marrying the likes of you." She eyed Maggie up and down with knowing disgust. The young woman sighed heavily, past experience dictated her mother would not be swayed from what she had resolved as truth, her stubborn obdurate nature disallowing other opinions to permeate her rigidly determined mind. It would mean she may be wrong, an unacceptable premise.

Jessica had masterfully dismissed the insufferable topic of Michael's behavior, by introducing a subject her daughter was ever ready to discuss in the hope of finally securing her mother's approval of the man she loved. Maggie, recognizing Jessica's favorite ploy, allowed herself to be put on the defensive, a strategy she felt best suited to the matter at hand.

"He's the mill owners son, Mama, as you well know, and he's ten years older than I, which if you care to think about it is not that much different than you and Papa. She scanned Jessica's face for some glimpse of understanding, but her mother, turning abruptly, began banking the fires in the coal stove. "I'm going to need a bucket of coal from the cellar, Maggie. I can't afford to let this fire go out, you know how much trouble it is getting it going again with all the wood, paper and smoke."

Not stirring from her chair, Maggie declined to fall victim to this next ploy, dismissal of both subjects. "In six months Bob is returning to Philadelphia, the mill is running smoothly and doesn't demand his full attention anymore. As a matter of fact, his father has a new project for him to take over that sounds really exciting."

Without turning around Jessica held out the empty coal bucket impatiently, summoning Maggie into action by the jiggling of the rusting handle.

"He has asked me to return with him as his wife, and I have accepted," her voice softened in an effort to lessen the blow.

The stoker fell from Jessica's hand, rolling noisily across the kitchen floor. "I knew it! I knew he could bamboozle you into anything, you stupid, stupid girl! Do you think for a moment he really means this? My dear God, think! If he does mean it why hasn't he ever come to me?" her eyes were incredulous. "That-- that great man of yours, with all of his high flatuin manners, and yet not gentleman enough to come and ask my permission. You're not twenty one, you know," her voice rose, "you can't do anything without my permission, and you'll never get it through deceit, sneaking around behind my back like two thieves, never once hinting to me what was being planned." Drawing a hand over her face, she bent to retrieve the stoker, then banging it sharply against the grate she screamed, "I won't put up with this treachery from either one of you." Striding to the table she forced a question between clenched teeth, "What is to happen to your brother now? How much you must hate him to be so callous, so unconcerned for his future, so willing to forsake us both over some manipulating promise made by some glib tongued fancy man you barely know."

Maggie, shrinking back into her chair, watched with relief as her mother lay down the stoker and began pacing wildly about the room mumbling, "I just cannot believe all this, it just cannot be true," her shaking head visibly denying the loathsome predicament just given voice to by her daughter.

"Mama, please, listen for one minute," pleaded Maggie as she rushed to her mother's side. "Bob is not the monster you think he is, Mama, quite the opposite as you will see once you get to know him. Neither, he nor I planned anything without first considering you and Michael. I love you both and never would I abandon you or do anything hurtful to either one of you, nor would Bob allow me to." Ignoring Jessica's suspicious glance, she continued, "We have thought about everything, Mama, and the truth is you have no need for this big house, which has gradually fallen into ruin around us with no man or the funds to keep it up. You could sell it, Mama, and take a nice apartment with---"

The voice was now a shriek, "You would have me give up our home, the home in which we were all born! You would have some stranger tending Isaac Hobbs garden, sitting in his grand parlor, or rocking on the front porch he loved so well?" Her eyes widened with the impact of her own words. Once again she strode convulsively around the kitchen, running agitated fingers through her tangled unruly locks. "Clearly this man has influenced your reason for his own motives. It is almost impossible to believe that someone with your academic brilliance does not have the wit to see through this guise of his, to not recognize deception----"

"Mama," Maggie's voice was firm, "Nothing is going to be resolved if you are going to insist upon being unreasonable. This house which I admit was once a treasure has unfortunately become a heavy burden, weighing you down with unnecessary liability, liability that can readily be turned into assets by the proper investing of the sale money, Mama, between the interest on your new found money, your widow's pension and a monthly allowance Bob is willing to contribute to you and Michael, you'll be just fine, maybe even better off than now." She smiled reassuringly. "We have six months to arrange all this for you, Mama, and then Bob and I are getting married with or without your blessing. You can't stop it, Mama."

Jessica stopped in the center of the room, her eyes narrowed as she stared at her daughter, resenting the determined voice and arbitrary features. This was not going to be one of their usual contests it would seem. The young girl was resolute and it would take all of her sagaciousness to fathom and fritter away at all her elections until methodically and meticulosity she made the optimal choice. No percentage saying nay to an offer not fully heard, she told herself, but city men were notoriously slick, quick to promise and slow to deliver. Well she could give him a test or two; she'd yet to meet the man who could outwit her, city slicker or no.

Seating herself humbly beside her daughter, she spoke apologetically, "You're right, Maggie, I'm just a selfish old woman trying to hold onto the past and expecting the whole world to stand still along with me. What are worn out memories of the dead compared to the adventure and challenge of living?" She sought Maggie's hand, "You deserve your chance same as I deserved mine, and you're right, my girl, I can't stop you, and shouldn't want to," then straightening with pride, she continued, "But, of course accepting all this generosity from a stranger is out of the question, no matter how well intentioned it seems, and I have no doubt it is."

Her lips forced themselves into a tight smile, "I think perhaps it would be to everyone's advantage if you invited him over to Sunday night supper. We need the chance to get better acquainted, to finally talk and see how we enjoy each other's company. If he's even half the man you seem to think he is, there'll be no problem."

"Oh, Mama, thank you," said Maggie joyfully. "I know you won't be disappointed, you'll just love him, and, of course, he you, because you're anything but an old lady, Mama, and I won't have you thinking that way about yourself, at least not until I've made you a Grandma."

Jessica quailed as her oblivious daughter jumped from her chair, bending to press her mouth into the matted auburn tresses. "Thank you, Mama, thank you." Then almost dancing out of the kitchen, she hummed happily to herself.

The tune offended Jessica's ears as she remained motionless with her bitter thoughts. "A perpetual optimist, just like her dear dead Papa," but she could handle her, just as she had handled him. Looking up, she addressed the ceiling, "Will this bane of caring for the irresponsible never be lifted from me?" She could not suppress a cynical smile.

The dining table was laden with Isaac's precious china, which had lain dormant in the cupboards garnering nothing but dust since the day of his funeral. The delicate pieces, still glistening, despite the gloom of a shade drawn room, lay elegantly adorning a decaying lace tablecloth, whose antiquity was preserved only by the benignity of the flickering candle light. Both mother and daughter shared a sense of pride unperceived by their guest as he joined them at the table.

As the savory dinner drew to an end, Bob Jennings tilted his wine glass toward Jessica, smiling, "My compliments, Mrs. McClellan, your meal was a true delight. I'd almost forgotten how delicious home cooking is, having accustomed myself to restaurant fare the past year or two."

Jessica, simpering sweetly, nodded in agreement. "Yes it was quite tasty, but I cannot accept all the credit. Maggie is an able and accomplished cook and was a great asset to me," adding pointedly, "As she always is."

"I don't like any of it," pouted Michael, toying with the food on his plate. "I want to be excused."

"Excused, indeed," answered Jessica, I was hoping you would be kind enough to help your sister clear the table so Mr. Jennings and I can have a little chat."

Michael banged down his fork, splattering it's contents over the fine lace cloth. Clearing the table is woman's work, I won't do it and you can't make me." His lower jaw jutted forward with stubbornness familiar to both women.

Embarrassed and anxious for Michael's disappearance, Maggie hastily began gathering the silverware. "I don't mind, Mama, you and Bob go right ahead and I'll join you shortly." Awkwardness prevented her glancing at their guest.

Grateful at his deliverance from such a distasteful task, Michael shoved his chair back and strode from the room in jubilant silence, pausing only to smile smugly as he passed his relieved sister.

Wearing her most appreciative smile, Jessica beamed at her daughter, "What a sweet lass," then addressing Michael's retreating back she announced, "And you, my little man, may spend the remainder of this evening alone in your room." The boy retaliated with a derisive sound that prompted all to feign deafness.

"Would you care to take a pipe in the parlor, Mr. Jennings?" Jessica asked graciously, trying to conquer her annoyance with Michael.

"Only if it's not an imposition, ma'am."

Motioning him to follow her she pictured an unsmiling Isaac, still clenching his unlit pipe in disapproval. "Both my husband and father looked forward to their after dinner pipe, I'm quite accustomed, Mr. Jennings."

The parlor seemed to have regained some of it's former elegance. All the sofa's mohair cushions had been fluffed and turned over, successfully hiding some of the more prominent signs of wear, while snow white doilies clung securely to the balding arms and backs of the overstuffed furnishings. Small bouquets of fresh garden flowers had been placed strategically, diverting one's attention away from the faded and fraying carpeting. Maintaining this aesthetic illusion prevented Jessica from turning up the lamp as she produced an ashtray from the end table drawer. Seating herself comfortably beside Bob on the sofa she could not resist eyeing the expensive Panama suit, the glistening patent shoes and pure silk tie. The smoke curled about the young man's precisely trimmed moustache and slightly arched brows framing his somewhat dreamy gray eyes. Quite a handsome figure she admitted to herself, easily understanding her daughter's infatuation.

"Maggie tells me you will be leaving our area shortly after the holidays, Mr. Jennings."

Removing the pipe stem from his mouth he gazed into it's bowl studiously. "I haven't had the opportunity to discuss this with Maggie, but my plans have been changed somewhat." Looking directly at Jessica, he continued, "My father has been in ill health these past months and I must return home sooner than was planned." His brows knotted together as he recalled his father's disintegrating condition. Each visit home had found the older man's stamina and ability to concentrate lessened by the onslaught of a debilitating and untreatable heart ailment. The effort needed to merely move about was increasingly punctuated by shortness of breath and frightening dizzy, spells, forcing him to take to his bed and look to his son for the completion of the deals he wanted set into motion.

"This war won't last much longer," he had confided to Bob, "And we must be ready to shift from the frantic race of war time production to the ambling pace of peace time production without stripping our gears." Smiling weakly he added, "It might take one hell of a lot of doing to get it right, but I have a couple of ideas." He tugged at the stubble of growth on his sallow cheek, deciding which conception might be most lucrative. "You know all the boys will be coming home to find jobs, get married and start families of their own." He mused, "Poor bastards, coming home to no jobs, no money and above all no place to live. Mark my words, Bob, the end of this war will see an unparalleled housing shortage, which in itself will escalate the cost of renting to an unbelievable all time high. The man wise enough to invest in low priced real estate now will soon be counting his profits, but never his vacancies because potential tenants will be lined up at his doorstep begging for accommodations. The landlord will be able to pick and choose only those he considers desirable and then subjugate them to law loaded leases beneficial only to himself. Sounds inordinately unfair after all they've given for their country, a sad testimony to one of the failings of a democracy. But so it will be, lasting years until the system gradually embraces this suddenly created flood of humanity." His filmy eyes seemed to clear somewhat as he questioned his son. I'm assuming you have established no ties that would make you hesitant about leaving Miners' Haven, so I want you to market the mill and devote yourself to the acquisition of real estate in and around Philadelphia. What do you say Bob, are you ready to become rich?"

Unable to deny his father's wishes and unwilling to introduce the subject of Maggie, he heartily endorsed his father's idea, agreeing to set things into motion upon his return to Miners' Haven. Every good business man knows that timing is the vital ingredient to success. This, he felt was definitely not the time to try focusing the old man's attention on his own personal life. People fall in love every day, empires originate only spasmodically. His thoughts returned to Jessica, and the need for her friendship.

"The factory here is up to expected production and will need only sporadic supervision. Your old friend Mr. Flynn is a very able foreman." Once again studying his pipe he decided for the second time in as many weeks not to divulge his plans. The sale of the mill and the permanency of his leaving could be brought out at a more opportune time. "As I've said Maggie is not fully aware of my decision so I welcomed this occasion to talk with you both."

So here it is already, she thought. A change of plans indeed! It was plain to see whatever the plan was or now is, it had never included her, just as she had suspected. This suave young devil was a danger to her. His manipulation of Maggie had been quite successful, but then stupid, innocent Maggie was hardly a challenge to anyone. Let me show you, Mr. Jennings, that your darling's mother is quite different, fashioned out of steel and grit, unmold able as granite with enough devious tricks and unscrupulous pride to best any unprincipled mischief you're about.

Jessica leaned toward him in a secretive manner, her guileless eyes wide with concern. "Before we pursue this further, Mr. Jennings, I must ask if Maggie has ever confided in you concerning her previous affair of the heart?"

Bob's head swung in her direction, "Affair of the heart?" he queried.

"Well I can see it's quite obvious she has not." She patted his arm with motherly affection, secretly elated by his dismayed features. "I must first have your promise you will never betray my indiscretion but a mother must do what she feels is best for her child, regardless of the pain it inflicts upon herself." Her eyes were now down cast, waiting.

Reluctantly placing his hand on her arm, he tried to assure her. "Of course you have my word, Mrs. McClellan." His senses quickened as he experienced a premonition of evil, watching closely as Jessica leaned back against the sofa cushions sighing, "Very well then, I shall put my complete trust in you." She paused theatrically, continuing only after she was certain she had created the exact amount of suspense. "It was all some time ago.

He was a miner, an unusually attractive young fellow." An unwanted note of nostalgia crept into her voice. "And both were totally devoted, one to the other. I'm sure you have realized by now what a sensitive child Maggie is, filled with romantic dreams and imaginings, retaining only deceptive memories while she dodges truth and reality. I just don't want her delving into some new relationship which may prove detrimental to her mental health. She is not a strong person, Mr. Jennings, given to moods of depression and sometimes even tirades against her own mother. She must constantly be protected and guided by those who best understand her. I'm sure it's not too difficult for you to see how important it is for her not to try replacing one affection with another merely to satisfy her fancies, or worse, to settle for something less than is necessary for her happiness. You're a very busy man I'm sure, and Maggie's well being demands much attention and abundant mettle."

Jessica rose, walking leisurely to the window. "Perhaps your leaving before schedule is opportune, Mr. Jennings. A short separation of a few months might prove to be the perfect answer. It will give the situation time to settle into its correct perspective. If Maggie is truly ready to transfer her affections, a little more time can only enhance that prospect. As a matter of fact--"

"Where is this fellow now?" he interrupted, a million questions battering against his brain.

Still facing the window, her voice was barely audible.

"He's dead."

"Dead! How terrible for her," gasped Bob with disbelief.

Jessica whirled around, rage in her voice, "How terrible for her," she echoed, "Did you not hear me, Mr. Jennings? He is the one who is dead!" Her eyes bulged from their sockets with uncontrolled resentment.

The young man's shocked expression forced her to regain her composure. "I must apologize. The entire episode has unnerved all of us. Even poor innocent Michael has been affected. His bad manners, I'm sure are only his childish way of attracting attention. I'm afraid I've neglected the lad by devoting too much of myself to Maggie and her problems. I couldn't bear going through another with her at this moment."

Bob, resting both elbows on his knees, stared into the carpeting. "This is all very difficult to understand, particularly since she has never once spoken of it. It's out of the question for me to leave without an explanation. She's expecting to go with me, we've made some wonderful plans. Plans that include all of us," he added.

Jessica was barely able to restrain a snicker as she took a few steps toward him. "My understanding was that she's not expecting to go with you for another six months. I do believe you're becoming overly concerned in regard to timing, or is there some other urgency about you're getting married that I'm not aware of?" Before he could utter a denial, she continued, her teeth almost clenched together.

"You gave me your word you would not repeat this conversation. Are you to be trusted or not, Mr. Jennings?"

"You can trust me, Mrs. McClellan," he felt his temper rising, "But all of this takes some sorting out and a decision arrived at on some reasonable course of action, not one dictated by you or anyone else." Jessica's sudden intake of breath did not deter him. "I must also say, Mrs. McClellan, that I feel, regardless of your assessment of the situation, whatever unfortunate tragedy transpired has long since been over for Maggie. Sensitive she is, but maudlin she is not. Your daughter is full of life and eager to live it, to live it with me." He paused significantly, "If it were still important to her, believe me she would have told me. I know her very well."

What the devil is he implying she wondered as she threw her hands over her face and began sobbing softly. "Please forgive the meddlings of a worried mother. If only it were true that you really knew her, but how can I, her own mother tell you things she herself should have said. NO I cannot, forgive me, Mr. Jennings, I cannot." She raised her head, the red rimmed eyes asking forgiveness, then once again her face fell into her hands. "I know now I should never have interfered, but surely you can sympathize with a mother's good intentions."

Spreading her fingers slightly, she watched as he placed his burnt out pipe in the ashtray, preparing to comfort her.

"My dear Mrs. McClellan, you must feel no remorse over this incident.

Everything will work itself into a happy conclusion I'm sure." His back was unnaturally stiff as he walked toward her, warily laying his hand on one trembling shoulder. "As for my repeating this conversation, please rest assured I will not as I have already dismissed it from my mind."

Liar, she thought as she raised her head, smiling sadly, "You're a very considerate man, Mr. Jennings," rancor raced through her every vessel, "And perhaps in some small way I can repay your kindness to me. Please feel free to leave without detailed explanation to Maggie. I will have a long talk with her regarding your father's health and, of course, your responsibility to him. I will tell her only what is necessary for her happiness, and then, when a short time has elapsed the both of you can, shall we say, reconcile, with a better understanding."

Her insistence was becoming irritating. "I'm sure that is not the answer. I feel no need for any reconciliation at a later date. Maggie's problems are mine, and we will work them out together, if and when there are any. I cannot believe you would expect me to leave her without a word. That is what you're asking me to do, isn't it?" His suspicions lay unmasked by the tone of his voice.

"Of course not, my dear Mr. Jennings. I merely suggest you put your confidence in me to make certain she understands fully, and doesn't feel abandoned or insecure by yet another unexpected departure. God heavens, are we not concerned about the same person?"

He determined to end this futile conversation and do what he thought best, without dishonoring his promise to Jessica not to echo her accounting of Maggie's past. He smiled feigning relief.

"Of course, you're right, Ms McClellan. I must admit that I will be needing a bit of time to put my business affairs in order, but I want you to know I am not a believer in the old cliché that everything happens for the best. I try making very sure everything happens the way I want it to, and I want this thing to happen for Maggie and me. I am prepared to totally devote myself to seeing to it that it does."

They stood glaring at each other as Maggie's flushed face peeped through the sliding doors.

"May I come in?" Her love filled eyes rested on Bob.

Jessica, rushing to her answered, "Of course, my dear, come in. Just look at my poor girl, all overheated from that dreadful kitchen." Pressing a hanky to her daughter's soggy brow, she inquired, "Have you heard, Mr. Jennings, some people are actually putting gas stoves in their kitchens? I for one think it's disgraceful. Heaven knows there's little enough work for the men now without their own kind turning against them. First thing you know they'll be thinking about converting their heaters."

"I'm sure it's only a matter of time, Madame. It's what we call progress." He wanted quit of this woman and her insipid conversation. Walking to Maggie, he gently pushed the damp hairs from her forehead. "And I must admit I for one approve of whatever makes a woman's life easier." His lips gently brushed her overly pink cheek.

"How gallant, Mr. Jennings," purred Jessica. "It amazes me you can bear to watch the poor souls treading their lives away behind your factory machinery, but then, of course, that's your living, isn't it?"

Insuring herself against his reply, she continued, "Dear me, just look at the hour. I must look in on Michael, and Maggie, remember tomorrow is a working day and you need your rest." She waited expectantly for Maggie to join her.

Bob took Maggie's hand, savoring the look in those resplendent blue eyes. "As always I hate leaving you, but your mother is right, I have overstayed my welcome."

Maggie's protest was smothered by his gentle fingertips.

"It's quite alright, dear Maggie, it's been an exhausting day for all of us. As you know I must return home tomorrow morning but I should be back by Wednesday evening. I would like to drop by about seven." Glancing at Jessica, he added, "With your permission, ma'am. We have much to discuss, Maggie," he added turning to the flustered girl.

"I'll be looking forward to it, Bob," she whispered with disappointment. Good night." Why is he so tense and formal, she wondered as she watched him turn to Jessica, bowing slightly.

"Again my thanks, Mrs. McClellan, for a most pleasurable evening." Had she imagined the animosity in his tone?

"Rest assured the pleasure was equally mine, Mr. Jennings."

No, not imagined, it filled the entire room.

As the young man walked slowly down the front porch steps, Jessica, feeling certain her voice would carry through the open windows, exclaimed sarcastically, "My, my, my, what a perfect gentleman."

"What in the world happened this evening?" asked Maggie following her mother up the stairway.

"Nothing, absolutely nothing."

"But something must have happened," persisted Maggie. "Why did he leave so quickly, and why were you both so--so overly polite?"

Jessica turned on the landing looking down the few steps between them. "When I said nothing happened I was mistaken. Actually it was less than nothing, if you must know. Never once did your hero choose to mention anything concerning Michael or me. Never a word about apartments, house selling or anything else even vaguely resembling what you suggested was going to be the subject of the evening."

Walking to the bedroom she called over her shoulder, "I think your young man is playing games with you, little girl, and as for his leaving early, I'm sure it was because he knew I was beginning to see through his charming charade."

Leaning against the door jam she waited until Maggie had shut and bolted the door at the top of the stairs. "Before making any more promises to me, I suggest you concentrate on checking out the promises he's already broken to you." Catching sight of Maggie's tear filled, eyes, her voice softened. "You're a wonderful young lady, Maggie, with every chance of having a wonderful life. To some day have your efforts recognized and becoming the first class writer you've always dreamed of being."

Maggie's unshed tears held her throat hostage with a grasp of grief, rendering her incapable of response.

"Please don't toss it all away for false hopes and distorted pledges of fidelity. You know you deserve so much more." Cupping the trembling chin in the palm of her hand, she begged, please promise you'll think over everything I've said, and above all remember how very much I love you and how important your happiness is to me."

Kissing the girl's cheek with exaggerated tenderness, she softly closed her bedroom door, leaving Maggie alone with her doubts, her unanswered questions and her ultimate disappointment in the evening's outcome. How could Bob have chosen not to approach Mama with the arrangements they had spent so much time concocting together? Wasn't that supposedly the aggregate reason for the invitation and his visit? Had Mama really seen through him or had he really seen Maggie for the first time when faced with their less than splendid way of life, perhaps realizing, at last, the magnitude of their differences, and finding himself unable to reconcile the incongruity, just as Mama had always predicted he would.

Bitter reflections paraded through her consciousness, accompanied by the solemn drum roll of her heavy laden heart. Walking to Papa's old room she gazed down at it's new occupant. The freckle spattered face, in repose, held the innocence and purity, common to all sleeping children, and she found herself envious, indignantly longing to be a child again. Once more to share this bed with Papa and feel again the ecstasy and blissful restoration his comfort had always afforded. Willing her ears to remember the sweet sound of his voice as it called her name, and longing hopelessly to feel anew that soothing, gentle touch, she finally released the pent up tears, sobbing with abandon until her brothers restless stirrings forced her retreat from the sanctuary.

Bob Jennings sat in his beautifully shining auto without turning the motor. A strange feeling engulfed him, depreciating the sense of security he had shared with Maggie. He knew he had been manipulated this afternoon, even to the point of being told when to leave. Shaking out the dead ashes, he relit his pipe, observing the enlarging glow. Every puff seemed to enhance his own growing glow of resentment until he resolved, regardless of promises, he would, indeed, need some sort of commitment from Maggie before leaving.

The intense heat had continued through the evening. Leaves hung lifeless in the stifling dry air. Even the cricket's happy song sounded stilted in the muggy night. Distantly he heard the constant creak of a porch swing, it's occupant vainly struggling for relief. Laying his head against the back of the seat he noticed a light flicker on in the upstairs window. Entranced, he watched as Jessica pushed aside the filmy curtains, leaning both hands against the sill. Her bosom heaved as she breathed in the heavy air. In the dimming light he imagined he could see her smiling. Despite the baking heat he shuddered.

Chapter Five

Annie Benfield's nose pressed against the kitchen screen door.

"Is that you in there, Maggie? There's a phone call for you."

Jessica turned wearily away from the stove. "She's not home from work yet. If it's that silly Miss Wingate tell her Maggie will be there at the regular time, although I can't see why a grown woman still sees fit to go to school. No earthly reason for it."

"It haint. I think it's her young man, the one from the factory. He sure is a swell dresser, ain't he? Seen him coming here on Sunday and I sez to Molly---"

Jessica shoved the door open interrupting the exasperating prattle. "I'll take the call for her if you'll just stay here for a moment in case Michael comes in for anything."

"The back door's open," Annie called after her, then shaking her head she mumbled to herself. "He needs something alright, and I'd love to be the one to give it to him. That young feller need a cat-o-nine tails across his behind every other day till he starts behavin', and then once a week as a reminder to keep doing it."

Jessica glanced quickly around Annie's house making sure she was alone.

"My dear Mr. Jennings, how nice to hear from you again, and so soon," she purred into the, phone.

The phone crackled, his voice coming from a distance. "Mrs. McClellan," she detected a note of disappointment, "I'm over in Eatonsburg on business today and just now received a call from home.

My father has taken a poor turn and I must return to Philadelphia tonight. I've tried reaching Maggie but she'd already left the office and must be on her way home. Would you be kind enough to tell her I will be by within the hour to say goodbye. I may not be able to come back for a week or two and I would appreciate seeing her alone before I leave." His emphasis on the word alone was not lost on her. Scraping her nails across the mouthpiece, she shouted above the sound.

"This is a very poor connection we have but I think I've gotten the message. Please give your father our regards and best wishes for a speedy recovery." She laid the phone in it's cradle without waiting for his reply. Rushing back to her own home she shooed Annie and an unfinished pilphered piece of pie out of the kitchen as the screeching iron gate announced Maggie's arrival.

"How wilted you look, Maggie, and just when I need you for an errand." Jessica was still somewhat breathless, but the exhausted girl did not notice as she sagged in the kitchen chair, fanning herself with the evening paper.

"What errand, Mama?" she asked listlessly.

"It would seem I've run out of just about everything this week, even coffee. There's not one tempting thing left for your lunch pail either." She smiled warmly at her daughter. "Some people can live on love, but not you, my girl. You're appetite is bigger than ever."

Maggie returned the smile shyly. "I hope I'm not eating us out of house and home as the old saying goes, so I'll cut back starting right now. It's too darn hot to eat anyway."

"Don't talk nonsense," Jessica chided, shoving a plate of creamed beef in front of her. "Just sit here and eat. We can't afford to waste what's already been made. Please do hurry along now so you can stop at the market before your lesson." It was the first time she had felt grateful for the existence of Mihara Wingate. "In just a few minutes Michael will be home and he can take his wagon and go with you."

"Oh, no, that won't be necessary, Mama, Maggie protested. "I can easily handle it myself." The thought of spending time with Michael only heightened her fatigue.

"One would thing you didn't enjoy your brother's company," Jessica answered wryly, placing a piece of paper on the table. "As you can see the list is quite lengthy so whether you like it or not you're going to need Michael to help pull the wagon up the hill. It's almost sinful you're not wanting to spend time with your own brother." She clicked her tongue in rebuke. What could the poor wee lad have done to you when he's hardly more than a baby?"

Maggie's eyes dropped guiltily. "I'm sure he won't enjoy waiting for me at Miss Wingate's, Mama. You know he's not too long on patience and will make a big fuss."

"So that's it is it! You're really worried about your precious Miss Wingate. Well just remember this, that old biddy is supposed to be an expert in the handling of children, so if Michael becomes restless just let her take care of it."

Maggie pushed the creamed beef around the plate. "But Mama, you know he doesn't listen, even to you. It will be embarrassing if he--"

"Hush, girl," whispered Jessica. "I'll not have him know his own sister is ashamed of him." Raising her voice she called to him. "There you are my darling. Come wash up, your sister wants you to accompany her on an errand."

Maggie's eyes darted to her mother with disapproval. Why did she have to be so insistent about Michael's tagging along when it was so unnecessary?

"I'm going to give each of you a few extra pennies for a frozen ice stick at the market." Jessica's voice held the magnanimity of a Papal blessing. "And then you'll have to wait like a good boy until Maggie has her lesson at Miss Wingates.

Instead of his usual tantrum when asked to perform a task, the young boy looked at Maggie with disbelief. "You really want me to go to Miss Wingates with you, really?" His usually piercing cat green eyes had softened, melting into the crinkles of a genuine smile of pleasure. Maggie, stunned by this unexpected reaction, instantly regretted her resistance to his company, feeling there was something almost pathetic in the incredulity of his question. She answered with affection.

"I'd love for you to come with me, Michael, if you have no other plans."

"I'll be ready in just a minute," he answered eagerly as he scrambled onto the wobbly step stool beside the kitchen sink.

Perhaps Mama was right. She never did give the boy any affection or attention, while she silently complained about receiving none herself. She remembered a fitting quote, "When you betray somebody else you also betray yourself." She wondered how many people unconsciously inflicted upon others the negligence they felt had been inflicted upon themselves. Vowing to make amends, she watched the boy as he diligently scrubbed his hands and face, then dried them on the towel reserved for dishes. The freckled nose and cheeks sparkled with cleanliness as he jubilantly ran to the yard to get the wagon. His enthusiasm was contagious, filling her with an optimism and responding vigor that was to wilt dramatically with Jessica's question.

"See how willing and cooperative he is? she asked, comparing her two children by the accusation in her voice. "Perhaps if you spent more time getting to know him instead of criticizing him, you both could benefit from it."

Maggie's memory of how Bob's sister had always supported him did nothing to raise her sagging spirits. She sighed wearily, getting out of her chair. She could no longer engage in this conversation that had been repeated over and over again, nor did she want her mother to recognize her guilt. Picking up the shopping list and money pouch, she brushed past Jessica, calling to Michael to wait for her.

Fanning briskly with the classified section of the Gazette, Jessica had barely stationed herself on the porch when Bob Jenning's car pulled to the curb. The young man smiled broadly as he climbed the porch stairs.

"How nice to see you again, Mrs. McClellan. You seem to be one of the few people holding up well under this heat wave."

Jessica beamed, "How sweet of you to say so, and just when I'm beginning to feel as wilted as last week's bouquet." Her eyes lowered flirtatiously as she indicated the seat beside her on the swing.

"Come, sit with me awhile."

The now familiar foreboding assailed him as he bowed ever so slightly, answering, I would enjoy that very much I'm sure, but I'm very pressed for time this evening. As I mentioned on the phone I must be in Philadelphia tonight, so if I could just visit with Maggie for a ---"

"Oh yes, how is your poor dear father coming along, Bob?" Her voice was filled with concern.

"Not too well I'm afraid. His condition seems to deteriorate daily and is now complicated by blood clots in his leg. I must get back to confer with his doctor first thing in the morning."

"That's what they call phlebitis, isn't it? I understand it's very dangerous. A friend of mine's husband, Bill Lewis, had that same condition. Have you ever met Bill?"

The length to which this woman could irritate him with her meaningless prattle only served to make him feel ineffectual and filled with petty ill will. Struggling to be civil, he answered.

"No, I never met Mr. Lewis and I don't mean to be abrupt, but as I've said, my time is limited this evening, so would you please call Maggie, now." He had not been able to conceal his annoyance.

"OH Maggie's not here, Mr. Jennings." She watched innocently as first surprise and then disappointment suffused his features.

"She had to run an errand for me, and I had forgotten when we were on the phone today, but this is her lesson night with Miss Wingate, which, as you know, she never misses."

His fingers drummed impatiently on the porch railing. "I know very well this is her lesson night, but I certainly thought that under these circumstances she would forego it."

"Well don't be peeved with me," Jessica answered sharply. "I'm merely a message taker and nothing more."

Torn between frustration and anger he began to question whether this detestable woman with the pouting mouth could possibly have been right about his minimal knowledge concerning her daughter. Maggie had always been so sensible and responsible, to the point that, only rarely had he ever been aware of their age difference. Why was she now acting like a belligerent child, punishing him for being called away?

Always alert to another's wavering, Jessica seized her opportunity. Leaning forward she stilled his impatient fingers with her own, speaking softly and with solicitude.

"Can't you see her predictable indifference only substantiates my fears? Please try to trust my judgment when I tell you that everything is happening for the best. By the time you come back she will have realized how much she's missed you and be grateful for your return. The separation will only serve to improve the entire situation, believe me."

Worn down by this repetitious conversation and an increasing sense of depression and melancholy, the young man stood, blindly studying the peeling paint beneath the porch rocker, and knowing in his heart he would never trust this woman.

"It's very difficult for me to accept she isn't here to say goodbye." Glancing up, he questioned, "You're positive she understood I was leaving tonight?"

Jessica stood up, sighing irritably. "I have found, Mr. Jennings that youth is both impetuous and impatient. Maggie's absence does not merit the importance you're attaching to it. After all it's not as though you were never going to see each other again."

Taking his arm she carefully began leading him back to his car.

"A phone call to the office tomorrow will straighten everything out I'm sure. You just be a little more tolerant and call tomorrow. You can certainly do that, can't you?"

The note of pettiness in his voice pleased her.

"If I get a chance I certainly will."

"Now, now, you must remember Maggie is just a child compared to us, so it's only natural that at times she acts like one. I'm sure you can forgive her being immature every now and again." Looking directly into his eyes, she added, "In reality, Mr. Jennings, you and I are more the same age." She kissed his mouth gently and swiftly. "That's goodbye for now from Maggie and me." Unable to hide a flicker of amusement, she turned, walking up the steps and into the house without looking back on the confused young man still standing on the sidewalk.

The eruption of one tumultuous event after the other in his normally complacent life left him unable to rationalize calmly. He dared not examine these obtuse but ever increasing sensations of doubt and uncertainty attacking his senses until he had first dealt with, and tried to resolve, the immediate problems of his father's health. Vigorously rubbing the back of his hand across his lips, he tried erasing the lingering feeling of Jessica's moist kiss. She, he decided, would no longer be an issue once he and Maggie left Miners' Haven. Easing the car down the hill, an eerie premonition forced him to look back at the old house as though he might be seeing it for the last time.

Returning home that evening, the children found Jessica heaving and moaning in her room.

"Maggie, oh Maggie, never have I been this sick," she cried, thrashing about the bed. "Oh, the pain. Everything hurts everywhere."

Maggie hastily dispatched her frightened brother to the kitchen for ice chips, then began pressing cool compresses against Jessica's forehead and cheeks. Their mother was seldom ill, and it was dreadful to see her suffering. Michael stayed in the shadows of the room, biting, his fingernails feverishly, the brown freckles standing out starkly against the pallor of his terrified face.

"Is she dying, Maggie?" he whimpered.

"Of course not, Michael, but it could be something like her having an appendicitis attack. Maybe you should run and get Dr. Salters."

The moaning on the bed subsided gradually. "That won't be necessary, my poor dears. I'm sorry to have frightened you, but the pain was quite intense. I think perhaps it was indigestion, it does seem to be getting better at the moment."

"Thank heavens," said Maggie with relief. "You scared the life out of both of us, didn't she Michael?"

The boy hung in the shadows, fearful of another outburst of wailing. "I'm tired, I want to go to bed," he answered sullenly.

"Of course you are, sweetheart. Lugging those groceries up the hill must have worn you out. Come kiss Mama good night." She opened her arms to embrace him.

He lowered his eyes guiltily. "I didn't help with the groceries, Maggie did it herself, and I don't want to kiss you good night." Stepping into the circle of light he shouted belligerently. "I don't like sick people!"

Flustered and embarrassed for her mother, Maggie tried calming the irritated child. "Mama's right, Michael, you're very tired. Come along and I'll tuck you in and listen to your prayers, okay?"

The boy ran to her as though released from some horror, throwing his arms about her waist with the gratitude of the delivered.

"Yes, please Maggie, I want you to luck me in."

Looking apologetically at Jessica, Maggie began, "He's just overtired, Mama. It's been a long hot day and he's out of sorts. Let me tuck him in and I'll be right back to take care of you."

The lids narrowed only slightly, the voice pitifully weak.

"Do you think you could remain at home tomorrow, Maggie? I feel too poorly to be left here alone all day."

Maggie, abandoning Michael, hastily returned to her side. "Of course, Mama, I'll stay with you tomorrow, and for as many days as are necessary, you know that." Touching the damp forehead to check for fever, and finding none, she again left the bedside. "Please rest now, Mama, and if you need me, just call.

Once Michael was settled in his bed she could not resist a recrimination. "It was not very nice of you to talk to Mama like that when she's so ill, Michael. I'm sure you hurt her feelings.

"Go on, Mama's feelings are unhurtable," he giggled. "I've said plenty of things to her before and she never minded, why does it matter now?"

"Because when people are sick they're more vulnerable. I mean more easily wounded because they're already feeling sorry for themselves. Do you understand?"

"Anybody that's feeling sorry for themselves deserves to be hurt!" The green eyes brightened with a glow of malignity. "I'll never feel sorry for myself, or anyone else for that matter. Pity is a waste of time, and only makes you weak. Like you said, vulnerable, or whatever that word was."

His short oration had fallen on deaf ears. Maggie, brimming with commiseration, tenderly tucked the thin sheet beneath his determined chin, wondering how someone so young had amassed so much cynicism. Her heart melted with deplorable sadness as her lips found his stiffly resisting cheek.

"I love you, Michael," she whispered into his ear.

Tossing the sheet aside, he turned his back to her without responding

Once in her own bed, she tossed from side to side with concern. What was to become of this pessimistic child, filling himself with misanthropic thoughts? A child alien to acts of affection and prone to sneering and surliness. Why does he feel the need to insulate himself against caring for another, and even against solace for himself? Her mother had been right. The child desperately needed attention. Her thoughts were diverted to Jessica. She could not recall ever seeing her mother so ill, and in some way the illness provoked the memory of dear Papa's misery. She squeezed her eyes tightly closed to shut out the unpleasant memory, not wanting to live through it again. Mama had to get well, that's all there was to it. Sitting up in her bed, she faced the mirror above the bureau.

"You are despicable," she uttered. "Worrying for yourself when it's poor Mama who is truly suffering. Her mother's voice interrupted herself condemnation and she bounded quickly from her bed.

Jessica had rushed to the mirror the moment Maggie closed the bedroom door. Turning her face right and left, she smiled at her reflection. "You should have considered the stage, my beauty, your talent as an actress is surprising." Filled with admiration she pushed the unruly auburn curls to the top of her head, then struck a bawdy pose, grinning wickedly. Abruptly the smile faded as she noticed how the hard lines about her mouth had deepened. The flesh about her eyes that once crinkled becomingly with laughter was now permanently etched with fine wrinkles. She released her hair, searching frantically through it for strand of gray. Moving back one step she surveyed the total image with dismay. Her once small waist had noticeably thickened. Her breasts had begun to soften and sag, even her stomach showed evidence of a bulge large enough to turn her silhouette matronly.

"You're getting old, Jessica McClellan," she said, speaking to her reflected image. And I can't say that it's one mite becoming,"

Slowly she returned to the bed, tucking the covers about herself in fidgety motions, then settling against the pillows she called out, "Maggie, Maggie, please come help me. I feel sick again."

Despite a sleepless night Maggie rose early, tiptoeing to her mother's room to see if she were needed.

"Is she alright?" asked Michael as he tried peeking into the dark room.

"Why Michael, whatever are you doing up at this hour? You're always the last one out of bed." She tried playfully ruffling the matted red hair, but he pulled away with distaste.

"Don't do that! he shouted, causing Jessica to stir in her bed.

"Whatever are you children doing out there so early in the morning? Come in, come in."

Maggie raised the shade allowing the morning light to flood the room. "We were worried about you, Mama, but I can see you're feeling better, today. I must run over to Annie's and phone Bob to say I won't be coming in for a day or two, but I'll be right back."

Jessica, contorting her features as though seized by unbearable pain, managed to utter through clenched teeth. "Just let Michael do it, Maggie. I need you here when I get these wretched spasms. They seem to leave me breathless." She punctuated this statement with a few short pants.

"I don't want to go to Aunt Annie's. She's an old witch. Besides why can't we get a phone of our own? Why do we always have to act like the poor relation?"

Jessica, raising herself on one elbow, answered bitingly. "Because we are the poor relation, Michael, and we can't afford the luxury of a telephone we don't really need."

"Maybe if Maggie wasn't always spending money on books we could afford it," he snapped.

"When you start making the money around here maybe you can start telling us how to spend it. Now you get over to Annie's this minute, and do as you're told."

The transparent green eyes smoldered with hatred as he glanced from one woman to the other, the brown freckles fading into the now flushed and ruddy complexion.

"This is the last time either of you will ever make me do something I don't want to do. The very last time." His voice was low and menacing, hypnotizing the women into a state of awe. Turning he ran down the stairwell and out the kitchen door, slamming it with a force that caused the old house to shudder.

He, had known since he was very young that Annie Benfield heartily disapproved of both he and his mother. Her accusing eyes and primly folded arms at his slightest misconduct had always spurred him on to ever greater deeds of mischief. Jessica seemed to enjoy his aggravating Annie, never once bothering to reprimand or deter him from continued provocation. Eventually his Aunt, occasionally being called upon to baby sit, and needful of the money, had formed a kind of silent pact with him. Reasonable behavior was rewarded and unreasonable behavior was ignored, leaving him bereft of any motive to continue his harassment.

Pounding on Annie's screen door he watched the old woman as she waddled through the kitchen, coffee cup in hand. "I'm coming, I'm coming.

What on earth could be so important at this hour of the morning?" Her throat was clogged with the residue of sleep.

Somewhat surprised to see who the intruder was, she questioned, "My goodness, Michael, what are you doing here? Is there a problem at home?"

"No, I have to call the factory to say Maggie's not coming in today."

"Is she ill?", Annie persisted

"No." He was determined not to give any information to this nosey old biddy, and the green eyes warned her not to inquire further.

Annie's bony fingers sought to relieve an elusive itch among her rollers as she led the boy into the dining room and dialed the factory's number for him. Stationing herself across the room, she stood with the familiar folded arms, as resolute as he to get the information by listening to this phone recital.

He began to despair after the fifth ring. If no one were to answer it would mean returning again later, an option he did not care to face. Turning slightly he positioned his body to block Annie's view of the phone, quickly depressed it's button, and began speaking into the dead receiver.

"I'm calling to report Maggie McClellan off today," he began. "Yes sir, that's right, sir." He continued his solitary conversation. "I'll tell her you said that, sir. Thank you, goodbye."

Placing the instrument back into it's cradle he faced Annie with malicious glee. "Thank you for the use of your phone, Aunt Annie. Thank you very much."

Knowing she was being taunted, and frustrated by her own failure, she decided to make one last attempt. "Tell your mother I might stop over this afternoon for that recipe we talked about last week."

The green eyes turned opaque and lifeless. "I wouldn't do that Aunt Annie." It was almost a threat. "No one will be home this afternoon."

Feeling intimidated and all but afraid, she was relieved when the sinister young boy marched victoriously out the kitchen door.

"He's the devil's own child if I ever seen one," she said aloud. Jessica was at last being sorely punished for the sins of her youth. The very thought of it brightened her day and she hummed happily as she freshened her cold coffee.

Joe Flynn's day had started off with his wife's usual and endless badgering about his weekly poker game, which he planned to attend that evening, and had worsened steadily as the day progressed. Neither Bob Jennings nor Maggie had appeared to man the office, leaving him with the dual responsibility of trying to supervise the line and listen for the phone, which was barely audible above the drone of the machines. Running once again to the office and fearing his efforts might again be thwarted, he yelled angrily into the phone.

"Hello, Joe Flynn here!"

"Hello Joe, you sound a bit upset. Is everything alright there?"

Recognizing Bob Jennings voice, the foreman laughed self-consciously. "Oh good morning, Mr. Jennings. How are you sir? Everything's just fine Mr. Jennings, it's just that without you and Maggie here today I'm having a bit of a problem keeping on top of the phone calls, that's all sir."

"Did you say Maggie hasn't come in today, Joe?"

"That's right, sir. I thought maybe she had reported off to you, but she didn't show up this morning." He could not see the entire line from the office and it made him nervous. "I was wondering sir, if I could pull someone off the line to catch these calls? It sure would lessen the hassle here today."

Bob's voice was pensive. "You do whatever you think is necessary Joe. I'm afraid I won't be much help to you for a while. My father is very ill and I'm unable to leave here at the moment. Put Mary Bolen on the desk, she seems the most capable and call me here if you need anything."

"I'm really sorry to hear that, Mr. Jennings. You just put your mind at ease there and don't worry none about this place. We'll all keep things going full steam until you get back. Don't worry, sir."

Joe Flynn was very convincing and Bob appreciated his assurances. Thanking the foreman profusely, and reminding him again to call if necessary, he hung up, his mind tormented and confused. It was one thing to exhibit personal displeasure, but carrying indignation into the working place was very unprofessional. How had he so misjudged this girl when spotting people of sound character and dependability always had been his forte? He felt obligated to impart his feelings and most certainly would do so when he spoke with her tomorrow. For now he would keep his scheduled appointment with his father's physician, report them back to his sister, and press for her coming home. His precise and meticulous nature demanded he deal with, and completely resolve only one problem at a time.

CHAPTER SIX

"I'm really getting tired of slaving over the pots in this heat and you're sitting nibbling like a titmouse every night. Are you ill or just trying to peeve me?"

Maggie tried to control her irritation as she looked up from her untouched plate. "I guess I'm not feeling up to par Mama. Maybe it's the heat."

"Or maybe it's because her boyfriend don't come around anymore." Michael, as usual had stuffed his mouth with food, somewhat garbling his speech.

"He's had to return home," said Maggie, defensively. "His father is ill and needs him. Besides, it's none of your business." She flashed her brother a look of disgust, to which he responded by sticking out his food laden tongue.

When Maggie had returned to work after three unscheduled days off Mr. Flynn had not reprimanded her, as he, like everyone else in the factory, was aware of her more than casual relationship with his boss. He did feel obliged, however, to inform her of and the reason for Bob's absence, an act necessary to continue the pretense of ambiguity. Her look of surprise was very convincing, he thought, then dismissed all these trappings of subterfuge from his mind, grateful to return to his normal job.

Maggie, sitting in the small stifling office, had tried vainly to fathom why Bob had not contacted her at Annie's, not only to tell her about his father, but to inquire concerning Jessica as well. The only answer she could arrive at was one she did not care to examine or admit to herself.

"Have you heard from him lately?" Jessica asked nonchalantly.

"He talks mostly to Mr. Flynn, but sometimes I answer when he calls." She did not want her mother to know the foreman had allowed Mary Bolen to remain in the office after her return. It seemed a reflection on her competence. To Joe Flynn it was insurance against any more truancy. An involuntary tear slid down her cheek, releasing a flood of recriminations.

"I don't understand it, Mama. He left without saying a word and finally when we did speak and I told him I understood and not to worry about me for now, he seemed to take offense, and assured me he would not. What could I have done differently Mama? Surely I could not complain about his caring for his father could I?"

"I hate being an I told-you-so," sneered Jessica, "But I warned you, against believing this man's intentions were honest. You're a lucky girl that fate has intervened. God knows what you would have been duped into had he stayed here much longer."

"But he loves me," objected Maggie, "I know he does, just as I love him." She was crying in earnest now, finding it difficult to speak.

"Well, look at this sorry sight," answered Jessica, the anger rising in her voice. You sit here, a sodden mess, mewling over a man who's seen fit to jilt you and are pitifully stupid enough to be mouthing words about his love. Have you no pride or self respect left?" Legs astride and hands on hips, she continued. "I want this moping about over and done with. I will not have you disturbing all our lives with an episode better forgotten. Always, always you put your confidence in the wrong people. Your father made you a dreamer and that school teacher only glorified those dreams by filling your mind with the impossible. If you had, from the beginning, listened to me, who had only your best interests at heart, think of the disillusionment you could have avoided already. I want you to think about what I've said and resolve to do better. Get some strength about you. You're nothing but a milksop." Her arms dropped to her sides in resignation. "Just remember, years wrinkle the skin, but to give up enthusiasm wrinkles the soul. You'd best get some spirit about you." She had read that line in one of Maggie's books and felt quite proud to have quoted it, not only accurately, but at a propitious moment. An unexpected stab of guilt released a flow of pity. Pausing she placed a consoling hand on one dejected shoulder.

"I know this is very hard for you, Maggie, but believe me, you're so young some day you won't even remember it. Life has a wonderful way of healing all wound either through time or by creating new and more important ones. Even when we think it's impossible we manage to live through every one of them. You'll be just fine in a week or so."

The liquid blue eyes were unbelieving and she could not confront them further. Motioning to Michael, the pair left the kitchen, abandoning the girl to her inner despair.

Maggie walked into the garden, weighing her mother's words. Maybe she had wasted much of her life dreaming, but they had all been wonderful dreams, and some had even come true. Her published words had not made the world stop spinning, but at least she had had the pleasure of knowing her thoughts were recognized and considered worthy of being conveyed. She had known love, and no matter how great the hurt, she would not care, even now, to relinquish the experience of it. Whatever reasons Bob had for his distant behavior she could forgive gladly, without explanation, if only he would come back to her. A deep frown creased her forehead. Perhaps Mama was right about one thing. It was time for her to become stronger, more grown up and realistic, more like Mama.

Bob and his sister gazed down upon the beloved man who had been both mother and father, and now lay grotesquely contorted by an irreversible embolism, his twisted features almost unrecognizable.

"I'm kind of glad now that I never told him about Maggie. I wouldn't want him to die thinking his son was a fool."

Still watching the agonized man on the bed before them, Jeanette gently slipped her fingers between her brothers, speaking in a whisper.

"I'm sure even father had at least one encounter with unrequited love. I believe he feasted heartily at the banquet of live with a taste for any experience, and relishing all of them." She squeezed his fingers lovingly. "Besides he never would have thought you a fool for any reason, least of all for loving."

"Thank you for saying that, Jeanette."

They faced each other in the hushed room, eyes radiant with affection and appreciation. Slipping her arm through his they wordlessly left the room, heading for the library in muted agreement, the room where all their important conversations had always been held. Jeanette was ten years older than her brother and after the death of their mother had willingly become amenable, responding to his needs with no thought of being a surrogate mother, but choosing rather, to be a friend and a confidante.

Seated before the unlit hearth she smoothed her fashionable pure silk skirt against thighs still taut and firm from hard fought tennis matches on the clay courts behind the house. Bob, looking down at the sun streaked, neatly coiffured hair, could not help thinking how very much alike they were. Both meticulous almost to the point of fetishness, with the same gray thoughtful eyes and ease of manner. Trying to picture Maggie in this setting he compared her simplicity, shyness and restraint to the elegance, grace, and polished refinement of his sister. His thoughts were interrupted by his sister's question.

"Are you thinking of renewing your relationship with Maggie before too much time elapses? I've always found time spent apart during crises has an unhappy tendency toward becoming a permanent condition. Or is that what you have in mind?"

"As I've already told you I'm not sure I could renew it." He spoke reflectively. "She has not been very receptive the few times we've spoken, except to tell me not to concern myself about her. God, I can't believe this has all happened. I tell you, Jeanette what we had was so--so right, so wonderful. I don't think I was ever so happy in my entire life as I was just being near her."

Rising to console him she kissed his distraught cheek, holding him in her arms. "My poor Bobby." Men like him deserved to be happy she thought, wondering if his assessment of this woman was accurate. Never having discussed his affairs of heart before left her powerless to gauge his naivety. This person could be as wonderful as he said, or just as wonderfully wicked. No matter which, she was obviously breaking his heart. Perhaps he was too old to be told what to do but just maybe young enough to be led in another direction. Holding him at arm's length she asked, "Do you remember that marvelous looking blonde gal who was the star of the courts a few seasons back? Well I bumped into her at the club this week and she's conducting some sort of cocktail party and white elephant sale combination tonight to benefit the U.S.O. It's a worthwhile cause and heaven knows we could use a break from this continual vigil. What do you say; it will do us both good?"

The shrill ring of the phone delayed his reply.

Mr. Keator, his father's attorney was jubilant. "We've got an offer on the Miners' Haven mill, Bob that's so good you won't believe it. I can hardly believe it myself. Your dad's timing has paid off again. That old rascal always did know instinctively, when and how to turn a buck. How is the old coot anyway?"

"Not very well I'm afraid, but as you know, I'm authorized to sign off on everything if you think the deal's reasonable."

"It's more than reasonable, Bob, and the best part is that they understand your situation and are willing to take over without any assistance from you. They'll be incorporating all of their own procedures anyway. All they really need is a guarantee of Mr. Flynn's cooperation."

"But what about the other personnel? I must insist on their retaining our people. They've all been loyal and can't afford to be unemployed." He thought of Maggie's illegal absences and did not want her to suffer any retribution by some stranger when he himself had still not reproached her for her actions.

Mr. Keator's joviality was endless. "That's not a problem, Bob.

Why would they bring in workers they'd have to train when they' surrounded with experienced ones. No, other than a few top management people of their own, everything will remain the same. Come by the office in the morning and we'll lock it all up. Believe me you'll be more than satisfied."

Looking at the dead phone in bewilderment, he spoke aloud.

"I don't think I'll ever be satisfied again. His sad gray eyes sought out his sister's. "I knew that day I left Miners' Haven I would never see her house again."

Maggie walked leisurely up the hill. She was in no hurry to reach home and subject herself once again to Jessica's harping disapproval of her continued lethargy. She had despairingly tried taking her mother's advise to put aside all thoughts of Bob Jennings, but had been unable, to do so. Facing his empty desk day after day had only increased her loneliness and longing for him. His old white clay pipe still lay in the desk ash tray, its dead ashes emitting the familiar odor of briarwood, while his fleecy soft cashmere jacket hung limp and abandoned on the brass clothes tree. Fondling these personal objects had, at first, been a pleasurable comfort to her, but as time went on their presence transcended into lofty obstacle, rising above her attempts to obliterate old memories.

His attitude had been very businesslike the few times she had intercepted his calls to Mr. Flynn. On each occasion, tempted as she might be to question his aloof and strange behavior, pride and the anxiety of hearing his reply, had always surfaced sufficiently, intervening with her good intentions, and permitting only polite inquiries as to the state of his father's health, and a growing disgust with the fact that he had not the sensibilities to reciprocate by inquiring about Jessica's. His apathy disarmed her and she found herself following his example of indifference which, she wanted to believe, served to prove her ever growing strength.

The stifling heat had relented a few degrees but the walk home was still arduous, and her steps slowed with every new block. It was evident that she would soon have to admit Jessica had been right. She could no longer console herself by blaming his position on business or health concerns when she, like Bob, truly believed adversities were meant to be shared. They had discussed the subject many times agreeing their definition of love was sharing. A sharing which would encompass all things pleasant or unpleasant, wonderful or woeful, delightful or disastrous. They would share life. Angrily wiping away a tear she felt might be testimony to her back sliding; she waved listlessly to Mr. Kramer, noting without interest that the ice can was unusually late today.

The old man and his horse drawn ice wagon were the last of a dying breed, and he had sworn this year, as he had sworn every year since Maggie was four, that this one would be his last. Too many people buying them new electric boxes to make it worthwhile anyway. Expertly shifting his wad of tobacco from one cheek to the other, he emitted a long stream of juice over his left shoulder while simultaneously laying the whip, not too gently, on Sally's back.

"Git up, you lazy old nag," roared the ice man as he again laid on the whip. "Me profits are turning to water along with me patience."

The horse had barely responded as they reached the top of the hill where Michael stood waiting for him with his usual group of rowdy companions.

"Blast them," thought Fred Kramer. "The fifteen cents I collect from Jessica hain't worth the pilfering I have to put up with from those rapscallions." Adamantly vowing to retire at summer's end he laid the whip even more soundly on the old horse's rump, and passed by the children without stopping. It pleasured him to hear Michael calling frantically.

"Stop, you forgot our house, you old coot. Stop do you hear me?"

The old man laughed aloud baring teeth turned yellow by years of tobacco stains. It was worth the fifteen cents to be able to irritate the rascal who had been a constant irritation to him, he thought snickering to himself. His elations was soon shattered however, as he turned to see his nemesis clinging to the side of the wagon, scooping into the chipped ice.

"Git off my wagon, you little pirate," he shouted. "Git off this very minute!"

Michael looked up; the defiant green eyes daring the old man as he repeatedly dipped his hand into the bowels of the dilapidated wagon retrieving yet another fistful of chips.

"Make me if you can, you old coot," the boy shouted above the noise of the creaking cart.

Once again shifting his wad, the ice man let go a stream of putrid juice, smiling with satisfaction at the precision of his aim as the filthy flow splattered over Michael's clinging hand. The boy shrieked in disgust as he felt the slimy liquid seep between his fingers. Automatically releasing his grip to escape the unsavory substance, he tumbled off the cart and into the street.

Fred Kramer's stomach convulsed as he felt the rear wheel pass over the small body. Successive obscenities poured from his lips as he pulled up the wagon and ran to the boy's side, turning him gently onto his back.

"Sweet Jesus," the old man whispered as he helplessly watched the blood's slow egression from the young lad's nose and mouth. Shaking with fear for himself as well as Michael, Fred Kramer lumbered to the nearest house, imploring it's occupants to call for help, then collapsed on the porch in a fit of uncontrolled sobbing and lamentations.

Maggie, jolted out of her despondency by the screaming children, found her brother spread eagled on the cobbles, his ashen features stained with blood. Kneeling beside him and cradling the small fiery head in her arms, she knew the same dread and apprehension she had known all those years ago with Papa. She prayed silently this time it would end differently so she might be given the chance to do the things with Michael she had always meant to do but had neglected through her total lack of patience with him and her complete devotion to her own life.

"Forgive me, Michael," unknowingly she spoke aloud.

The once defiant eyes opened slowly, looking up at her with pleading. His weakened hand slid lingeringly across his mouth, smearing the crimson trickle over his pallid cheek.

"She told him bad things about you," he whispered. "That's why he didn't come back."

Running her fingers through his hair caressingly, she cautioned,

"Shhh, Michael, don't try to talk. Everything will be alright as soon as the doctor gets here. Please just rest, sweetheart."

Unhearing, Michael continued slightly louder. "She sent me to bed but I didn't go. I listened in the stairwell and I heard her tell him you loved somebody else better than him." He coughed lightly, becoming almost limp in his arms.

Maggie's shocked fingers ceased their stroking as she looked deeply into her brother's face. "What are you telling me, Michael? Are you being inventive?"

A sickly smile passed over the small wan face. "That's a word Mama uses when I'm a liar." The pale green eyes appeared almost sad. "I'm not lying. I have no reason to lie now."

How many times had she marveled at how one so young always managed to simulate the thoughts and actions of one much more mature? He had never really been a child in the manner children have of demanding love, attention and caring for. Rather his demands had been to be left alone, to do his own bidding, never caring about love or being loved. How lonely and unhappy he must be, she mused.

As though able to read her thoughts, he smiled his usual mischievous smile. "I'm glad I told you, Maggie. Maybe it will make you happy again."

A long wistful sigh escaped him, filling her nostrils with the suffocating smell of death. Pulling him closer to her bosom, she rocked slowly back and forth in reparation for all the things they had never been allowed to be to one another. For the many times she had resented him and his audacious behavior. For the few times she had bothered to venture into his world only to be rebuffed. For the sacrilege of cradling him in death after ignoring him in life. Her fingers automatically resumed their stroking as she pressed her lips against the cooling forehead. Distantly she felt Jessica's arrival, hearing the screams of protest without commiseration or compassion, continuing to hold her brother fast, even after their mother, fainting, had crumbled into a heap beside them.

The decidedly distinguishable odors of dying flowers and decaying flesh once more pervaded the antiquated parlor. Once more Jessica sat mourning on the well worn sofa, alone and filled with self pity. Totally consumed with the emptiness of her life, she sat oblivious to Maggie's presence in the doorway.

Her benumbed mind sluggishly retraced the past, never acknowledging blessings or good fortune, dwelling only on adversities and pain. Deciding life had been unnecessarily cruel to her, she suffered the thought that she had been slighted by God. The incongruity of the idea startled her. "Just retribution, I must admit," she spoke aloud. "He most certainly has been slighted by me." But what about the people in her life she had selflessly devoted herself to, demanding nothing, desirous only of their approbation and respect. Neither Michael, her father or her son had seen fit to grant her both, and each, in his own way, had deserted her long before they had deserted this life.

Surely she had not been that bad a daughter, wife and mother, yet in some unfathomable fashion they had all set out to punish her. Issac through his incessant and stubborn disapproval, which he had taken to the grave without repentance. Michael by his inability to love and honor her. Steadfastly preoccupied with other more significantly important things. His child, her father, and even the damnable union had taken precedence over her, while she, in turn, had made him the consummation of her life. And now her dear son, who, during his short life, had never respected anything. A lad so bent on malevolence and destruction he had succeeded only in destroying himself. His dying, the ultimate disappointment, had devastated and ravaged her soul beyond enduring.

Was it possible that she was the appalling person, driving away, by her clinging and tenacious nature, the very ones she had wanted to hold fast? Was she the solitary enigma, standing alone, her untainted and sincere intentions misunderstood by everyone? The thought, too horrendous to pursue, was promptly dismissed and replaced with one more palatable.

Her life had, indeed, been a series of misfortunes, bad luck and other people's weaknesses, which, unfortunately even she was not able to help them overcome.

Well now it's just me and Maggie. Unthinkable that it would have come to this, but it was the way of it and there was nothing left but to see it through. Her human nature, that part within all of us that enables survival, sprang to her rescue, forcing her to remember, if not with exacting recall, with at least a reasonable semblance of past realities. She smiled involuntarily thinking of the happy times they had shared together while Maggie prepared for her new promotion.

How they had studied so assiduously, neglecting both the house and the meals, munching only on sandwiches and candy bars, in their intense effort to acquire for Maggie the maximum aggregate of education in their minimally allotted space of time. Breakfasts had been balanced with spelling bees, and shampooed hair, normally set and primped over, was left unfettered, hanging free to dry out to the ever quickening tempo of the borrowed typewriter. Weekends, rather than a respite, were looked upon as an opportunity to devote two full days, without interruption, to the complicated study of time cards, payroll and the seemingly undecipherable mathematics dictated by piece work. Sweet nostalgia glorified the retrospection until she saw them inseparable, still vying for that same small plum of happiness, dangling from the tree of life, managing always to remain just barely out of reach. Together, perhaps with a renewed and concerted effort, they may be able to surmount these hideous times, and pluck that tree dry by their very persistence and undaunted eagerness to prevail. Hadn't they both already arisen above crushing odds?

Her weary eyes fluttered closed with relief. Sunny reflections on the past and an optimistic search for a plausible future had dutifully ministered to her need for surcease from this detestably odious present. Unknowingly Maggie was about to shatter that temporary respite as she interrupted Jessica's hard fought for tranquility.

"Mama, I'm leaving now. I've come to say good-bye." The somber black hat and painfully plain mourning dress made her already pale face appear almost ghostly. Deep gray circles of grief surrounded the determined blue eyes as she stood resolutely in the center of the threadbare carpet, gazing at her bewildered mother.

Pins of fear pricked Jessica's heart as the gravity of her daughter's words penetrated her already troubled mind. Noticing the packed traveling bags resting against the sliding door, she pointed rigidly.

"What are you doing with those valises? What do you mean you're leaving? Maggie where would you go?" The jerky successive questions had sallied forth without pause, voiding all means of separate response.

The girl's voice was calm, but firmly determined. "I haven't quite decided yet, Mama. I only know it's time for me to leave, and I'm doing it today. She lowered her eyes. "I wish you would say nothing to try to stop me. I want us to part without any bitterness."

Jessica almost leaped from the sofa. "I haven't quite decided yet, Mama," she mimicked. "To hell you haven't! I know what you're up to, throwing yourself after a man that doesn't want you, and never did, no matter what he told you. "How in God's name can you debase yourself like this? How can you possibly consider doing such a thing? Just remember when you get there and he turns you away, you can't come crawling back here, because I won't have you. Do you understand that?"

The sudden clamor of her distressed voice echoed about the stilled house, reverberating it's anguish through the quiet rooms. Waiting for Maggie's contrite reply, she observed that the usually empathic blue eyes remained icy, the lips had compressed in frozen silence, the impassive expression unchanged, despite her raucous outburst. She would not allow herself to be bested by this obstinate child. A new approach was called for.

"And what about me, Maggie?" Her hand flew to her breast. "Surely you don't plan on leaving me here all alone?" Tears conveniently glistened on the rims of the faded brown eyes. Why I've just this moment been sitting here making all kinds of plans for us. Oh, Maggie, we've both been through some hard times lately, but together we can make it all good again, just the way it used to be, remember?" She took a step forward intending an embrace, but something in the girl's demeanor caused her to hesitate. "Just look at me, Maggie. I'm getting old. I don't know what I'd do if I were all alone."

Maggie, noting the slumping shoulders and haggard eyes, the lusterless hair and slowly thickening body, mutely acknowledged the verity of her mother's words, but her tone was as cold as her answer.

"You've always been alone, Mama.

Picking up the sparse luggage, Maggie walked through the door and down the weathered porch steps for the last time. Breathing deeply she gratefully accepted the uplifting sense of finally being free, of a freshly reawakened inner spirit, a rejuvanance of her lost enthusiasm, and above all, the cognizance that she would readily adapt to her new found energies without guilt or retrospection.

Racing to the parlor window, Jessica shouted through the tattered screen. "Maggie you come back here this instant. Do you hear me, Maggie? Come back here!"

She stood screaming, the desolate tears gradually drying on her flushed cheeks, long after her daughter had disappeared into the distance.

From some remote region a church bell hesitantly began it's joyous tolling, only to be shortly joined by another, and very soon, yet another. The fire stations siren made it's announcement by repeatedly releasing it's ear splitting wail, while the fire horn from the almost deserted colliery emitted short happy toots of elation. The Great War was over.

THE END

CPSIA information can be obtained at www.ICGtesting.com
232656LV00002BA/124/P
9 781456 744687